gorse | *Number Three*

GW00634698

Published in Dublin. The first 150 copies
are individually numbered.

gorse | art in words

Published in Dublin March 2015 by *gorse*
ISBN 978-0-9928047-2-5
ISSN 2009-7093

GORSE, NO. 3
www.gorse.ie

EDITOR Susan Tomaselli
EDITORIAL ASSISTANT Therese Murray
COVER ART Niall McCormack | home.hitone.ie
PRINTER Naas Printing | naasprinting.ie

The editor would like to thank Christodoulos Makris; Galley Beggar Press; Paula Meds; Derbhla Leddy; Maria Zvereva & Evgenia Kozhina; Colm O'Shea; Stephen Crowe; Linda Fallon; Maria Dickenson; Vinny Browne; Louisa Earls; Steven Maybury & Ángel Luis González at The Library Project.

Contents

.

A merican artist, illustrator and adventurer Rockwell Kent wrote that Glenlough, County Donegal was 'a place never to be forgotten – a place, indeed, to be remembered with nostalgia.'[1] Kent sojourned there in 1926, 'painting in a remote and all but inaccessible coastal valley ... lived there in a tiny one-room house, painted the surrounding countryside and the great cliffs that dropped almost a sheer thousand feet into the sea.' It was in Dan Ward's[2] converted cow barn he completed some of what are now considered to be his best paintings: 'And Women Must Weep,' 'Annie McGinley,' 'Dan Ward's Stack.' It was also in this year that Kent was approached that year to produce an illustrated edition of *Moby-Dick*.

A failure on publication in 1851,[3] Melville's magnum opus was enjoying something of a comeback with ex-pats in

1 *Of Men and Mountains*, Rockwell Kent (Asgaard Press 1959)

2 If Glenlough is famous, it is perhaps for Dylan Thomas, who stayed in the same outhouse a decade later—'ten miles from the nearest human being...and as lonely as Christ'—though, absconding without settling rent or setting his bar tab, he is thought of less fondly than Kent.

3 'We have no intention of quoting any passages just now from *Moby-Dick*. The London journals, we understand, 'have bestowed upon the work many flattering notices,' and we should be loth to combat such high authority. But if there are any of our readers who wish to find examples of bad rhetoric, involved syntax, stilted sentiment and incoherent English, we will take the liberty of recommending to them this precious volume of Mr. Melville's.'

United States Magazine and Democratic Review, January 1852

twenties' Europe (and Kent's handsome edition, published in 1930 with its two-hundred-and-eighty woodcuts, assured *Moby-Dick*'s rebirth). *Moby-Dick*, says Nathaniel Philbrick, [4]"in its wilful refusal to follow the usual conventions of nineteenth-century fiction, … possessed the experimental swagger that so many authors were attempting to capture in the years after World War I,' and D.H. Lawrence was an enthusiastic admirer: '[Melville] was a futurist long before futurism found paint.' 'At first you are put off by the style,' Lawrence concedes. 'It reads like journalism. It seems spurious. You feel Melville is trying to put something over you. It won't do. And Melville really is a bit sententious: aware of himself, self-conscious, putting something over even himself. But then it's not easy to get into the swing of a piece of deep mysticism when you just set out with a story.'

Rockwell Kent tried to purchase Dan Ward's cottage in the fifties but was refused a passport by the US State Department and became embroiled in an eight-year battle against his government, who he claimed were keeping him in 'continental imprisonment,' a struggle Melville would have approved of (he won in the end, but the cottage was sold to another). We know of Kent—of his radicalism, his popularity in Moscow, his appearance before the House of Un-American Activities ('believing that the world should live at peace and that atom bombs could never prove the instruments of peace')—because we were *failing* to engage with *Moby-Dick* and were *reading around the text*. Not uncommon—'all over the world people are taking notes as a way of postponing, putting off and standing in for,' says

4 *Why Read Moby-Dick?*, Nathaniel Philbrick (Viking 2011)

Geoff Dyer in *Out of Sheer Rage*, his failed attempt at a 'sober and academic' study of D.H. Lawrence. We tried a different tack. To paraphrase Dyer, we picked up *Moby-Dick* and put it down, thought about doing some writing and watched the movie instead.

Director John Huston and writer Ray Bradbury[5] wrestled with Meville's text in 1956. Filmed on location in Ireland, the pair eliminated characters—including throwing Fedellah overboard—combined elements of the one-hundred-and-thirty-five different chapters (and an Etymology, Epilogue and Extracts) into single scenes, and added material, most notably the masterful embellishment of Father Mapple's speech delivered brilliantly by Orson Welles. Despite these credentials, Gregory Peck's Lincolnesque Captain Ahab just doesn't cut it. It may have been more advantageous to allow Huston to take the lead, as Bradbury joked he had wanted to: 'Have you tried to read that novel? ... John Huston didn't know any more about it than I did. He wanted to play Ahab. Give him a harpoon, and he would've done it.'[6]

We considered hunting down a 2007 abridged edition of the book, *Moby-Dick in Half the Time*, but were discouraged after reading Adam Gopnik's review[7] which said it was 'all

5 Filmed in Ireland, Bradbury was to revisit the agonising experience in his 1992 novel, *Green Shadows, White Whale*.

6 'How Ray Bradbury Wrote the Script for John Huston's *Moby Dick* (1956),' *OpenCulture*, December 2013: http://www.openculture.com/2013/12/how-ray-bradbury-became-herman-melville-and-wrote-the-script-for-john-hustons-moby-dick-1956.html

7 'The Corrections: Abridgement, enrichment, and the nature of art,' Adam Gopnik, The *New Yorker*, 22 October 2007· http://www.newyorker.com/magazine/2007/10/22/the-corrections

Dick and no Moby.' As Gopnik noted, 'all abridgements and additions are part of their period…the Orion *Moby-Dick* is not defaced[8]; it is, by conventional contemporary standards of good editing and critical judgment, improved. The compact edition adheres to a specific idea of what a good novel ought to be: the contemporary aesthetic of the realist psychological novel.' You can see the appeal. However, 'the subtraction does not turn good work into hackwork; it turns a hysterical, half-mad masterpiece into a sound, sane book.'

We stopped reading it as an editor. As Damion Searls pointed out,[9] 'what makes Melville Melville is digression, texture, and weirdness.' Searls wondered what was missing. His *; or The Whale*[10] is composed of the bits culled from the Orion edition, so there's a chapter that's one single word ('hapless'), another is pure punctuation. Shorn of excess wordage *; or The Whale* is 'avant-garde by being as rearguard as possible,' says Searls.[11] 'In our present age, after the collapse of literary authority, rewriting or even rereading a nineteenth-century classic—the classic American novel—is as radical as it gets.'

The International Necronautical Society (INS) might agree.

---

8 The 1851 British edition was defaced, however: it has a rearranged and incomplete ending. Writing to Nathaniel Hawthorne, Melville lamented: 'So the product is a final hash, and all my books are botches.'

9 'Carving the Whale,' Damion Searls, *The Believer*, September 2009: http://www.believermag.com/issues/200909/?read=article_searls

10 *; or The Whale*, Damion Searls, *Review of Contemporary Fiction*, Vol. XXIX, Summer 2009, Dalkey Archive Press

11 'The Other Half of Moby-Dick: The Damion Searl Interview,' *The Quarterly Conversation*, 2008: http://quarterlyconversation.com/half-of-half-of-moby-dick-the-damion-searls-interview

The semi-fictitious avant-garde art organisation, of which novelist Tom McCarthy is a member, sought in their *Founding Manifesto*[12] to 'map the spaces that open around the sign of death in the fields of literature, art, science and culture; to plot and to follow the paths that lead to these spaces.' 'Navigation Was Always A Difficult Art,' their contribution to Hans Ulrich Obrist's *Mapping It Out: An Alternative Atlas of Contemporary Cartographie*s, may borrow its name from *The Hunting of the Snark* ('the only genuinely accurate map ever drawn,' McCarthy says; a 'perfect and absolute blank,' Lewis Carroll's crew sing) but places Kokovoko native ('It is not down on any map; true places never are') and the Pequod's harpoonist Queequeg (his tattoos a map to the heavens) at its centre. *Moby-Dick* is a major codex for the INS (their Twitter feed, @necronauts, used to default to *Moby-Dick*, tweeting the text 140 characters at a time). And no wonder: Melville's book may well contain nothing less than 'the genetic code of America' but it *is* one 'of suicide and murder, as C.L.R. James[13] puts it, 'destroy yourself and everything you can take with you rather than submit.'

For procrastinators, *Moby-Dick* is the perfect text to shilly-shally with, and Ishmael a good (or bad) example: 'God keep me from ever completing anything.'

---

12 http://necronauts.net/manifestos/1999_times_manifesto.html
13 *Mariners, Renegades and Castaways: The Story of Herman Melville and the World We Live In*, C.L.R. James (privately printed 1953; reissued, Allison & Busby 1984). Trinidadian James struck on the idea of writing an analysis of *Moby-Dick* while interned on Ellis Island awaiting deportation. It was a valiant attempt to prove his credentials for citizenship, but proved a failure: he was deported for his 'subversive politics' (he had been involved in a Trotskyist group) in 1953.

In 2009 Matt Kish's began an ambitious project to illustrate 'every single one of the 552 pages of the Signet Classic paperback edition. I'll try to do one a day, but we'll see.' Kish's *Moby-Dick in Pictures*, drawn on pages torn from repair manuals and engineering textbooks[14], and finished in 2011, is a fitting tribute both to Melville and to Rockwell Kent: 'Friends often question my obsession with the novel…and the best explanation I have been able to come up with is that, to me, *Moby-Dick* is a book about *everything*. God. Love. Hate. Identity. Race. Sex. Humor. Obsession. History. Work. Capitalism … I see every aspect of life reflected in the bizarre mosaic of this book.'

As Philbrick says, '*Moby-Dick* is a long book, and time is short. Even a sentence, a mere phrase will do. The important thing is to spend some time with the novel, to listen as you read, to feel the prose adapt to the various voices that flowed through Melville during the book's composition like intermittent ghosts with something urgent and essential to say.'

Rather than a outright refusal a la Melville's Bartleby (we would prefer not to), submit to it we will.

'Call me Ishmael…'[15]

---

14 "Something about those old diagrams fascinates me because their symbols and all those lines and drawings and letters look almost alchemical to me. Magical. So the thought of all that unfathomable information, a bit buried but lurking just beneath the paint and ink really spoke to me. It hinted at the deeper themes and mysteries of Melville's novel as well as the mysteries lurking beneath the sea."

15 As Philbrick points out these are not actually the first lines in the book, but no matter...

Limbed
David Hayden

A journey of light ending and ending and everything feeding off this, in one way or another, but the light just arriving, warm and buttery, letting us see; shapes, shadows, colours and a cottage and a field and a cottage garden with cornflowers, eye blue, heartsease, winking violet, delphiniums, risen purple, primroses, tooth yellow, upgazing, sightless, calendula stars, thyme, tight green spicing curls, and daisies, scattered wings, open palms; over all, fattening bees swing boozily in the warm air. A man or a woman stands smiling once upon the day. All the motion of the living world above and the worm-turned earth below and the breath of life rushing from warm to cool, from damp to dry, adds up to a seeming stillness, a closeness to silence in which one may be wise, be idiot, be almost nothing. If not for the faint tapping, heard and then not heard, and then the man—it is a man—turns to the sound, which is where it is not, and turns again, to where it is not, and turns again; but the knocks have stopped.

He sits on a cool, slate bench and pulls on his socks and boots, then, standing, raises a left-hand L of thumb and forefinger to the white O of the sun, and reaches around the sky with the memory of the sound and, again it comes as a *tap, tap, tap*. Across the field Lo walks, crossing ridges of newly-turned soil, birds dip their olive beaks and lift their pied tails; hopping, swinging, flighting ceaselessly, feasting on tiny seeds and beetles.

Heat rises up from the dirt in fat waves that are visible, not in themselves, but because Lo's sight through them is warped and rippled; nothing solid moves; nothing at all. Noticing this Lo stops and considers his clothes; green, heavy, folding over his mass, touching him in a way that could be disallowed as excessively intimate, as meaning that things have claims over selves that they should not have; but they do. And a *dat, dat, dat* sounds, only a little louder given the distance he has travelled. The sun is in itself, pressing hard against the sky, being orange, and beneath, at the field's end, a copper river runs; loud at once, thick and reaching up its banks; there are ranks of sharp, black trees beyond this and beyond and beyond a blue mountain dabbed on the horizon.

Lo walks on and sings and the words run backwards out from his mouth in coloured ribbons and back into his mouth; or so he sings—the song being a song of a voice both pressing outwards and being drawn from the air; taking its many textures and scents and shaping words from there that fly out in coloured ribbons. The words are: 'one day I will be.' And there is no melody as the words are both words and music.

He raises his hands, palm out, and falls flat onto the river still singing and is carried across on the fast flow of thin mud, sticks, window frames, fenders, boots, dresses, disposable razors and long-playing records. He rolls his body and stands, dry, on the other side where the earth is blue.

The black woods shoulder together, swaying and cracking, from time to time they flash white with lightning. Lo skirts the trees, averting his eyes but seeing the blanking seizures reflected in his polished boot-caps.

There are no roads and Lo has gone past his furthest

boundary. The land out here is untilled; on the surface fragments of porcelain, shards of twisted metal; chunks of masonry in blocks and cones are risen in the dry ground; where the land falls away irregularly are great circular hollows filled with stinking green water, floating over which are violet clouds of midges that gather round his ears and neck, dancing on their tiny feet but not biting. Lo stays his hand, deciding neither to kill nor to provoke them and as he passes by the sound returns. This time as a wetter *thap, thap, thap.*

Lo hears the gasping and slurping of feet or mouths; many, many of each—two to one; but he sees no one except what he imagines of many, many people striding sexless towards the mountain and Lo wonders if he might be one of these phantoms but senses his head thinking, his trunk big and loose, his delicate fingers flickering at the ends of his arms and decides that he is curious; real.

The wind works percussively through the grasses, short and tall; a music complicated enough to seem random, progressionless, alive, machinic, marine, unintended; restful. The air changes direction and there's a sudden stink of estuarial mud. Lo looks around even though he knows the river is behind him. Gulls are nowhere in sight but he imagines their white evacuations falling from the sky, their cries, cracked, trapped in a bottle, the tips of their hooked, yellow beaks stained scarlet-orange. Lo turns the sky over by lying down and the grass sizzles and the not-there gulls grow frantic and silent; as the birds wheel above, their stone eyes shrink and tumble from their sockets, scattering down into his hair, eyes and mouth. Lo rises spitting out the eyes and at the end of the sky sees three mountains, not one, that might be purple or red or brown.

Lo's first new steps are loud and beyond them is the skitter and pound of other feet and a long, wavering roar. On a large green, boundaried with long, proper lines of white paint, people become more and less themselves by gathering as a crowd, shouting, and on a small platform, like a table, draped with a pale canvas, like a table cloth, two women, naked but for black aprons tied in front with red bows, face each other stamping their feet and grunting. One slaps gently, more a stroke, the other floats a measuring punch towards the chin and withdraws her arm. The women each make a solid, low, broad-legged stance a few inches apart from one another and begin to rock from foot to foot in a counter-motion, shoulders rising and falling, breathing irregularly through the nose and out of the mouth until they find each other's rhythm.

The crowd silence themselves.

The women belt each other with well-moulded fists, left then right; skin bursts soon around the eyes, cheeks and lips split, noses crack, creamy blue-white milk pours down their heads and arms staining their aprons. The crowd are screeching and crying like colicky babies. None of them can make words.

The punching is heavy and continuous and the canvas becomes soaked, the milk washes to the edges and the spectators get on their hands and knees and crawl forwards, pushing their heads to the platform and, with teeth and gums, clamp to suck. They settle and quieten.

There is room for everyone.

Lo gazes up and sees a woman taking off a black apron. She looks tired.

The canvas is dry. The crowd stop sucking and stand up one by one and turn towards the mountains and the *chab, chab, chab.*

'I worried that I'd be overdressed,' says Lo.

The woman looks down at herself and laughs.

'Everyone has to go now. I know why but I don't *really* know why.'

'I've thought that often… It seems a shame now that we've just met.'

'You knew me before.'

'I know, but you were quite different.'

'Not so different.'

'And so was I.'

And now?'

'Now we're not so different.'

'Goodbye.'

Lo feels a breath in his legs and he stretches off through the crowds joined by other crowds all heading across a stony plain to a forest. Up above the out-in-the-open bruise-coloured clouds get over-heavy and begin to make torrents of rain. Some of the people are dashed to the ground while others walk on amused or saddened, or feeling blessed or lucky or pleased with their good judgment. Some of the battered sodden get to their feet and carry on, while others remain, clinging to the dirt, immobile.

The stones and weeds glitter.

There are indirections in the woods and people can be an arms breadth away from one another without realising.

Beech and oak and elm make up the forest, with pine interlopers planted and forgotten, ferny undergrowth and brackish streams that run clear in places where the water tumbles down rocky beds. People crouch and sup. Shafting sunlight drops into the open where there is a clearing and some gather to talk.

Lo stands back to listen.

'In my house I have a chair next to the fireplace that's like the only place in the world.'

'When I go to work I miss my kids and, for a moment, when I see them again at the end of the day I miss them even more.'

'Every night I would feel her hand on my forehead just before I fell asleep.'

'I have a shed on my scrap of land and when I'm not digging or weeding, or what have you, or if it's raining fit to flood the world, I brew up and then I just sit there and look out at nothing in particular.'

'The two of us going around the house at the end of the day, unplugging, closing windows, locking up; and then we meet, maybe, in the dark at the foot of the stairs; but I can still see her eyes, see. That's the best.'

'We leave each other alone for the most part. It's better that way.'

'I re-decorate the bedroom every couple of years but always the same colours. We like it the way it is.'

All the men sit; on rocks, on tree trunks, on grass, and some close their eyes the better to feel the sun on their faces.

Lo is one of these men.

An old one rises, exclaiming wordlessly; among them in the clearing is a stag, stamping, snorting, turning; heat and a meaty odour rising around the beast; it thumps into the wood and after, at speed, cutting across and across each other come four hinds; and hard on them countless long-limbed, quicksilver hounds; heads raised or pressed to the lower foliage; yapping or silent. Lo watches their faces for smiles—they run past without any.

Everyone takes to their feet and passes through the trees. Persistently now there is a beat and a *snap, snap, snap*; a *thrap, thrap, thrap*. The wood's edge is thickened with chest-high brambles and Lo, and the others, push their way through; parting the sharp-spined boughs with their toughened hands, avoiding the springing rods that slash back at face height; still clothes and skin are lashed or gripped, shins and backs and cheeks are striped with stinging lines.

Lo breaks out unmarked. There is a tower that is an axe, three mountains and a twitching hillock. The air is sweet with honey and bitter with iron. Crowds of men shuffle where they stand. A body flies up into the air, howling, his clothes flake away and fall to the ground, the axe swings *chuh, chuh, chuh*; blood, viscera and shit spray the air; arms, legs and trunk dump onto different mountains and as they separate the penis and scrotum fly too and flop onto the hillock. The head drops onto a pile behind the mountains.

Another man loses his footing on the ground and the axe pivots and rolls, making the parts. The blade is double-headed, clean but not shiny, the shaft made from a single piece of wood. Lo imagines the tree from which it must have come, a cloud-reaching tree as old as dry land; a tree filled with sunlight, sap pulled from the lower earth, boughs and limbs that nodded, heart-shaped, serrated leaves that trembled while the trunk stood almost still in a high wind that crossed the plains from the early ocean.

The head thumps onto heads and another man rises into the sky. He calls for his mother. She doesn't answer.

Lo runs from man to man touching hands, shoulders; his mouth dry, unspeaking, his eyes asking and not finding. The ones become rising hundreds, thousands, tens of thousands; become parts; become rising mountains that settle and compress, finding an angle of repose. Lo turns to the forest but the bramble breaches have closed. No more men come through; the fields are emptying, the sky darkening. The axe swings and the ground drinks up the gore; froth floats on the earth.

The woman in the black apron appears in the sky, floating. She calls out, raises a hand and vanishes.

Lo is alone with one man who turns to shake his hand. Lo reaches and the man's heels are where his face was and the last of him is scattered.

Lo removes his boots; strips off. Rain falls and it is clean and warm. The axe stops moving and Lo dries in the new sun that appears over the mountains. And Lo rises slowly and the axe cuts him and the limbs go to rest and his head falls onto the tallest peak and it coughs and spits and raises its voice and sings:

'One day. One day I will be made whole.'

A Fine House

The Irish & Their Bungalows by Oliver Farry

I was two years old when I saw what was going to be our new house, and it is one of my earliest memories. We were living in rented accommodation—an old Victorian terraced house—in my father's native village, Ballymote, County Sligo, and by the time my parents had managed to scrabble together the means for a mortgage there were three children —my newly born younger brother, my older sister and me. One Sunday afternoon in November, my mother's aunt and uncle were visiting from Mullingar and my father offered to show 'Uncle Mick'—a man we all loved because of his amazing ability to perfectly replicate the sound of almost any farm animal—the new house that was then under construction. I must have canvassed strongly to be brought along, probably by threatening to cry, and I was allowed come.

The new house was located on the eastern edge of the village, no more than a five-minute walk away, surrounded on three sides by fields, as it still is today. The original intention on the part of the developer was to build a mini-estate of a dozen or so houses but by the time building had started, the recession threatened by the oil crisis of a few years before had become a reality. Families began returning to England and elsewhere as the jobs dried up in Sligo. Only two of the planned houses would be built, ours and the one next door, which was to be occupied by the Kennedy family, who, like my parents, still live there today. I grew up, then, on an unfinished housing estate, looking out onto fields that were mostly untended, except in the summer when the developer, who was also a small farmer, would save hay. When I was old enough to understand things such as metaphor I thought this a good one—if not exactly sure for what—and I resolved to use it in a story or a screenplay someday. Unfortunately, Atom Egoyan's 1991 film *The Adjuster*, set on an unfinished suburban estate in Toronto, beat me to it.

The house was still a long way from being finished that November evening, though the roof was on and the floors had been laid. The only light came from naked bulbs that glared harshly in each of the rooms. Curls of uniformly perfect pine shavings littered the cold concrete floor. The inky darkness of the night (I have never in my life seen skies as profoundly black as during a Sligo winter) hulked just outside the windows, which were, to my untravelled eye, enormous. The night nudged the panes, just as I would discover a dozen or so years later at school, as it did in 'The Love Song of J. Alfred Prufrock,' a maleficent thing seen through those huge uncurtained apertures that dominated the front and the back of the house. And the front and rear of the house were much longer than the one we were living in at the time; in addition to this there were no stairs in what was to be our new home. We were moving into a new type of house, with a strange name: a bungalow.

That name 'bungalow' came into English originally from Hindi and its meaning in that language was prosaic, being attributive to the housing styles of Bengal. Those Bengal-style dwellings, cheap and easy to construct, were used by the British colonial power to house its soldiers in the days of the Raj. In the late nineteenth century demobbed and retired officers brought the style back to Britain but while it had a brief period of popularity in the latter part of the century, it never really caught on in either Britain or on its neighbouring island. In the 1970s that all began to change in Ireland.

Work on the house dragged on and our move didn't take place until the following June, a few days before the World Cup final between Argentina and the Netherlands. According to my parents, I kicked and screamed as I was bundled into the car to begin the shortest of house moves. I would spend the next fifteen years of my life in that house, though, in retrospect, it seems like it was a lot longer. The construction was not yet complete; the builders maintained a presence for a few months, setting up camp in the garage while they laid the tarmac drive. They had their own kettle with which to make tea—which I seem to remember thinking was luxurious—and they ate either corned beef or salami sandwiches, both of which they called 'mate.'

The driveway subsided, so did the floor of the kitchen, and the situation was not rectified for a long time after. To say the house was jerry-built would not be a wild exaggeration and a number of improvements were necessary in the years that followed. In 1985 we got patio doors that were sold to us by the only living professional footballer I had ever met: Paul McGee, formerly of Queens Park Rangers and capped fifteen times for Ireland. True, by then he was playing for Galway United and earning most of his money from selling windows and doors, but he had played for Ireland against Kevin Keegan's England at Wembley. Later, while Ireland were performing heroics at Italia '90, the attic was converted and three new rooms added to the structure. Both the walls in my bedroom and the scullery, which had been built of cavity blocks, were dry-lined, and the persistent problem of dampness resolved.

Our house was within the town limits, which I imagined were set by the position of the welcome sign on the approach road, but surrounded by fields and with a few of the rolling drumlins that our part of the country was famous for in the school geography books. Because of this location I was never sure if I was a 'townie' or a 'country.' When football games would be played in the schoolyard between the two, I would plum for the country, out of contrariness more than anything else, so I would line out alongside all the farmers' sons, many of whom couldn't kick snow off a rope. Frank McDonald, recently departed environmental editor of the *Irish Times*, and a trenchant critic of bungalows and the 'one-off planning' that has facilitated the construction of many of them, has written that the first major effect of the spread of bungalow-building across the country was to suburbanise the countryside, leading to a land where the town never ended and the country never began. Not that distaste at unchecked rural development is anything new: Michael Collins noted in 1922, shortly before his death: 'the fine, splendid surface of Ireland is besmirched by our towns and villages—hideous medleys of contemptible dwellings and mean shops and squalid public houses.'

McDonald's point considered, the house I grew up in was an 'ethical' bungalow, if it may be so called, as it was located in the semi-urban environment that good planning would call for it to be. It might not have been a beautiful edifice but it did at least fall within the town's boundaries, was originally intended to be accompanied by a dozen or so other houses and, most crucially, it was linked with the village's sewage system rather than to an independently maintained septic tank, the prevalence of which has caused untold environmental damage to groundwater sources in rural Ireland.

I had no particular love for our bungalow, or any other bungalow for that matter; they were simply the most practical option for dwellings in Ireland at the time. I never thought of them as either ugly or beautiful, but then there are few people anywhere in the world fortunate enough to have lived in domestic surroundings that might be considered idyllic or beautiful. Many Irish, though, thought of bungalows as admirable, if only because they conferred a certain patina of prestige, a sense of modernity and of financial well-being—and well-being, for most people in Ireland throughout the 1980s, was the best you could expect in life. Bungalows were built by anyone who could afford them, from farmers to public servants, from small businessmen to teachers, such as my parents. All but a few were built to prefabricated specifications and many looked identical. The source for many of the designs was a book, first published in 1971, with the ingenuous title *Bungalow Bliss*, written by an architect from County Meath by the name of Jack Fitzsimons a man who was later to become a Fianna Fáil senator and an unlikely anti-bloodsports campaigner. (The first edition of the book was printed in a garden shed in Drumcondra, adjoining one of James Joyce's numerous homes, which features in *A Portrait of the Artist as a Young Man*.) There was no bookshop in Ballymote, only two small newsagents, and there were rarely books to be found in either of them. One book that was on the shelves for years though, strapped in behind the elastic ties in Cassidy's newsagents alongside copies of *Ireland's Own*, the *Farmer's Journal* and the *Sacred Heart Messenger*, was *Bungalow Bliss*.

The bungalow might have been introduced to Ireland by way of the British Empire but the main impetus behind the blaze of one-off housing came from across the Atlantic. More than anything else, the houses that were built from the 1970s on resembled—or at least in a cut-price fashion —the spacious suburban houses that the cousins of many Irish people had come to inhabit in the post-war United States. Low, single-storied dwellings with a stretch of lawn and a generous drive in front, the only major difference was that the Irish bungalows maintained fences, or, more commonly, low surrounding walls, as, unlike suburban Americans, their lawns were at the mercy of stray cattle. This, too, was responsible for the ubiquitous cattle grid placed over the gateway threshold to deter any adventurous bovines. In the same way that our family, and, no doubt countless others, received the hand-me-down clothes of their older American cousins, the Irish people received hand-me-down American planning and the untrammelled sprawl has continued to this day.

Fitzsimons' book itself is an ostensibly benign expression of civic architecture. While he undoubtedly knew that he stood to do very well out of the prospective spread of buildings based on his designs, Fitzsimons also presented a bright-eyed altruism—akin to Graham Greene's Quiet American. In the introduction to his book he quite sensibly advises his readers to 'engage an architect' if they can afford it, before proceeding to accept that many people would avoid the 15% extra cost by copying his own cheaply available designs, of which there were sixty. The bonhomie of the introduction to *Bungalow Bliss* goes so far as to give a wryly tacit approval to the government's floor area limits for grant entitlement as a type of non-sexual contraception (to encourage smaller families). Fitzsimons signs off with a wish that the prospective family would 'live happily ever after' in their new house and he also asked them to send them 'a snap of the building,' as if the new homeowner were someone the architect had met on holiday at one of Ireland's windswept seaside resorts.

The success of *Bungalow Bliss* and several other imitators such as Ted McCarthy's *The Irish Bungalow Book* (1979) led to a rash of bungalows being erected across the country, many of them privately built over the course of a few months with the help of family and friends. The book's fifth edition published in October 1975, the month of my birth, also came with the imprimatur of the then Minister for Local Government, Jimmy Tully, in whose Meath constituency Fitzsimons lived and worked. In his preface Tully declared that 'it is heartening that the pace of building shows no sign of slackening.' (Tully would later, in his capacity as visiting Irish Defence Minister, escape death sitting just a few feet away from Egyptian President Anwar Sadat as Islamic Jihad gunmen sprayed the president with bullets, on my sixth birthday, as it happens.) The bungalows were popular because they were relatively cheap (even our house, which was contracted, and designed by an architect, cost £19,000, which even in those days was not an enormous sum). Few people thought of the aesthetic effect of the housing —less were probably even conscious there was an aesthetic effect. The paramount concern was of owning a home, something that was of particularly high importance for an Irish rural population that was still only a generation or two from the peasantry. Gladstone's Purchase of Land (Ireland) Act of 1885, following the Land Wars led by Michael Davitt and Parnell, started the redistribution of small plots of land to previously tenant farmers and the new proprietors zealously took to their new status as landowners. At the height of the economic boom, Ireland had, at 83% home-ownership, the highest such rate among OECD countries, a figure that had, by 2011, slumped to 69%.

It did not take long for people to object to the flurry of bungalows that spread across the country. The new buildings were reviled by many, though these were mainly people from outside Ireland or Irish people that didn't live in bungalows themselves. I remember reading a letter to the editor of the *Irish Times* in the early 1990s, from an English woman—whose name was sufficiently remarkable for me to note her later career as a novelist—deploring the epidemic of bungalows with their 'gravel drive scars' defiling the Irish countryside. What I saw as the arrogance of this woman hurt; what did she expect us to live in? Mud huts? Cabins? In her letter she had suggested using many of the fine quarries that one sees the length and breadth of the country, which was a recommendation to eat cake if there ever was one. The only people that had stonework on their houses were doctors, solicitors or other such professionals and even they only used it as cladding, the rest of the structure being made of concrete blocks like any of the humbler houses in the area, and the additional stonework scarcely made the houses any more attractive. No, there was no prospect of building a stone house. Nor mud cabins either as the experience of one Dublin architect showed. The said architect jokingly applied to construct, on the Lake Isle of Inisfree, 'a small cabin, of clay and wattles made, with nine bean-rows and a hive for the honey-bee.' He received a po-faced refusal from Sligo County Council, which may or may not have been aware of the provenance of the lines, but had by this time begun to take a firmer line on granting planning permission in scenic locations. The architect keeps the refusal framed on his office wall.

The historian Kevin Whelan has remarked upon how Ireland is structured both spatially and psychologically like a Russian doll: first there is the national territory, then the four provinces, then the counties (which, in the Republic, with the exception of Dublin and Tipperary, are still administrative entities), then the parishes, then the townlands and finally the private plot of land. People will refer to others at a distance, starting with a man from another townland, such as Clúid, Emlaghnaughton or Ardnaglass in the parish where I grew up; even someone that has moved from a neighbouring village will be considered by some to be a 'blow-in.' The only aesthetic judgement that was ever proffered on housing by people in the west of Ireland was that somebody had built a 'fine house,' 'fine' being a moral judgement as much as anything else, an indicator of material rude health.

As the London woman that wrote to the *Irish Times*,

many tourists abhorred the ribbons of bungalows that were spread among the previously unspoiled stretches of land. Most of the houses gleamed brilliant white against their background of sodden, jagged pasture and raw heath, their bug-eye windows agape, looking onto the road, cheap dry-dash finishes and orange Wavin drainpipes further dulling the visual impression. The windows, though, were the most remarkable things about the bungalows. All of a sudden windows got wider; it was as if Irish homeowners suddenly wanted to view the world outside in widescreen. Gone were the lace curtains that allowed a greater degree of furtive snooping—famously recounted in Brinsley McNamara's 1918 novel *The Valley of the Squinting Windows*. The new long windows afforded grand, elongated vistas to the bungalow dweller, sometimes it might be of sumptuous landscape, as was the case with our house, from which we could see Keash Hill, famous from the ancient Celtic sagas of Diarmuid and Gráinne—the pair fled here when on the run from Gráinne's betrothed, Finn McCool, and her father Cormac Mac Airt had been raised in one of the hill's caves in Romulus & Remus fashion by a she-wolf. Sometimes the view might simply be of a front lawn that was invariably a pride and joy second only to the house itself. The irony is that many people located their houses in certain places to drink in what they no doubt recognised as beautiful scenery, while simultaneously scarring the same landscape.

But there was also a hubristic, Promethean nature to much of the building; many houses were built on ridges with their windows and driveways facing roads, displaying the new house—if not quite a new-found wealth—to those that passed. As with any form of hubris, it was misguided as houses built without any shelter were, of course, prone to heat loss in the windy winters, without the protective buffering offered by trees or hillocks to the farmhouses of previous generations. Frank McDonald, in his now-famous series of *Irish Times* articles from 1987 'Bungalow Blitz,' fulminated against this trend of building to face the road, claiming that the 'wild individualism of the Wild West' had turned into 'rabid individualism' in the West of Ireland, that the insensitive location of many of the bungalows was a 'screw-you' to the outside world, a two-fingers up to the environmentally-concerned. McDonald's language was intemperate and erroneously ascribed mean motives to ordinary people, but he was right about the desire to master the surrounding countryside. An outsider might have possessed the critical distance to see the developments for the eyesores that they were; the locals, on the other hand, saw the countryside as a place to dwell.

In some parts of the country, such as Clare, for some reason, pastel colours were popular—the sight of green, pink and yellow buildings would punctuate the drive down to Limerick. In the nineties as the economic boom took hold the bungalows got bigger and bulkier, adding floor upon floor to the original 1970s model that by now seemed puritanically restrained (a Swedish girlfriend of mine compared some of them to JR's Southfork ranch). But the sight of bungalows in the countryside did not sicken all visitors: in the early nineties, an amateur football team from Northwich, in Cheshire came over to Ballymote to spend a weekend and play a friendly match. As well as being thrilled to see the Atlantic Ocean on their visit they were also impressed by the large, bright housing they saw on the bus journey down from Dublin. I can imagine that working-class lads that grew up in two-up two-downs or who now lived in featureless suburban estates might have been surprised by the apparent luxury that Irish people lived in, in these large exotic houses, that were much less widespread in their own country.

Amid all the objections to what many saw as the destruction of the natural environment, some local authorities began to take a tougher line on planning applications; the lack of proper planning procedures being applied was the chief cause of much of the indiscriminate one-off housing. Some councils, such as Cork County Council, were more sensitive to the problem than elsewhere, while others, such as Sligo applied a selective policy of planning restriction, forbidding construction in some of the more popular scenic areas, places like Glencar and Knocknarea. An Taisce —Ireland's National Trust—also began to campaign against one-off housing and to oppose certain planning applications. Members of An Taisce have been vilified by rural Irish people for their often well-founded objections, and the same rural folk have claimed persecution at having been refused permission to build on land given them by parents or other relatives.

Today a debate rages between the conservationists and the planners on the one hand and developers and rural politicians on the other, the latter often pulling strings to advance planning permission for constituents. The division between the two camps is often clear-cut: the conservationists are portrayed as snobs out of touch with the reality of rural living, while those wishing to build see themselves as the little man fighting against urban elitism and restrictive bureaucracy. The pro-bungalow lobby, among its number many members of Fianna Fáil with close ties to both builders and auctioneers, has used cod-historical theories about dispersed settlement being prevalent among inhabitants of Ireland since the early Celts, and it has also employed populist rhetoric to oppose suggestions of importing sensible planning measures from Canada, continental Europe and, the greatest sin of all, Britain.

While local culture was evoked as a rationale for continuing to build bungalows, the reality was that the short-term interests of certain sectors of society were the ones that drove this anarchic development. While people naturally want to build as close to their homeland as possible —and few can afford, or desire, to build anything more prestigious than a bungalow—it is the developers and the auctioneers that profit from unscrupulous rezoning of land and laissez-faire planning. There are also farmers, who, tempted by the opportunity to make a quick killing by selling off land that has been rendered unprofitable by diminishing returns on dairy and beef produce, sell land on having secured the planning permission that they only by law are entitled to build upon.

The damage done by one-off housing runs far beyond the scarring of the landscape too. According to McDonald, [1]the public costs of installing services for one-off dwellings

---

1 Frank McDonald and James Nix, *Chaos at the Crossroads* (Gandon Editions 2005)

is exponentially higher than for buildings grouped in even small urban areas. Similarly, the scattered dwellings have produced a dependence on private car use, which, as well as having its obvious environmental effects, is beginning to affect obesity levels among the generations of local people that grew up in bungalows. American experience is being replicated in more ways than one.

A 2007 Environmental Protection Agency report[2] stated that 36% of group water schemes in rural Ireland are infected with e-coli. One of the chief causes of this is the proliferation of inefficient and under-maintained septic tanks, and every few years people in towns and villages in the west of Ireland are advised not to drink the tap water because of the high risk of infection.

Though many Irish people—including some that grew up in them—have fallen out of love with bungalows, they continue to be built, cursorily impeded only by planning restrictions. Meanwhile the small towns have themselves come to be suburbanised, in the way that was originally envisaged with the building of the mini-estate on which I was supposed to have grown up. Ballymote has seen its population double, as the fifteen-mile journey to Sligo town has been cut to fifteen minutes by improved roads, making it a more attractive location to commute from. Curiously, the house I grew up in is still in much the same physical location as it was when it was built almost thirty years ago, still surrounded by fields on three sides.

When the bottom fell out of the housing market in 2008,

---

2 Environmental Protection Agency, *The Provision and Quality of Drinking Water in Ireland* (2007)

bungalows were replaced as *bête noir* by a planning catastrophe which, ironically, had it been properly implemented, might have spared the Irish countryside the bungalow blight. Towns and cities across Ireland found themselves with undersubscribed, often unfinished, developments—the notorious ghost estates. The metaphor I had imagined as a teenager became a ready-made one for the country's calamitous crash, as everyone from the *Guardian* to the *New York Times* plastered wide-angle shots of abandoned new homes on their front pages, preferably with wild horses in the foreground to accentuate any misty Celtic ambience. Many of the estates were conceived as suburban extensions of small towns, eating into the countryside but, in theory at least, being a more economical use of land than one-off housing. Many of them, though, were in truth no better than the much-reviled bungalows: hobbled together with as little regard for aesthetic value, and small and squat in comparison. Another letter to the *Irish Times* printed when the builders' credit had not yet run out suggested that we had not advanced too much with our attitude to either planning or housing: a Dublin architect wrote of the remarks of a visiting Dutch counterpart on the new housing estates in West County Dublin, Meath and Kildare. The Dutchman was impressed by the standard of social housing that the Irish authorities were building, only to be told by the embarrassed Irishman that what he saw was private, and not social housing. That anecdote is indicative of a social outlook that informs both the disdain that the urban middle-classes feel for the bungalow phenomenon and the pride that the rural lower middle-classes feel for their own houses.

It also explains why the working-class lads from Northwich were so impressed by the endless string of Irish bungalows they saw on their visit. Nobody was using the same aesthetic compass.

My attitude towards bungalows changed after I moved away from Ballymote, but the growing awareness that visual culture did not have a strong foothold in Ireland rendered me resigned in the face of what many people viewed as environmental vandalism. I spoke to Frank McDonald and he was similarly resigned, saying that 'only when bungalows become as environmentally unacceptable in Ireland as SUVs have become in southern California will things begin to change.' By then, it will be too late anyway. In fact, from a simple visual perspective, it is already too late: the landscape has been irrevocably altered. The feeling I have nowadays is one of sadness that the Irish countryside has been changed in such a radical, and none too pleasing, fashion. The west of Ireland has, since the Celtic revival of the late nineteenth century, been the locus of Irish identity and the model for the ideals of national purity and even the idea of the rugged Irish character, and now it is been slowly eroded by dwellings that intrude upon the landscape like the clutter of Seán Hillen's gaudy photomontages.

Personally, I can live with the bungalows themselves, and the fact I grew up in the West means I can't view them with the same damningly critical eye as outsiders or planning and architectural professionals do, but the feeling of what the countryside might otherwise look like is overbearingly lamentable. I return home at least once a year to the bungalow I grew up in. It is a more comfortable house now than back then, but growing up I had just assumed any discomfort was due to the drab constancy of the Irish climate. The house has also got prettier over the years—my mother has worked on the garden and planted trees at the front of the lawn, the once-subsided driveway has been paved like a pedestrianised street. The fields in front, where we used to light our bonfire every St. John's Eve, have been tidied up a bit. Keash Hill still looms majestically in the distance, the row of caves notched high into its forehead and a fake, non-antique cairn sitting atop it. And in the foreground of this vista, resting placidly on a small drumlin a half a mile or so from our own house is the humble gable of a 1970s bungalow, one that, from a distance, looks the part.

Five Poems

Georg Trakl, translated by Will Stone

SILENCE

Above the forest glows
The waxen moon, that has us dream.
By the dark pond the willow
Drips tears soundlessly in the night.

A heart relinquishes life – and gradually
The fog rolls in and rises –
Silence, silence!

THE THREE PONDS OF HELLBRUN

VERSION II

Passing along black walls
The evenings, silver sounds the lyre
Of Orpheus in the dark pond
But spring scatters in droplets
From branches in wild showers
The night wind sounds silver the lyre
Of Orpheus in the dark pond
Dying against the greening wall.

In the distance shine castle and hill
Voices of women who died long ago
Woven tenderly and dark their colour
Over the white nymphs' mirror.
Lamenting their bygone fate
And the day flows into the green
Whispering in reeds, in waves returning –
And with them jokes a song thrush.

The water shimmers greenish blue
And calmly breathe the cypresses
And their measureless melancholy
Drifts upwards in the blue evening.
Triton emerges from the flood,
Decay trickles across walls
In green veils the moon is swathed
And slowly passes above the flood.

DELIRIUM

Black snow that runs from the roofs;
A red finger dips into your brow,
Into the cold chamber blue ice snow sinks
The naked mirrors of lovers.
Into heavy shards the head shatters and senses
Shadow in the mirror the blue ice snow,
The cold smile of a dead whore.
In carnations' scent weeps the evening wind.

IN WINTER

The field gleams white and cold.
The sky is lonely and vast.
Jackdaws circle above the pond
And the hunter steps down from the wood.

In black treetops a silence dwells.
A fire's light darts from the huts.
Sometimes sleigh bells sound from afar
And slowly climbs the grey moon.

Game bleeds softly on the border
And ravens splash in bloody gutters.
Reeds quiver yellow and shoot up.
Frost, smoke, a step in the empty copse.

SUNFLOWERS

You golden sunflowers
Deeply bowed towards death,
You humility filled sisters
In such silence
Helian's year ends
Mountain coolness.

Then with kisses grows pale
His dark brow
Amongst those golden
Flowers of melancholy
By silent darkness
Their spirit determined.

So earnest the summer twilight.
From a weary mouth
Sank into the valley your golden breath
To the place of shepherds
Sinking into leaf.
A vulture rises at the forest's edge,
The stony head –
An eagle's glance
Beams through grey cloud
Night.

Wild glow
Red roses by the fence
Glowing dies
The loving one in a green wave
A perished rose.

I. GO WHEN YOU SEE THE GREEN MAN WALKING—STORIES BY CHRISTINE BROOKE-ROSE

The first story in Christine Brooke-Rose's 1970 collection, *Go When You See The Green Man Walking*, 'George and the Seraph,' opens with an eye. Someone is looking not through, but onto the eye. 'My blue eye, which was myself, blinked again into wavelengths that suddenly rippled with laughter,' and the image vanishes. The speaker is the possessor of the eye, who, as a seraph, is only occasionally embodied, and looks, (from the perspective of what?) simultaneously onto, and through his (her, its?) occasional physical functions. At first it's quite difficult for the reader to orientate her (him?) self in relation to the narrator, and the subjects, and objects he (she? it?) is seeing. 'Naturally,' says the seraph, 'it's all

---

II. EYE AM A CAMERA - A PERSONAL NOTE ON WRITING[2]

...and I've been wondering where one stops and the other begins: I mean seeing, and writing, that is, or perhaps I mean myself, and everything outside, if any such division (or union) exists. For instance, I sit at my writing desk looking out of my eyes and I can see my hands on the keyboard doing something quite mechanical that I cannot exactly put into words. They are doing it almost without my having to think at all. I cannot see my eyes looking, or even my face which must be showing something related to what my hands are doing. I can only, if I cross my

an optical illusion. There is nothing here but a large dark vacuum.'

The difficulties of the eye are at the centre of the stories of Brooke-Rose, who, from 1957 to 2006 published twenty-six books of fiction, theory, and criticism, one for each letter of the alphabet. She addresses these difficulties in her book of essays, *Invisible Author*: 'The difficult thing I have been doing on and off for the last thirty-six years,' she wrote in 2002, 'has a technical name, a lipogram, though I'd prefer the word constraint... a refusal of the narrative past tense.' Consequent upon this constraint is a rejection of the narrative past's prescient closure—'It has to say 'then' for 'now,' 'there' for 'here,' 'the next day' for 'tomorrow'—and its author/narrator's omniscient perspective.

The conventional literary solution to this problem has, Brooke-Rose writes, been the use of 'Free Indirect Discourse' which implies an inner monologue while preserving all the privileges of third party narration (e.g. 'He walked... would

---

eyes a little, see the end of my nose which, a number of people do not hesitate to point out to me, is pointed.

Which bits of me are sitting here?

Who am I where I am writing?

For a long time I didn't want to enter into the world in writing, can still scarcely believe that the world is somewhere that I—folded here inside this thing I mostly cannot see—might be able to take such a form. I am only, after all, quite an ordinary person, and words are things that ordinary people mostly brush off: they're showy, and some of them are dirty, and if they stick, they can be dangerous. Thinking (or perhaps feeling) this, I spent as much time as I could withdrawn into this thing,

he find courage?'), but this does little more than shift the problem. 'Nobody speaks here,' (she quotes linguist, Émile Benveniste) 'events seem to narrate themselves.'

'Who is speaking?' wrote Roland Barthes, quoting Beckett, in his essay, 'Death of the Author.' Brooke-Rose, who counted members of OuLiPo and Tel Quel amongst her friends and colleagues, and who held a post in the literature department of the University of Paris Vincennes at the same time as Barthes was teaching at the Sorbonne, was concerned 'with the whole question of the so-called death of the author and the author's authority.'

This idea translates fairly literally in the *Green Man* stories, many of whose narrators are, if not actually dead, disembodied, abstract, incomplete, mutable, or ill. In 'On Terms,' a ghost haunts a landscape that is ghostly: the 'vampiric jaw' of a Regency crescent where her ex-lover still lives with his wife. She waits outside his house, remembering, or is she experiencing for the first time: 'Have you ever stood

---

using words as little as possible, only looking out at my hands which, on the keyboard, naturally, continued not saying a word but only appearing in front of me, wearing different sleeves, and sometimes nail varnish, or rings, and doing something with words, as if they had a will of their own.

How do the hands do the seeing?

How does the seeing do the words?

Why are the words to do with the eye (and not the ear or—rather more ridiculously—the nose)?

(Do I have to write about the hands at all?)

I type. The words appear, so I must have written them, though

he says once when we are still on terms?' This Schrödinger's cat of a narrator, who may be dead, or may be still living, if only just, on one final trip after overdosing in her rented bedsit, is, understandably tense. Lacking the boundaries of punctuation, she's confused by what is past and what is present. 'Like any constraint,' wrote Brooke-Rose in *Invisible Author*, 'the present tense is a limitation, but one that allows greater concentration on one aspect, simultaneity.' Time cycles; the (possible) ghost haunts her lover's street with 'my repeated presence.' Brooke-Rose was bilingual, a native speaker of both French and English. I think of the French verb, *ressentir*, which ties memory to sensation (and, doing so, points out their Cartesian difference, perhaps). Sensations are recognised because they have been experienced before. 'There are ways to recreate distress,' says the patient's phantom limb that is the narrator of her story, 'The Foot.'

The *Green Man* stories are full of repeat phrases that serve to anchor the passage of a being through time, and also

---

not with the biro which my six-year-old primary-school friend suggested I suck when it ran out so that the ink would flow again, and at that moment I thought I had found the secret of writing.

I asked her whether I should keep this portentous information to myself. She looked at me oddly or, no, not oddly, as though I were odd.

But how can the words belong to anything except the black marks on the page? Once on the screen, I cannot use my hands to scrape them off, and I need another machine to extract them onto pieces of paper. Even transferred to pages, the words still have not gone anywhere near me, or my hands, not even as near to them as they would if I'd used a biro though, even then, its slim length would have separated us, still.

of a being through the body, which it seems to live beside and, though affected by it, touches upon it only at intervals. How does the mind know it is in the body? Mostly, in these stories, by its aches and pains, and by their expression. The body is a symptom, both of itself, and of consciousness, which it in turn partially controls. 'You are cherishing your symptoms my dear says Mr. Poole,' the seductive surgeon in 'The Foot,' to his patient, the victim of a car-crash. 'And are you occupying your mind?' Well, there's a question. Who, in Brooke-Rose's writing, consistently can?

The floating, narrative 'I' of 'George and the Seraph,' which is also, if only sporadically, an eye, so insistent, and yet so absent, tells us that wherever there is some body to look at, there must also be an 'I' to be looking. And eye is a feminist issue. Used to being evaluated by their looks, the eye affects the 'I' of women differently. 'The victim to be haunted is female,' says the phantom limb that narrates 'The Foot,' using a telling passive construction bracketed

---

How am I linked to them? It is through an attempt to link?

Put two words on a screen. There they stand, a hawk *and a* handsaw, *or maybe a* raven *and a* writing desk. *Each pair is nothing alike. They are too far apart even to be a decent joke but, reading, my mind tries to couple them notwithstanding, to find anything that will bring them closer together. I can hardly help myself. I might notice that a hawk and a raven are birds; I could mention that a handsaw might be used to make a writing desk—but, in this case, those are the wrong pairs for these questions. I have, after all, been asked to find out how a raven is* like *a writing desk, whereas I'm looking to know a hawk* from *a handsaw. These are sensible questions, and maybe there is a reason for*

with a future intent. 'It is also important,' Foot says, 'that the victim is beautiful.' Before her accident, the patient was a model, and her looked-over body has given her the 'habit of confidence,' which makes Foot's job of creating the ghost of physical pain a challenge, but the patient's involvement with beauty is also her weak spot. 'I knew then that the visioerotic element of her inner eye would always help me despite her intelligence or perhaps because of.'

'It's best to haunt the intelligent,' says Foot. 'They are not used to responding fully with their bodies and the shock is greater.' The (nameless) patient's intelligence manifests by her ability to tie ideas together: 'She winds me round with other thoughts like boring details of hospital routine that loom larger than life or intrinsic worth and wrap each phantom fibre of me like a medullary sheath at times.' In Brooke-Rose's stories, the body is seldom experienced cheerfully (an exception might be the body caressed by clothes in 'Go When You See The Green Man Walking')

---

their being asked in the world outside the screen where real ravens can be put next to solid handsaws, and flighty hawks removed from heavy writing desks, but it's difficult to pry them off the page so, instead, I notice that the 'aw' in hawk is calling to the 'aw' in handsaw, and that the 'r' in raven is echoed by the 'wr' in writing desk. I might say that, under the right circumstances, almost anything can be made to rhyme, and I could say, as British philosopher and poet Denise Riley does,[3] that rhyme, with its 'tendency to constantly glance over its shoulder and in its rearview mirror,' creates meaning, and that meaning is perhaps retrospective, depending, as rhyme does, on the eventual answer to its questioning first half.

and it is not a path to liberation, but a constraint, a restraint, at best an illusion. Sicknesses of the body, or of the mind, are present in most of the stories, even if only in the background. In 'Red Rubber Gloves,' one telling reference to 'my relapse' (physical, mental? We're not told) immediately complicates the narrator's authority. But Brooke-Rose is not at heart a Gothic, a sci-fi, or a horror writer. If her work contains elements of these genres, it is down to her mistrust of what manifests as flesh. Several of the stories ('They All Go To The Mountains Now,' and 'Medium Loser and Small Winner') —avoiding the 'he said' 'she said' parentheticals proscribed by Robbe-Grillet—consist almost entirely of dialogue.

Words may be a way out of the body.

'As a matter of fact,' says the patient in 'The Foot,' 'I thought, perhaps, I could write.' 'Oh yes,' replies the 'sexy-eyed' surgeon, 'Love stories you mean? Or spies?' But no, she means a translation of her pain into words. 'She is

---

But this is not the question I have been asked to answer. I naturally want to accomplish the task I have been given, of bringing one pair (the raven and the writing desk) together, and of keeping the others - the hawk and the handsaw - apart. The trick, to facilitate both actions, is in negotiating the abyss between them. There may be no way to keep the hawk apart from the handsaw, or to bring the raven nearer the writing desk, but it might be enough to see the gap between.

The eighteenth century philosopher, Johann Georg Hamann, whose double nns stagger through Heidegger's essay, 'Language' (in Poetry, Language, Thought) is, 'still waiting for the angel with the key to this abyss.' The abyss, says Heidegger, is something that opens when

thinking of me to write about in order to get me out of her system as they call it,' says Foot, 'not sympathetic or parasympathetic autonomous but cerebrospinal out of her midbrain on to paper instead of aching there fifty-three and a half centimetres away from her stump.' Words may trump flesh, but they are double-edged. 'Nice word, intractable,' says Foot, 'in view of the way we phantoms infiltrate ourselves down the pathways of pain, down the spinothalamic tract to be precise, not that I'm partial to words, they can be enemies too, but I like words that bring alive my task.'

The phantom Foot is neuter, so far as we know, but falls for his 'victim.' Could Foot be male? Heterosexual seduction (usually via conversation) is Brooke-Rose's paradigm. The patient in 'The Foot' is patronised, and flattered by Mr Poole. Barely compensated for by same-sex friendships, heterosexual romance is almost the only relationship played out in these stories, with the genders so polarised that the lovers are also always enemies. Brooke-Rose, who self-mockingly labelled

---

Hamann asks, 'how do I know reason from *language?' (or maybe he's asking, 'why is one* like *the other?'). Even sitting in front of my screen, folded into this thing with hands on that perhaps contains what I have to say (or maybe it doesn't), I can see there are some problems here. Since when did an abyss have a key, so that it can be locked and unlocked? Surely Hamann should have waited for something more practical, like a writing desk, which he could have stood on to climb out of the abyss, if it wasn't too deep, or which, with the help of a handsaw, he could have made into something that functioned as a ladder, or a bridge. Or maybe he should have asked for the help of a hawk or a raven which, if he had been very light, or if they were very big, might, like the chicken, have*

her sexual/intellectual partners 'mentowers,'[1] concluded, in her fictionalised autobiography, *Remake,* that she, like the narrator of her story, 'The Trogladyte,' who ends up serving the man to whom she also pays rent, was on the whole better off without them.

Many of Brooke-Rose's male characters are doctors, or lay claim to their diagnostic privileges, but the sickness of the doctor is also always a possibility: 'Why don't you go and eat?' says the Scent Maker to his exhausted and eccentric acupuncturist, the eponymous Needle Man. 'I like it when it hurts,' says the Needle Man, as he sticks pins into the Scent Maker's buttocks. Like Foot, the Needle Man is there to produce a physical effect on his victim but, as in 'The Foot,' suffering is a flexible power relationship. The married lover in 'On Terms' says to his ghost stalker that he'd 'got the impression you rather enjoyed' suffering. 'Suffering,' Queenie (fat, then thin) tells her doctor 'friend,' is how she lost all that weight and became a celebrity spiritual guru.

---

been able to get him to the other side. Instead, he waits hopelessly for something that will unlock the rock door of his very solid prison.

The abyss, says Heidegger, goes up, not down,[4] which makes it all the more confusing. What is the point of writing something into existence that does not go the same way as what we have seen?

The Austrian writer Elfriede Jelinek's 2004 Nobel Prize acceptance speech[5] is all about trying to keep up with language, and it is full of words that go nowhere. First, she's doing her hair, then, quite suddenly, she's standing on the side of the road, then she's sliding, in danger of falling into Hamann/Heidegger's abyss. She is not actually in the abyss, but, being out of it—as she's not a dead philosopher but is

Spurious or not (and, as the doctor/narrator is anything but trustworthy, who's to say that Queenie isn't the real thing) the spiritual is opposed to flesh, and also to the 'I' (and, perhaps, therefore to the eye). Brooke-Rose, brought up nominally Catholic, though she claims it never took, said, in conversation with Lorna Sage, 'The most important [religions] advocate annihilating the self in favour of Nirvana, God, thy neighbour, the other, and though none of us succeed in doing that, I believe it's the only important teaching. It's just possible that women have always been slightly better at it because they always have to follow a new clan and learn its language,' language being, here, directly linked to authority, as well as transcendence.

The seraph, in the opening story, uses such earthly language that at first I'd expected the narrator might be George. It (he? she?) employs qualifiers 'of course,' 'I myself' 'certainly' that tell the reader there are some standards to be adhered to, but simultaneously imply the opposite:

---

still quite alive, and mobile with her little quiff and the strange hairball pinned to her blouse, both bobbing as she speaks on video in the full view of the Nobel Prize committee, as well as the little china dalmatian on the table beside her - she is at the mercy of any live encounter between her own language and anything she can see, or be seen by. She admits to being on unsteady ground, is in fact unsure as to whether she is actually on the road or its sidelines, or in the 'sideline pitfall' that she says is always running beside it. Luckily her concern with her locks buoys her up, as some kind of distraction, or deferral. Language makes a leap that is in no way logical. She is not, after all, concerned with finding a key, but she is concerned with how to get from one side to another.

that—unreliable—they need to be constantly reaffirmed. They suggest to us that the seraph, and Foot, are not final authorities but psychological (or spiritual) middlemen; we never glimpse their own watchmen. Perhaps language itself is in control and, if so, what hope is there for either its perpetrators or its victims?

The last, and title, story in the collection, is perhaps Brooke-Rose's most successful experiment with Robbe-Grillet's third person, present tense 'speakerless' narrative voice. A 'foreign' woman (though we identify with her, and, instead, feel her setting's strangeness) buys a new, expensive suit that becomes her: 'It is difficult in a strange country,' says the mysterious stranger who takes her shopping (an angel, a seraph?), 'Or perhaps difficult always yes? You make mistakes? They hang in cupboard not put on for years?' Nevertheless, the woman makes a choice. 'It's a good buy says the elegant foreign lady you will not regret.' The language of clothes as the shrouds of identity has already

---

Before I began to write, I didn't know where to put myself. I tried to stay very still, folded within this thing I could not see thinking, perhaps, that if I could not see myself, then no one else would see me, and I would not be pushed into an abyss. I was 'genuinely tranquil,' as Heidegger says creative stillness is not, whose tension holds it 'always more in motion than all motion and always more restlessly active than any agitation.' If I took no stand on where I was, I would, I thought, be in no danger of falling into any category that I might be unable to climb out of. Denise Riley complains: 'The best-intentioned classifications can result in obscurantism and comedy.' How else though, she admits, but by them, can those already categorised begin to exit them?

been explored in 'The Religious Button,' and 'Queenie.' In 'On Terms,' the ghost lover is 'acting out a fantasy that I can wear my temporal body and move about as if I existed.' Clothes are only a step away from a phantom limb, and can be put on, or off, with similar ease or difficulty.

The woman in 'Go' watches from her hotel window. She sees the green man, who tells her when to stop, and when, to go, when to return, and within what boundaries to walk. The woman watches a prostitute, who is eyed up by the passing men, though she does not look like a prostitute, but is 'scholastic' in a prim navy skirt. The woman watching from the hotel room 'opens the wardrobe and with a screech of agony her image vanishes.' She puts on her new clothes, 'She stands and sees a stranger framed in the strange room itself in the strange city. She opens the cupboard, the stranger screams and vanishes… She looks at the stranger who is beautiful.' The woman in turn descends to the street in her expensive get-up, to feel the caress of its silk, and of

---

How did I get out? Really, I have no idea. Perhaps I climbed up from my writing desk, which, being constructed entirely from words, could be made to fly like a raven. Language was key, even though it did not fit any door in my abyss which, of course did not have a lock, not even the lock of a writing desk, which is frankly usually flimsy and only for show, or a lock of hair which, we all know, means something else altogether, and, unless I were in a fairytale, could hardly be relied upon to get me out into the world. Or rather, I was already there in the world (as all abysses are) but was not able to see myself (or therefore be seen). Words let me let myself be seen and heard, so that when I got out of the abyss I began to wave and shout, 'here I am!' to the people I saw on or by the

the gaze of the men on the street. A man flashes her. 'She inclines her head politely to thank the man for the display.' All Brooke-Rose's themes are there: authority, control, identity, body, vision, choice. 'One could walk miles and miles,' says the narrator, 'obeying the code.'

And, if one does not obey?

In her essay on gender and experimental writing, 'Illiterations,' Brooke-Rose claims there is no space for women within the traditional parameters of artistic practice. 'All she can be is beautiful, and hence not understand beauty,' or create it. Like Foot's patient she must, by force of necessity, write experimentally, which is the only way to defeat, to control, to get past the problem of the eye, which is also the problem of the 'I' and, especially for women, the body.

'Nathalie Sarraute,' says Brooke-Rose in 'Illiterations', might have 'reversed the realist/formalist opposition and said that the true realists were those who look so hard at reality

---

side of the road. Then I turned and looked behind me to see if my abyss rhymed retrospectively, so that I could find some meaning in it, and I saw for the first time that it looked like what it was, that is, something that went down instead of up, or perhaps that's only how it looked from my new perspective because, by now, I am already in quite another abyss, one that, because I can't see that it goes down, must go up. And, because the abyss I am presently in does not rhyme, I wonder whether I haven't got to its second, answering part yet, and if this is something that the things I can see in front of me (my hands, the screen) could provide.

I look at the screen, at my hands. The screen is not a mirror. I cannot look myself in the eye.

that they see it in a new way and so have to work equally hard to invent new forms to capture the new reality,' but 'today one would push it much further and say, not that new ways of looking necessitate new forms, but that experiment with new forms produces new ways of looking, produces in fact the very story that it is supposed to reproduce, or, to put it in deconstructive terms, repeats an absent story.'

Go When You See the Green Man Walking was first published in 1970, the heyday, perhaps, of literary theory as practice. 'Illiterations' was published in 1991, and *Invisible Author* in 2002. 'Difficulty,' wrote Brooke-Rose, in those last essays, 'has now become unfashionable… the pleasure of recognition being generally stronger than the pleasure or puzzlement of discovery.' Contemporary writers, she thought, had constructed a 'blur' (a tellingly visual metaphor) that gives writing the 'illusion' of being easy. 'It's as if literary people didn't want their subject tarnished with difficult thinking,' said Brooke-Rose in her interview with Sage. 'But it'll come

---

That's just as well.
'The inadequacy that enters the writer's field of vision,' says Jelinek, 'is still adequate enough for something.'

back. It always does. In a renewed form—like everything.'
Perhaps now is the time to begin to appreciate the nature of
Brooke-Rose's achievement.

'Let us play,' as she wrote, in 'Stories, Theories, and
Things,' 'there are more theories in heaven and earth…'

ENDNOTES

1 "The old lady is long past needing mentowers." *Remake* (Paul &
Company Pub Consortium 1996)

2 Part II for Rachel Genn: thanks for the Jelinek.

3 Language's 'tendency to constantly glance over its shoulder and
in its rearview mirror… The whole affair runs only by means of a
settling retrospect in which the machinery of the achieved rhyme…
will usually close down the suspended instant, which had to have
been held momentarily ajar.' *The Word of Selves.*

4 'We do not go tumbling into emptiness. We fall upward, to
a height.' Heidegger: 'Language,' from *Poetry, Language, Thought*
(Harper Perennial Classics, translated Albert Hofstadter)

5 http://www.nobelprize.org/mediaplayer/index.php?id=721

At Home in the Unheimlich

An interview with Deborah Levy by Andrew Gallix

At the close of *Swimming Home* (2011), Nina Jacobs confides that she only enjoys biographies once the subjects have escaped 'from their family and spend the rest of their life getting over them.' This confession could be dismissed as of little import, were it not for its strategic appearance in the penultimate paragraph. As well as providing a metafictional commentary on the preceding narrative—and a thematic template for much of Deborah Levy's fiction —it also gives us an insight into the author's writing process. In *Things I Don't Want to Know* (2014), Levy likens her 'literary enquiry' to 'a forest': an annex of the unconscious, where she contrives to lose her characters Hansel and Gretel-style. Everything begins with this sense of disorientation and dislocation; wrong turnings taken and lives gone awry. Deborah Levy is at home in the *unheimlich*—this is where she poetically dwells. I picture her blindfolding her dramatis personae and spinning them round, before peering at them (while paring her fingernails) from behind some venerable tree. I picture it all wrong, of course, because the novelist should also appear blindfolded, or, at the very least, squinting quizzically. She too is at a loss, like the guests in *The Unloved* (1994) who become 'unwitting players' in a drama they remain unaware of. Levy has written about the 'sheriff's notebook' where she was wont to gather 'evidence for something [she] could not fathom.' A crime that was yet to be committed, perhaps, unless the evidence-gathering itself constituted the crime, like that tortured portrait, in *Beautiful Mutants* (1989), which captures by happenstance the very instant when a priest loses his faith. This unfathomable 'something' time-lapsed, over the course of two decades, into *Swimming Home*, as though the Booker-shortlisted novel had been there all along, in potentia, written in the stars or invisible ink.

In their quest to find their own form, Levy's works attempt to throw off the shackles of dominant discourse and narrative determinism. 'What kind of language will (re) create us?' wonders a character in *Swallowing Geography* (1993), before positing that 'classic rules of form and structure' may not 'fit this experience of existing and not existing at the same time.' What kind of speech could express the experience of being spoken when speaking? What kind of narrative could convey the experience of losing the plot as a result of being trapped inside it? Such questions are of particular significance to women, who are specifically referred to in the quotation. A prime example is that of Kitty Finch, who inspires poems in her conventional capacity as a muse, but fails to be recognised as the poet she aspires to be in her own right (*Swimming Home*). The author constantly flags up the essentially fictive nature of notions of womanhood and femininity, even chronicling how she first made this discovery as a child: 'The fact that lipstick and mascara and eye shadow were called 'Make Up' thrilled me. Everywhere in the world there were made up people and most of them were women' (*Things I Don't Want to Know*). Cass, in the exquisite short story entitled 'Cave Girl,' wants—and indeed undergoes—a sex change, not in order to turn into a man, but into a 'pretend woman' (*Black Vodka*, 2013). The thrilling allure of the real (that is to say pretend) woman is probably best embodied by Luciana, whose glacial glamour is part Stepford wife, part femme fatale. She is described in mock-Ballardian terms as an 'Italian suburban supermodel, catwalking the white surgical aisles of hypermarkets in Frankfurt. Clasping soap powder and pâté to her beautiful breasts as if they were Oscars' (*The Unloved*). For her female characters, Levy strives to 'find a language that is in part to do with learning how to become a subject rather than a delusion; unknotting the ways [they have] been put together by society' (*Things I Don't Want to Know*). Monika's subversively made-up face takes self-effacement into camouflage, or even war paint, territory: 'She looks like a Noh mask: black kohl eyes and lips the colour of a recent massacre' (*The Unloved*). The character called The Poet mistresses (as Levy puts it) the art of metamorphosis by turning to advantage her lack of identity as an individual: 'If she had no identity she would have many identities' (*Beautiful Mutants*).

One of the dangers here, of course, is to fall back on clichés about the protean, mutable character of women. Deborah Levy is acutely aware of the archetypal narratives that shape our identity and aspirations, chief among them motherhood. Fairy tales endure in the disenchanted world she depicts, even though they no longer cast a magic spell. Take this example from *Billy & Girl* (1996): 'If Girl had tried to kiss him better, this frog Dad, nothing would have happened. What could Dad have changed into? The world has changed and he needs a new story.' Or this very similar one from *Swimming Home*: 'She had turned into a toad in old age and if anyone dared to kiss her she would not turn back into a princess because she had never been a princess in the first place.' Billy clicks his heels thrice, like Dorothy in *The Wizard of Oz*, but nothing happens. 'Take me away from here. Take me home,' he mimics, before remembering that 'this is home' and that there is no exit. His sister, a connoisseur of 'American sitcom moms,' longs to inhabit a perfume commercial: 'She wants to dream herself into peachness because she wants a happy ending. Like in the ads' (*Billy & Girl*). 'Life is only worth living,' echoes Kitty Finch in *Swimming Home*, 'because we hope it will get better and we'll all get home safely'—an unlikely outcome in the absence of pebbles or even breadcrumbs.

Deborah Levy is one of the first novelists to have truly taken stock of the radical changes, not to say ravages, brought about by the neo-liberal revolution. Her early nineties novels herald our 'age of the migrant and the missile.' They already depict the 'splintered times' we live in 'when whole worlds and histories collide' and everyone is 'separated and afraid' (*Beautiful Mutants*). Stupefied by late capitalism, passengers at airports no longer know if they are 'an arrival' or 'a departure'—if they are coming or going —although it makes little difference when everywhere is a non-place ('Pillow Talk'). Worse still, 'we have been robbed of a language to describe the bewildered brokenness we habit.' Levy's fiction is thus an exhortation to 'leave and learn a new language' (*Beautiful Mutants*) in order to be 'in exile from exile' (*Things I Don't Want to Know*). In this spirit, Gemma writes letters backwards, forcing the addressee to read them 'through the looking glass.' 'Backwards letters are my escape,' claims the little minx—and perhaps ours too. The free bus tour around the Thatcherite enterprise zone turns into a kind of Situationist *dérive* due to the disjuncture between the guide's commentary and the cityscape being travelled through: '…where she said you were, you were not—she'd point at the waterfront and it would be the railway station' (*Beautiful Mutants*). The whole scene feels like a rollicking *Carry On* remake of Marguerite Duras' *Le Camion*. There are more psychogeographical high-jinks in *Swallowing Geography*, when J.K., having established that 'maps correspond to reality as seen at a particular time,' wonders what would happen if she observed 'a number of realities at the same time'…

A couple of hours after *gorse* editor Susan Tomaselli had sent me a message to see if I wanted to interview Deborah Levy, I met up with a friend—Adam Biles—in a Parisian café close to Shakespeare & Co., where we were going to attend a reading by Joanna Walsh. As I was telling him about the interview commission, he pointed out that Deborah Levy had just sat down at a table outside. As we went out to join her, I remembered that line from *Billy & Girl*: 'Life hurts more without magic.' Suddenly, life hurt a little less.

•

In *Beautiful Mutants*, The Poet urges Lapinski to 'ask the present what it's got to do with the past'—sound advice that Deborah Levy follows to the letter throughout her work. Take Nina Jacobs, whose mute conversations with her late father on London buses testify to the porousness of temporal borders. She confesses, in the bittersweet coda to *Swimming Home*, that she has 'never got a grip on when the past begins or where it ends,' thus failing to make it 'keep still and mind its manners.' As a result, the past 'moves and murmurs with [her] through every day' unlike the statues—'forever frozen in one dignified position'—with which society commemorates history. The sudden shift from time to place in the above quote points to the survival of the former in the latter. The angel, in *An Amorous Discourse in the Suburbs of Hell* (2014), hears 'the historic echo of yesterday's lambs' beneath 'the tarmac of the ring road.' In 'Black Vodka,' the hunchbacked narrator muses, as he walks up Exhibition Road, that 'under the twenty-first-century paving stones there had once been fields and market gardens.' Later, in South Kensington's posh Polish Club, he unearths a dark forest, complete with prowling wolf, beneath the plush pink carpet. This primeval forest —rooted in the author's tragic family history, as well as in Dante or grim fairy tales —is, as we have said, the primal scene from which Levy's entire oeuvre seems to draw its inspiration. It finds its fullest fictive expression in Joe Jacobs, whose father 'had tried to melt him into a Polish forest when he was five years old' (*Swimming Home*), but also resurfaces through numerous, seemingly incidental, lupine and sylvan references: The Banker who 'sobs like a wolf cub' at night (*Beautiful Mutants*), Magret's accent that her lover cannot place but 'makes him think of wolves' ('Vienna'), the woods outside Prague whence Alex emerges as Aleksandar ('Shining a Light')... The pivotal road trip in *Swimming Home*, which recurs like some kind of repetition compulsion, establishes a direct link back to prehistoric times: 'Early humans had once lived in this forest that was now a road. They knew the past lived in rocks and trees and they knew desire made them awkward, mad, mysterious, messed up.' When the zoo is torched in

Beautiful Mutants, the gibbons 'make loud whooping calls that echo through the city, into nightclubs and cinemas and traffic jams; the call is 65 million years old…it is answered in the dense forests of the gibbons' origin, it breaks the windows of the local police station.' Like gibbon, like man. Seeing his estranged, abusive father again sends Billy 'primal': 'Whirling through the caveboy vortex into fire, fat and flint. Demon terror' (*Billy & Girl*). A character in *Swallowing Geography*, who has contracted AIDS, recognises that he 'still has the same sort of fears people had in the Iron Age': 'Fear of the dark and certain kinds of animals. Things lurking under the sea, under my bed, inside my skin.' The 'Stone Age girl''s brother would like to ask 'an Ancient' if 'he's scared of the dark things lurking in the sea' like he is ('Cave Girl'). The Banker dismisses The Poet as 'the dinosaur trapped in ice from the age of slow-moving beings' (*Beautiful Mutants*). The alleged 'beast' inside J.K. is described as 'a mammoth, frozen in ice' (*Swallowing Geography*). FreezerWorld Louise, who works in a frozen-foods store, is said to be 'trapped in the ice age because she is frightened of the future. Which is the past' (*Billy & Girl*). It is possibly this terrible truth that explains why we can't see the primeval forest for the ring road—why the presence of the past is swept under the plush pink carpet, or tamed into a genteel doorknob bestiary:

> I have grown to love the bronze doorknobs in the shape of jungle beasts: a lion's head, a tiger, a snake. These seem to me to be caveman icons on the doors of the bankers and dentists who live here, a way of keeping in touch with The Divine ('Cave Girl').

AG Deborah, could you talk to us about the parallel you seem to draw in your work between childhood—which you describe as 'a primitive culture' (*Billy & Girl*)—and prehistory?

DL Well, it's all about attempting a temporal fuse and fizz in the present tense, interrupting chronology: what are we connected to? Of course, like Ballard, who was working from Freud but who was also a futurist, I'm interested in the ways in which the psychological past is preserved in the present—in architecture, commercials, landscape, everyday objects, ideologies, the human body. In my story 'Black Vodka,' I wanted to find a way of getting to twentieth-century Eastern Europe in the twenty-first century: how could I make them happen simultaneously? So I have the male protagonist conceptually roll up the genteel faded pink carpet in the Polish Club, South Kensington, and find a Polish forest in 1942 beneath it. While customers are eating plates of goose and handing their credit cards over to the waitress, wolves are digging up human bones beneath them in the forest. He hears silver spoons stirring cappuccinos, and he hears insects thrumming in the forest. It's tricky to pull this off without it sounding like a fairy tale; it took a few drafts to tune the reality levels. But that's my job, and I'm happy to spend my life solving this sort of problem.

The Polish Club has this sort of time warp about it anyway, because it was opened in 1940 and became the cultural meeting place for the Polish community in exile. I used to take my students from the Royal College of Art there when I taught writing in the Animation Department, and found myself over time beginning to mentally dig beneath the carpet and plot what would become *Swimming Home*—also the hunchback in 'Black Vodka' whose own body becomes a site of excavation.

I believe we are all anthropologists, and the primitive culture we know most about is ourselves—from infancy to adulthood. I have just reread Conrad's *Heart of Darkness*. I'm still recovering. On the one hand, the writing is just incredible: what a piercing record of these depraved white primitives out on the steal (ivory, minerals, oil) in the guise of civilised European gentlemen, yet where Conrad positions himself in all of this is too unsettling for me. I don't understand his intentions. Here is one of my favourite writers, Chinua Achebe, on this matter: 'Conrad saw and condemned the evil of imperial exploitation but was strangely unaware of the racism on which it sharpened its iron tooth.' Steve McQueen's masterstroke in *12 Years a Slave* was to make the cotton plantations of the American South cinematically beautiful, and the picking of it totally brutal. It is my destiny to adapt *Heart of Darkness* for the big screen, and I have a trick up my sleeve to turn the subjectivity in that story inside out. But, you know, if we're looking for a savage culture, why not take the train to Kent, and interview Nigel Farage?

Those who are robbed of their childhood, never grow up: **AG** are they more likely to become writers or artists? Does the writer remain more in tune with that 'primitive culture' of childhood than most other people?

No one is entirely robbed of a childhood: we experience **DL** life in the mindset of our age whether it be two, five, seven or seventy. Oliver Twist had a childhood. So did Jane Eyre. Children are wise because they feel things so intensely. I have never believed in the advanced wisdom of the old —that's just experience, which isn't the same as wisdom. In my view writers can be in tune with anything they like so long as their attention is in an interesting place. It is what we pay attention to that makes a writer worth reading—or not.

AG Writing, for you, is associated with childhood rebellion. You were beaten at school because you never wrote on the first lines of your exercise books. The same thing happens to Philippe in *The Unloved*: 'I had a horror of the top of the page, it seemed to me right to begin a sentence on the second line.' Stanley—the boring accountant of *An Amorous Discourse*, who refuses 'to live in a grey area' or 'read between the lines'—is, naturally, a stickler for methodical page-filling: 'Love must start on the first line / Continue on every line / No line without love.' Could you tell us about this 'horror of the top of the page'?

DL Writing on the top line of the page in those school exercise books, starting in the far left-hand-corner (no margins), working across to the end of the line in the far-right-hand corner (no margins) and on to the next line so that the writing comes out in a dense square block: I just couldn't organise my thoughts like that. There were no spaces or gaps allowed. We were told not to waste space. Starting on the third line seemed a good idea to me—and then there are things called paragraphs, where we might be sinful and leave a little gap, maybe indent half a line, etc. Well, for some reason, we were not allowed to do paragraphs in my junior school. It's odd to think this was probably the moment I truly had some sort of intuition about language and form: I was seven years old, and I know it sounds a little romantic, but actually the anxiety I had about this was quite intense. If you have a facility with words, it's not hard to cover a page, but then I have never thought that writing is about covering a page.

Is the future the past (as it is for FreezerWorld Louise) **AG** because we are condemned to spend our lives trying to get over the traumas of childhood—perhaps even the trauma of being born itself? Billy pictures himself inside his mother's womb, thinking, 'I don't want to be born. I'm never coming out' (*Billy & Girl*). Tatiana, in *The Unloved*, wants to sue her parents 'for being born' and, in the same novel, consciousness is described as a curse...

I regard Tatiana as one of my best characters. Tatiana is the **DL** unloved child, and this makes her very interested in love. As for consciousness being a curse, it costs us to know things: knowledge is not a free ride. Talk to any war correspondent, and they will tell you they have seen things they wish they could unsee. The opposite of this would be what Lacan described as a 'passion for ignorance.'

In *Beyond the Pleasure Principle*, Freud wondered if the goal of **AG** life were not to return to an initial inorganic state. I wonder if this isn't one of the things we don't want to know your work revolves around—*Swimming Home* seems to indicate so...

DL The message in *Swimming Home,* in its exploration of the death wish, is that life must win us back. That uncanny Leonard Cohen song, 'The Night Comes On,' seems to agree: 'I wanted the night to go on and on / But she said, Go back to the world.'

Faber have reissued Sylvia Plath's *Ariel*, in a very nice edition. I know my twenty-year-old daughter enjoyed *The Bell Jar*, so I bought it for her as a small present to put under the Christmas tree. Before I wrapped it I thought I might write a few words inside the book—like you do—so I had a quick browse. Well, I thought I knew all about these sad, brutal, beautiful poems, but they seem to sting me differently in every decade of life. It is incendiary writing. That poem about folding her children back inside herself—it got to me all over again. Plath was at the top of her game as a writer in these poems, yet what she seems to be anticipating is her future suicide. What kind of inscription was I going to write in that book to my daughter? I wanted to make a joke—*Don't try this at home!*—and then I thought, well, there's no way I can write anything in this book: there's nothing to say; no words will do. And that made me wonder how Plath would have spoken to the world about these poems if she had lived. You know, let's say she had a few book tours and readings, and a sweet young woman, like my daughter, in the audience asked her, 'And what were you thinking when you wrote these lines?':

The frost makes a flower,
The dew makes a star,
The dead bell,
The dead bell.

Somebody's done for.

What kind of conversation would have been possible for Plath? These poems feel like the final words and I'm sorry to write this, and wish she had believed the conversation didn't end there.

Time and again, your characters are confronted with **AG** information that is too painful to process. For the protagonist of 'Vienna,' living without his children is 'a grief he knows he cannot endure but he must endure' (which reminded me of Beckett's famous 'you must go on, I can't go on, I'll go on' in *The Unnamable*). The short story 'Placing a Call' opens in similar fashion: 'You are telling me something I don't want to hear. You are telling me the honest truth.' 'What am I supposed to do with the information?' wonders Billy apropos of his mother's absence (*Billy & Girl*). The five-year-old Joe Jacobs faces the same excruciating conundrum when his father informs him he can never go home again: 'This was not something possible to know but he had to know it all the same' (*Swimming Home*). Your own sense of homelessness is described in almost identical terms: 'I was born in one country and grew up in another, but I was not sure which one I belonged to. And another thing. I did not want to know this thing, but I did know it all the same.'

There seem to be two options. The first one is to go mad and be sedated with syringes filled from 'Lethe, the River of Forgetfulness' ('Stardust Nation'). The second option, which you describe in your memoir, entitled—precisely—*Things I Don't Want to Know*, is to write. When you first put biro to paper, as a child, 'more or less everything you did not want to know' came pouring out, but you felt, simultaneously, that writing could provide an 'escape to somewhere better.' Please tell us about your conception and practice of writing from this ambiguous perspective…

DL The writing I enjoy reading is both knowing and unknowing without being faux naïve. There is a sense that the writer herself is discovering something so potent it could just tip her over the edge, but the point is that it doesn't. As Duras points out, the writer has to be stronger than her material. At the same time there is nothing more exhilarating than writing a book. It's not all a downer, Andrew! I think you're in a mournful mood. Let's have a pick-up: do you want a beer, or perhaps a Bloody Mary with horseradish and celery salt?

AG Sounds like I could do with both!

DL In my story 'Stardust Nation'—which is to become a graphic novel, in collaboration with artist Andrzej Klimowski—there are two swans that are always asleep on the moat which circles the psychiatric institution. I had this idea that the water in this moat was Lethe, the river of forgetfulness, and the nurses fill their syringes with it and inject their patients with oblivion. This is not just a surreal image—although I can't wait to see how Klimowski works with it—it is also a critique of medication that coshes the patient into unmemory. I repeat this idea in *Swimming Home* when the Hungarian doctor says to Joe, 'Give me your history and I will give you something to take it away. I'm interested in the ways we forget as much as the ways we remember—or what Freud called simulated forgetting. I'm interested in defeated desire as much as realised desire, and every book I write starts off as an enigma. Writing is sometimes like a snake-charming act: the writer is both the charmer and the snake.

Billy, in *Billy & Girl*, stands in for the writer as chronicler **AG** and interpreter of pain: 'Pain is a black box full of mystery and one day he will unpack it for the reading public.' Is the writer's role (or justification of her calling) to suffer on behalf of the rest of society?

No. That's the job of Jesus Christ, isn't it? **DL**

In your memoir, you relate how your father had advised **AG** you, in a letter, to say your thoughts out loud rather than in your head, and go on to explain that you decided to write them down instead. This put me in mind of Marguerite Duras' remark that 'To write is also not to speak. It is to keep silent. It is to howl noiselessly.' Do you agree with her on this point?

Noiseless howling? Maybe it sounds better in French. Duras **DL** made a beautiful noise in her books, that's for sure.

AG The most famous passage in *Things I Don't Want to Know* is the one where you explain that in order to become a writer, you had to learn 'to speak up, to speak a little louder, and then louder, and then to just speak in [your] own voice which is not loud at all.' It's true that earlier novels like *Beautiful Mutants* or *The Unloved* were characterised by a high-octane spikiness that has gradually given way to a more subdued, but also much more self-assured, narrative voice. Now that you are speaking in your own spellbinding voice 'which is not loud at all' (and which we recognise from readings) —now that you are howling noiselessly and beautifully— people seem to be paying far more attention…

DL I totally stand by the high-octane spikiness of my earliest fiction. You know, I'm so glad I was properly young in that writing and not wearing sensible flat shoes. I made mistakes, there was more work to do. For this reason I'm happy I didn't have a creative-writing tutor telling me to calm down and get to grips with narrative. It would have been better for my career to have done so—but not better for my future writing. I don't regard my books as becoming more subdued, but it is probably true that in a long writing life you gain some things and lose other things.

AG I wonder if the discovery of your 'own voice' isn't also due to the adoption of a less theatrical style. Were you more influenced, in the early days, by your playwriting? Many people who discovered you when *Swimming Home* was shortlisted for the Man Booker, in 2012, had no idea that you had been a successful playwright for many years: did this give you the feeling that you were starting over again as a fiction writer?

Yes, I trained as a playwright. Oddly, my two favourite plays **DL** written in the 1990s, *The B File* (an erotic interrogation of five female personas that has been performed all over the world) and *Honey Baby: 13 Studies in Exile* (performed at La Mama Theatre in Melbourne) are not theatrical at all. Read those plays (*Deborah Levy: Plays 1,* Methuen) and you will see I'm starting to slip into prose. I can't begin to convey how hard it was to be a female playwright in the mid-1980s, writing in the way that I did—yes, the whole gender thing—but mostly because I wasn't writing social realism which was very much in vogue, nor was I writing didactic feminist theatre which was also having a moment at that time. I was much more influenced by Pina Bausch and Heiner Müller than anyone else, though Pinter and Beckett were influences too. Writing for the theatre taught me to embody ideas.

I was giving a reading somewhere recently and a woman came up to me to say she had trained at drama school, and the play she had put on for her graduation show was *The B File*. I asked her if she remembered her lines, and do you know what, she did! She began to recite them to me, there and then, almost word perfect and with such power. That was the biggest tribute ever, because I knew they had meant something to her. The best actors are incredibly open-minded, shamanistic and playful: I loved those qualities in the rehearsal room.

The prose that is most theatrical is probably my first novel, *Beautiful Mutants. Things I Don't Want To Know* is where I pulled open the theatre curtain and switched on the house lights, but obviously that's not the same thing as saying there's no artifice in its construction. There is a peculiar relationship between writers and readers—but then all relationships are probably a bit peculiar, aren't they? For example, I know that Virginia Woolf trusted me when she wrote *To the Lighthouse*. I was never going to laugh at the seriousness of Lily Briscoe's struggle and ambition to create a visual masterpiece. There was no nasty little voice saying to me, *ooh she's a bit above herself, isn't she?* I understood the class analysis Woolf made with the angry student Tansley waiting for his toff tutor to talk to him about his dissertation. I understood that domesticated Mrs Ramsay was Woolf's bid to understand the rituals available to women of her generation, and to have a go at finding something good in them—despite rejecting them herself—via the avatar of Lily Briscoe. I understood that the form of the book was as radical as its content and that Woolf's vision for her novel was complete. That is what a successful writing-reading relationship should be like. Strangely enough, I'm not the biggest fan of Oscar Wilde's plays, although I am a big fan of his sensibility. I feel I have a writerly relationship with him, an attachment to his idea that 'Being natural is simply a pose, and the most irritating pose I know.'

AG Language can take on an Adamic quality for your characters. Its purpose is to 'record and classify' the world, as the narrator of 'Black Vodka' puts it. This often leads to a quasi-Oulipian desire to exhaust reality by enumerating its component parts, as in 'Vienna,' for instance: 'She is Vienna. She is Austria. She is a silver teaspoon. She is cream. She is schnapps. She is strudel dusted with icing sugar. She is the sound of polite applause. She is a chandelier,' and so on until the end of that long, delightful paragraph. The world becomes a kind of litany, as in this example from *Swallowing Geography*:

> In Washington the currency is dollars, the bread yeasted, breakfast waffles and maple syrup, coffee filtered and decaffeinated, golf is being played on slopes of green grass and yellow ribbons hung on taxis. In Baghdad, the currency is dinars, the bread unleavened, breakfast goat's cheese, coffee flavoured with cardamom, foreheads scented.

Ebele always describes J. K. in this enumerative fashion, much to her annoyance, because 'That's what strangers do. When they are in an unfamiliar place they describe it.' This sends us back to the question with which *Swallowing Geography* opens: 'When you feel fear, does it have detail or is it just a force?' Giving detail to fear is an attempt to master it, to defuse its power. Shortly after, Gregory explains why he collected stamps as a young boy: 'It was my way of naming places and conquering the world.' Language, here, is conquest: a means of controlling the world and endowing it with meaning. Jurgen thus views Kitty Finch's poem as a map that will show him 'the way to her heart' (*Swimming Home*). Is this neurotic, stamp-collecting approach a masculine way of writing?

DL I am a stamp collector too—the skill is placing one stamp against another. For myself, when the writing is going well, I love the smell of the smoke! Here are some things I dislike in various types of books written by men. I don't like it when girls and women have no point of view or intelligence or wit or interior life or subjectivity that doesn't always serve the desires of the male world and its arrangements.

My favourite male writer is Ballard—then Houellebecq, which probably contradicts all of the above, but all his characters are so wrecked that I forgive him. I always buy his books in hardback and now we share the same publisher in France, so wish I could read fluently in French because I could get the book for free. I also love Apollinaire and Nietzsche. I've just read Lou Salomé's gentle and fascinating portrait of Nietzsche translated by Siegfried Mandel. He was in love with Lou Salomé (what a beautiful name) who wisely declined his offer of marriage and wrote a book about him instead. And I admire Burroughs, who was endearingly fragile under that stylish hat. When I'm old and grey and have nothing to do except sit in a hot water spring in Iceland entirely naked (apart from my nose jewel) I think I might write about how Burroughs is often misunderstood by the heterosexual men who have been influenced by him. On the other hand I might write a murder mystery set on a cruise ship.

AG It seems to me that there is another conception of writing at play in your work—one which is not concerned with mapping, but with unmapping. In *Things I Don't Want to Know*, you describe how your journey to recovery from a midlife breakdown began when you strayed, as it were, from the straight and narrow, finding yourself in a dark wood: 'The night before, when I had walked in to the forest at midnight, that was what I really wanted to do. I was lost because I had missed the turning to the hotel, but I think I wanted to get lost to see what happened next.' Deliberately wanting to get lost—attempting to escape narrative determinism—is something a character like Madeleine Sheridan could probably never understand: 'It was impossible' for her 'to believe that someone did not want to be saved from their incoherence' (*Swimming Home*). Perhaps there is a kind of writing that does not want to be saved from its incoherence; that shuns the 'why the how the when the who and all the other words [you are] supposed to ask to make life more coherent'...

The writing that interests me lives in this ambivalent **DL** relationship with coherence and incoherence. Duras gets closest to this. A writer like Gertrude Stein is baffling and exhilarating, but mostly baffling—yet I love her anyway, especially the way she drove a motor car without knowing how to reverse. These days my aim is to find an innovative narrative design that snares my own attention, and rewards readers for their attention. It seems to me that in the end coherence is going to win in my books, because it would be dishonest to pretend I have gone through the journey of writing a book and am only left with incoherence. It sounds good, but so far it's not true. I can't stand fake incoherence, or fake coherence for that matter. Back to *Swimming Home*: my point with hyper-rational Madeleine Sheridan is that she might have a point—perhaps Kitty Finch is really very ill. But what is it she is so afraid of? Madeleine Sheridan holds on very tight to a rigid concept of coherence—her knuckles are turning white with the strain. As Disney tells us in the animated film *Frozen*—let it go let it go let it go.

ten thousand tiny spots

Sheila Armstrong

In the city, there are ten thousand thousand mouths. But a mouth is a terrible thing. A gash across the skin; a slit that has been widened and then healed so that two lumps of scar tissue trace the wound on either side. And inside, inside some instinct has caused lumps of calcium and carbon and bone to protrude out, sprouting in some awful facsimile of symmetry; each lump pointing upward, anchored with a cruel hook below the jaw, their surfaces blunted and ground down into flat planes that crush and grind. And the tongue —that flopping, shape-shifting, pocked muscle—oh, the tongue. And surrounding it all is a liquid; not the primordial liquid of the sea, or some fresh mountain spring, but a glooping, filmy lubricant that ebbs and flows like some unholy tide; gushing in the present of an enticing aroma, and fleeing in time of stress. A mouth is a terrible thing. And the things that come out of a mouth—things that are wrenched from a slit in the very self, puked upwards and rolled around those awful teeth and bulbous lips—have no worth, can have no worth when they come from that awful place.

It's the pauses in between that matter.

Coffee swirled around the man's mouth, and he felt it keenly; felt each gollup of fluid swish and blend with his saliva, coating his teeth in a greasy, tacky veneer. That was the sweeteners, he knew. At the coffee counter in the newsagents, there had been a new slot filled with yellow packets featuring a smiling young woman, one of those models that you can't imagine ever having a real life; ever waking up hungover or taking a shit or losing her keys. She was trying to convince everyone who passed by that you should dump a load of this white powder into your coffee and you will magically become that size eight that you were at seventeen, before your tits came in and your arse started to crinkle and bubble under the surface. He wasn't aiming for a size eight, or a young, or middle-aged (or even recently deceased—he knew his limits) Arnold Schwarzenegger. But the sweat patches that began in the embarrassing crease under his breasts were beginning to cause him concern, especially since they showed up if he wore the colour grey. He told himself he hated the colour, but chose grey-tinted clothing too often. Grey should do a better job of camouflage than white or black, seeing as it occupied that middle ground between colours that people had put a name on for fear of it going around unchained. Sometimes it was just ten thousand tiny white spots and ten thousand tiny black spots, laid down in alternating patterns so that the eye did the hard work of mushing them together, and sometimes some faithful dyer, or more likely some faithful machine, had already mixed them together into Cloud Grey or Steel or Metallic Sheen, before dipping the cloth in and letting it soak up the stain. But no, it was the colour that most often let the shame bleed through; outlined sweaty armpits and the nervous wiping of fingers. He decided then and there that he would start running, become one of those people who find joy in exertion, who compare race times and runner brands and muscle supports. If he did so, everyone would look at him, just everyone, and think, doesn't he look well? They'd all see his body grow taut and affirmative and watch as he answered the office phone with one hand instead of two, and they'd all think: doesn't he look well. And then he could look at the pert brunette on the sweetener packet and meet her eyes. He shifted his weight to the other side of his body as the electronic notice board declared the bus was due.

Each person waiting at the stop paid his or her fare in a fumble of coins, except for a tourist who argued with first the machine and then the driver about an expired ticket. None of the passengers on the number seventeen were inclined to acknowledge the others, so they sat on their own, in seats made for two, and refrained from looking outside of a conservative ninety degree field of vision. Some chose to stand and sway in time with the bumps along the road, anchored to the ceiling by yellow flytrap handles. The bus was not full to bursting as it usually was at this evening hour; a twin had pulled up just thirty seconds ahead of it and had taken the brunt of the load. But the brakes screeched horribly at each junction. Those on the back seats were uneasy, raising their faces each time the bus slowed; willing the brakes to sound more like the ageing hydraulics they were, too afraid to look out the window in case they saw toes caught under wheels or little fingers lodged in screw-holes; screams teased out on the evening air as the bus pulled off again.

There was a woman, middle aged, although she seemed nearer to the beginning than the end, one-thirds age, maybe. She bounced a baby on her knee, an infant of indiscernible gender that seemed to find the other passengers' polite indifference fascinating. It stared with eyes that were crusted with old tears and some bovine sleepiness. It did not cry. The mother jogged the child idly on her lap and thought about dinner. There were frozen peas in the ice-box, so that was all right. She felt like a bad mother if she did not provide her children with something green at least once a day. Most of the time she failed, or convinced herself that a smattering of dried herbs on the top of a frozen pizza counted towards her quota, but she had the right idea, or so she told herself. She stared out the window, but the darkening light meant that her reflection kept getting in the way, surging forward and melting away, until she was trying to discern the pub and shop names through an ineffably thin image of her own face, one that would slice and slice her into pieces if it was ever permitted to switch planes and dally in a new dimension.

They trundled out of the true heart of the city and into its arms and legs; through streets that had been laid out crooked, born of some celestial spewing of tarmac. A splash of vodka from a squidgy topped bottle broke free and stained the floor a darker grey as a trio of students —two girls and one hopeful boy—got on the bus and climbed the stairs. Laughter trickled down from the upper level, slopping and overflowing downwards a step at a time, in putrid waves of glee. A twenty-something in a stained hoody and a prematurely receding hairline looked up in barely suppressed rage, furious at missing out on the joke. His hands disappeared into his pockets and the gentle thud of a bass beat rose up to keep time with the thrumming of the bus. The man in a suit beside him slowly raised a foot to wrap the strap of his satchel around his ankle, a gesture too close to the dividing line between furtive and obvious to be deemed offensive. The bus pulled up at the next stop, and the door sprang open for a moment and air poured past, into the cracks and wedges between arms and feet and torsos. No one got on; the red button had been pressed in error and the driver *fuck's sake*-d loud enough for the lower level to hear and join together in a collective humanitarian shame at having caused this minor distress to the man. A pigeon, made bold from a concussive encounter with a car or some inherited stupidity, hopped onto the bus, looked briefly up and cocked its head to one side before the doors began to close and it danced away like an overweight and ageing boxer.

Another woman, younger, peering through a raised yellow bar at the child on its mother's lap, considered what it was, in fact, that babies were crying about. She had seen it happen before; an infant that was dry, fed, warm and loved, would suddenly look to the side, as if at something diverting, and then howl and howl and howl for hours on end. She wondered what floated over there, just past the vanishing point, that caused them such distress. The one who sat on the bus had not done this, which seemed to emphasise its absence even more. She wondered—although she didn't really wonder, because the thought was too abstract to wrap in words, and the blip of her mobile distracted her as soon as the thought dipped in below her skull—if anyone else had noticed this. If there would ever be a moment, then, when each person on the bus, each person on the street, in every damn tiny office and alleyway and apartment block would all turn their heads in unison and look—just look—at what lay over there beyond the vanishing point, to see what it is infants see. And then they would return to their chores, to typing and pissing and shouting, and never mention this little anomaly, and nothing would have changed, except that the churning great entity of the city would have recognised that something, *some thing*, lay just out of sight and needed to be acknowledged.

An older man turned the corner just as the bus pulled away from anther stop and caught a lungful of warm and gritty air in its wake, snorting out the foulness as he considered the shrinking yellow mass that was slowly picking up speed as it moved away from him. His face was melted. Perhaps the distortion came from a burn, or an accident, or simply old age and gravity had caused it to drip and slide so. He could have raised an arm, attempted a half-run, shouted for the driver to wait, but he preferred lateness over any unseemly loss of dignity. He sat down on the narrow bus shelter seat to wait for the next one, then shifted in his seat, rising up on one hipbone to release a gentle flow of gas that was inoffensive enough to go unremarked upon by those passing by. Soon, it began to rain. Not heavily, but as if the sky hadn't fully decided to commit to the action, and was losing drops in erratic bursts. It never fucking rained properly, just a half-arsed thing that greyed the sky and stained pavements and windscreens, distorting and magnifying everything. A couple of pre-teen girls ran screaming up the street, hands over heads and bared bellies flashing pale, squealing at each other to run faster, to get out of the rain. Their hair swung in auburn showers and he quite carefully did not follow them with his gaze, just filed the image away for later perusal. He scratched at his head, a shower of flakes dusting his shoulders. He rubbed his skull against the back of the bus shelter, trying to ease the itching. The eczema was a trial. He would try the new tea tree oil stuff tonight. Usually, he wore a hat to hide the scaly, balding patches on his head, but the damp mugginess of the day had made the sweat cling to his scalp and the wool had made the prickling unbearable. His wife had tried her various creams on him, but the itch never quite went away. When he finally left, having given up on his imagined errands, on another bus ever appearing, seven thumbnail-sized flakes of skin remained stuck to the beer poster; seven white smudges that eventually dropped and were ground up under feet and wheels.

On the next street over, a child sat in the evening drizzle, impressed by his own daring at risking damp trousers and his mother's wrath. He was twelve, and precocious, and knew how to spell words like precocious. A fireman was hosing blood from the concrete steps across the road. It looked like a waterfall; a pooling that had spilled out and over the edge of the step, once, twice, three times, or maybe a crimson slinky like the one his baby sister had chewed and then left in the garden. The blood wasn't exactly sent anywhere—just diluted and allowed to run down the street in a gutter river, thinned enough so the responsibility for it was everyone's and no one's.

Later, the boy would overhear a lady in the shop saying that it had been a dog, a big one, shouldn't have been loose anyway, a boxer or a pit bull, one of those animals that were more muscle than fur. Ran right in front of the bus, it did. And the kids coming home from school and all. I tell you, it should have been chained up, and I bet it was the one that had been barking these last few weeks and tearing at the bins. Keeping everyone awake. Splat, it went, splat (and this would be punctuated by a gleeful meeting of the hands) and into the gutter it went. And did the bus driver pull over? Not on your life. Just drove off with the blood still staining the grill, turning on his wipers as casual as you like. Later, much later, the boy would remember the dog, remember how it had walked around the neighbourhood with such assurance, confident of every step, ready and capable of dodging buggies, thrown stones and traffic alike. And he would wonder if the dog didn't in fact know what it was doing.

But for now, as he watched the bored fireman hose the pavement clean, he created a thousand scenarios in his head. A mugging; a syringe that had ripped and torn at the skin, causing the blood to spurt uncontrollably away. An older person, a woman maybe, who in his mind wore the face of his dead grandmother, who had slipped and the crackling of the hip had sliced open the femoral artery—he knew that from the telly; the one in the leg, *f* for femur and *f* for feet, although it was the thigh, really—and had died, there on the pavement. Or a child and a truck, come together in a crashing, stupefying mess. Two children. Six. Or, with as much likelihood, a van carrying supplies of red paint or vampire blood made out of sugar and crimson dye had hit a speed bump too fast and had dumped its load. He played around with possibilities, letting them form and merge, form and merge, never deciding on one or minding which one was the truth.

The red fire engine stood quietly idle, as if attempting to be unobtrusive and to avoid causing alarm, distress, even curiosity. The fireman was embarrassed at this slow day bereft of real emergencies, at his bad luck in drawing such a mundane chore. He had downloaded a new US TV series last night and was considering whether his girlfriend would have started without him. So he tried to whistle as he washed, to distract himself, but he wasn't very good at it, pressing his lips together into a tiny little bum-shaped hole through which half-notes and puffs of untuned air escaped.

And then, so suddenly it appeared to reach backwards in time and take up some of the most recent past, he succumbed to one of those uprooting moments where everything is heard, every screech and bark and word falls on the eardrum in equal, terrifying intensity, upsetting his balance, causing the liquids in his inner ear to swirl uneasily. And because everything was equally loud, everything was equally soft, and the gaps in the noise weighed heavier in their echoing emptiness, a vacuum that sucked at the ears, begging to be filled, please, with anything, anything to stop the silence from spreading like a grotesque fungus. So he cleared his throat, and again, the muscles in his neck clenching and unclenching in a racket that sounded loud, so very loud, in the confines of his head.

And then was silent in the city, or as close to the breach as silence can get in the press of humanity; grazing its fingers along the plastic sealant on windows, over neon lights and dull chalkboards advertising today's specials, before stooping to cower in the gutters, scratching at ankles and disregarded shopping bags. But there were pockets of noise that could be approached and broached; spillings of words *in potentia* that were there to be claimed, if a mouth could be found.

But a mouth is a terrible thing. A hinge; a frightful one that separates the face, and gapes and distorts to produce sounds. And the worry is in what shape those sounds will make? Why not worry that all there is to stop the top of the head continuing to rise and flip back, until a terrible flat plane is created, is a few flaps of muscle and a stubbornness of bone. And bone can be broken, and muscles torn. And the hinges that keep the mouth together and the self cooped up within would snap, and the upper jaw would flop backwards until it was a flat plane of a maw, and something would leak away. And if that were to happen, the self would be laid open to the world, and it would pour out in a putrid rush that leaves the shell of the body, slumped and hollow, but still upright; walking and talking and kissing and eating and dying and sleeping and being.

So it's the pauses that matter.

Father of the Man
Terence Davies' Trilogy by Bobby Seal

'Cinema creates a loop that preserves memory, and through the artful use of music and unexpected juxtaposition, Davies communicates the intensity that belongs to those memories. The re-enactments of *Children* are transcended. *Death And Transfiguration* is a powerful and deeply moving experience for the audience as well as for its creator. Robert dies in a crescendo of rasping, heaving rattling breaths, and as death comes, the last memories bubble up; of mother and son walking hand in hand, of two seagulls a-wing over the Liverpool skyline. And for all the Catholic indoctrination, this is a godless death. Redemption lies in cinema.'
– Matthew De Abaitua

Terence Davies' *Trilogy* sequence comprises the three short films *Children* (1976), *Madonna and Child* (1980), and *Death and Transfiguration* (1983), the most autobiographical of his works. They chart the life of Davies' alter ego Robert Tucker, from unhappy childhood through to sexually-repressed adulthood. In the final triptych Davies imagines an elderly Tucker looking back on his life as he lies in bed facing a lonely death. This was the kind of old age and demise that Davies believed would have been his, had he not broken away from that particular trajectory in his late twenties.

The image of the child is central to Davies' view of life: inside we are all still children. The first film in the trilogy, *Children*, opens with a soundtrack of schoolboys at play and slow, tracking close-ups framing the faces of Robbie and the three older boys who are tormenting him for being effeminate: 'Who's a fruit then, eh? It's Al Capone isn't it, eh? Your name's Al Capone, isn't it?' In Davies'world, though, these are not just children, not simple beings who have yet to become fully-formed. Each, Davies implies, is a complex individual with a rich inner life. Thus, the child does not grow up and become a man, or a woman, in the sense of being transformed into another being; the adult is still, underneath it all, the same child he or she once was. We are all, in that sense, still the child we once were.

Terence Davies, the youngest of ten children, was born into a working-class Catholic family in Liverpool. His father was a violent bully, driving the young Davies even closer to his loving but downtrodden mother. His father died when Davies was seven, but cast a shadow over the rest of his life. Davies realised he was gay when quite young and suffered terrible feelings of guilt and confusion because of the dissonance of his sexuality and his faith. The themes of Catholic guilt, repression, bullying and loneliness are integral to all three films. But underlying everything, as was the case for Davies himself, is Robert Tucker's unwavering devotion to his mother.

Terence Davies' *Trilogy* is an exercise in memory. But memory, Davies insists, is episodic, a kaleidoscope of images which do not follow a conventional narrative arc. We are shown the world through the eyes of Tucker, but Robbie's Liverpool is not an objective reality, it is a projection of his memory. And as is the case with memory, feelings and moods are just as important as narrative. Narrative, after all, is very fluid: each of us constantly constructs and revises the story we tell about ourselves.

Although the films are set in Liverpool, we see very little of the city. Robbie's is essentially an interior world: home, school, office, church, hospital. Looking at Davies' work as a whole, there seems to be an association of interior space with the female: safe, warm, comforting. Exterior space he seems to personify as male, and thereby harsh and threatening. All the dynamism of Liverpool in this period, the maritime links with America and the joyous musical and artistic creativity, are absent from the *Trilogy*. Or, more correctly, they do not feature in Robbie's life. Snatches of people happily singing and laughing are there in the films, but always at the periphery, rarely directly involving Robbie. But Davies does use music in his films, often to very powerful effect. Chamber music, folk songs, children's hymns and songs from Hollywood musicals are used sparingly but to haunting effect, an aural seasoning to the stew of visual images. The choice of music is never obvious, which sometimes produces breathtaking juxtapositions. In the opening of *Death and Transfiguration*, for instance, the last film in *Trilogy*, the middle-aged Robbie travels to his mother's funeral, alone in the back of the funeral car, overlaid with the strains of Doris Day's 'It All Depends On You.'

Children, Madonna and Child and *Death and Transfiguration* move relentlessly through the three stages of Robbie's life. But Davies consciously breaks the rules of linear time as he moves backwards and forwards exploring the jumble of Robbie's memories, his youth, adulthood and old age. Davies does not want us to just look at Robbie's life, he requires us to witness it, and presents each fragment as if part of a body of evidence.

Although at one level we know that these are films set in the Liverpool of the 1970s and 1980s, because that is when they were made, *Trilogy* is essentially set in a perpetual present. We all live our lives in that way, never questioning what we mean by 'now.' And yet the past is always present and, through memory, we re-enact it, again and again.

In one of the most ineffably moving scenes in *Children*, an eleven-year-old Robbie and his mother make a journey through Liverpool by bus. In one's memory the scenes one plays out operate from just one point of view. And so it is with this journey: the camera, still and unblinking, observes Robbie and his mother from one side as they sit, mother looking ahead and Robbie writing in the mist of his breath on the window.

Courageously, Davies holds this shot for a full two minutes. There is no dialogue and no sound, other than a haunting oboe lament. Then he switches the angle and we are face on to the mother and child. The sound clicks in, first the labouring engine of the bus and then a sob, and we realise that Robbie's mother is crying. She continues to look ahead as the tears stream down her cheeks. Robbie looks at her, confusion and fear in his face, but neither of them say anything. The scene switches to Robbie in his early twenties getting off a bus, alone but burdened with his memories.

Davies offers no explanation of the scene on the bus. How could there be an explanation? This is a childhood memory and so many of those memories, things one is too young to understand at the time, remain locked in mystery forever. Mam cried, and that is all Robbie remembers. It is all he needs to remember.

In *Madonna and Child* we find a middle-aged Robbie living at home with his mother; his father died many years before, and so the mother and son live quietly together, each providing the other with companionship and support. By day he crosses the Mersey and keeps the books in a stultifying shipping agent's office, just as Davies did for twelve years before he went away to drama school.

By night, Mam safely in bed, Robbie creeps out to find something he hopes will fill his void of loneliness and frustrated desire. He seeks casual sex with rough, hairy men, just like those in his collection of pictures of wrestlers. One is left with the thought that these are men who bear an uncomfortable resemblance to his late father.

There is no joy in Robbie's sexuality; just pain, humiliation and an overwhelming sense of guilt. A guilt that he carries with him to the confessional box, but even there it is something he cannot face, sublimating it instead for a meticulously kept log of other more acceptable sins.

By the time we reach *Death and Transfiguration* Robbie's mother is long-dead and he is an old man alone and dying in his hospital bed. Memories bubble up and burst in his mind throwing out aoristic juxtapositions: the nurses decorating a Christmas tree in Robbie's ward become the nuns at his primary school nativity play and the fire consuming his mother's coffin summons up a cheery blaze in the grate from a childhood Christmas.

Wilfrid Brambell, in his last film role before his own death, gives an outstanding performance as the elderly

Robert Tucker. In a hospital bed, unable to move or speak because of a stroke, his cadaverous face and sunken eyes seem to carry the whole story of a wasted life. Davies clearly loves faces: in one scene he lights Terry O'Sullivan, playing the middle-aged Robbie, from below and in close-up to give his face an alarming resemblance to Edvard Munch's *The Scream*. Valerie Lilley, painfully sublime as the young Robbie's mother, might have been chosen just for her face, which seems to carry the beauty of her youth at the same time as the tribulations of her married life.

The *Trilogy* is about looking back: in *Children*, Robbie Tucker, now in his early twenties, is tortured by memories of his childhood; in *Madonna and Child* it is the middle-aged Tucker who looks back to his earlier years; while in *Death and Transfiguration* an elderly Robert Tucker surveys his whole life.

Davies breaks a number of cinematic conventions in the way he portrays Robbie's life. It is likely he would have been taught at film school to avoid empty space and dead time on the screen; such errors are said to interrupt the narrative flow and risk losing the audience's attention. In *Trilogy*, and indeed in his later Liverpool films, Davies ignores this advice; he presents sustained shots of characters saying and doing nothing and even shots with no characters present at all. This is life and not a performance, he seems to be saying, there is a world beyond the frame and these characters will continue to live their lives when the camera is not rolling.

Davies was to return to some of the themes covered in *Trilogy* in his later Liverpool films *Distant Voices, Still Lives* (1988) and *Of Time and the City* (2008). *Distant Voices, Still Lives* is another exercise in 'memory realism' and continues to mine Davies's Liverpudlian working-class Catholic background.

Though this is a return to some of the same ground covered in *Trilogy*, Davies now opens up the story. Memories are played out before us once more, but this time they are the memories of an extended family of characters, not just Davies's alter ego. Each memory is, seemingly, picked up and dealt out at random, as if from a hand of cards.

Twenty years later, now a critically-respected writer and director, Davies returned his creative attention to the city of his birth. *Of Time and the City* uses archive footage from the fifties and sixties with a voice-over by Davies.

But this is not the tourist-trail Liverpool of football, Cavern Club, Tate Liverpool and Albert Dock. Davies selects footage to reflect his own reminiscences of Liverpool in that period; memories of a city of dirt, poverty and brutally enforced ideas of gender roles and sexuality. Rather like Eliot's *Four Quartets*, from which he quotes liberally, Davies transcends a mere documentary study of a particular place and time into a series of ponderings on the very nature of time, place and memory.

Because of the restrictions of his budget, Davies had to shoot *Trilogy* in 16mm black and white. *Children* was made before he went to film school and *Madonna and Child* was his graduation piece. Yet Davies' vision seems to supersede the technical limits of his medium and his lack of experience as a director. He seems to coax the monochrome film to the point where it shimmers with the haze of memory. He makes the maximum use of natural lighting too; many of his indoor shots are lit just by windows.

We have been conditioned to associate black and white film with the forties, fifties and sixties. Thus, for those of us who were children during that time, our childhood memories have taken on monochrome tones. For Davies, having to use black and white film, albeit for financial reasons, produced the happy accident of his *Trilogy* seeming to exist outside of time; he makes no attempt to create period settings. The effect is a remembered life in a perpetual present.

Trilogy ranges back and forth through time but, whatever stage of Robert Tucker's life we are asked by Davies to bear witness to and whichever of the four actors playing him is on screen, he is still the child we first saw in the opening scene of *Children*. Davies eventually lost his Catholic faith, but he still seems to share the Jesuit conviction that the first few years of a child's life, the early influences and experiences that affect him or her, will determine the course of the rest of that life.

The young Robbie Tucker is cowed into passivity by an abusive father, brutal teachers and bullying school-mates. His ability to function, to express emotion, is locked into petrification from an early age by the shame of his sexuality; homosexuality was not just forbidden by the Church when Robbie was young, but by the law.

The quiet passivity we see from Robbie as a child when spoken to by his teachers we see again and again throughout his life: with doctors, priests and other authority figures. He even walks meekly away when refused entry to a gay club, as if accepting that he does not belong even there.

Through the course of the three films we see no friendships in Robbie's life. Any sexual encounters he has are completely without any tenderness. The only love in his life, the thread that runs through all three films, is his love for his mother. He loves her to the end with childlike faith and sincerity.

In the final part of *Trilogy,* as Robbie lies in his hospital bed rasping out his last breath, the torch of the patrolling night-nurse playing on his face, the film closes with the voiced-over words: *When the light goes out, God is dead.*

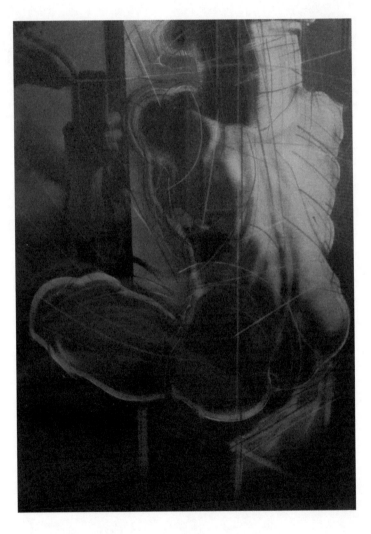

'Photography is a means of appropriating something.'
– Susan Sontag

Selfie

Paula McGrath

1.

—But what is art? Who gets to decide? And why are there always so many MEN in charge? My voice grows shrill to be heard over the near-closing volume of Grogans. It's because women don't get past the GATEKEEPERS. Two more PINTS, please.

The cloudy beers arrive in front of us in their own good time, followed by a pause I can't bear so I take out my purse.

—Are you paying yourself? the barman asks mildly. Maybe he throws a look in Aidan's direction, or maybe I imagine it or am misremembering.

—Women drink pints. Women pay for pints. It's the nineties, for chrissakes. I slap the money down, the last of this week's. It means there's none for a taxi, and the buses have stopped running by now. Shit.

Aidan takes a long draught.

—I'll get you back tomorrow. I sold a drawing at the Jo Lane.

My annoyance melts away. So there'll be another tomorrow. With Aidan, I'm never sure.

Anxiety kicks back in. Will that tomorrow begin with a jokey co-stagger out into the night. Or will I be walking down Kevin Street and the Coombe and Cork Street by myself at closing time?

2.

My writing style is tense and prissy, but I don't know what to do about it. On my Women's Studies course I write articles and essays on women in the arts, and why there aren't enough women in the arts. I've counted women poets in *Poetry Ireland*, and complained all the way to the top, to the nodding, tutting disapproval of my peers (despite terse, left-aligned paragraphs).

My Women's Studies women, Rachel and Claire, don't like Aidan. Aids, they call him.

–That's not very nice, I say without conviction.

–*He's* not very nice, they toss back quantities of dark, dismissive hair.

I agree.

–He's an arrogant git, adds one.

He is an arrogant git. The other thing we agree on is that he's very handsome.

There's more to it, but I don't explain because I haven't figured it out yet.

3.

Our eyes met across a crowded room. Roll yours all you want, but that's what happened. The same bar, actually. I was leaving Grogans, and his leopard yellow eyes followed me as I passed his table. I turned and held his gaze steady, brazen. I don't know if it was recognition of kind, or simple physical attraction, but the rest of the room—his circle of friends, the crowded bar—faded out around us, and weeks of flirting and game-playing were dispensed of in one, long look. It was game-on. Full on. Very French, very Miller-Nin, very Betty Blue.

4.

I gather up alcohol-loosened limbs, climb off the barstool, look around for my bag, all the while wondering if he's coming with me. The last moment I can possibly string out my leave-taking, he drains his pint and stands.

–Take care, the barman says without looking up from the glass he is polishing. Or maybe he does look up, from me to Aidan, then back to his glass. Or maybe I'm misremembering.

We emerge from the smokey bar into sudden cold, but dilated blood vessels make us immune. As we weave along the road to my Liberties cottage I resume my diatribe and he listens, sort of. Only when we're rounding Ardee Street does he say anything. He sounds bored.

–Why not make something yourself. Make some art instead of talking about it.

Make art? Me? I can't think about that so I dwell instead on his tweed-trousered legs which kick out ahead of him as he walks. (Oxfam. £2 on the tag. *Mm, wool,* he observed, peering at the label. *And lined too.* He was not taking the piss. He talked them down to £1. It's the only pair I've seen him in since. He's the only man not my father's age I've ever seen wearing woollen, lined tweed trousers.) I'm:

pleased (Aidan thinks I could),
angry (he probably thinks anyone could),
angry (he obviously doesn't see the point of my articles
or essays),
and pleased (could I? Make art?).

I don't know what to say.

5.

My 205 belts up the N11, diesel, loud and proud. Stillorgan,
Cabinteely, Kilmacanogue, it zigs and zags past the quarry,
up the hill, turns for Calary, goes past the tiny church. Slows
for the lane, a pot-holed dirt track, scutch grass down the
middle. Sceacs and furze, words from childhood I thought
I had forgotten, press hard against the paintwork. Slo-o-ow
and stop. Handbrake on, change into rubber boots, a farm girl
after all. Slam the door. Hello, curious sheep. Ah, smell that
sheep shit. Swing leg over gate and jump. Continue straight
past the 'studio', a rust-roofed shed, without stopping. He
knows I'm coming. He'll be in when he's in.

6.

I made the mistake of going out to his shed once, the first
time I came up here. We'd had too much to drink the night
before, so it was close to ten when I woke, hungover and
shivering in the heatless cottage. Aidan was nowhere to be

seen. I had a vague memory, I'd thought it a dream, of him getting up and going out and me thinking, but it isn't even light yet. I yanked the ancient eiderdown back onto the bed in an attempt to get warm, but it was useless. From under the scratchy blankets, I pulled on my clothes, and a thick jumper I found on the floor which smelled of mildew.

Outside, a light drizzle fell, backlit by a pale yellow sun. I could smell the furze from the ditch, sweet and thick. There was a moment... I can't explain it very well... where my breath stopped. Or, I think that's what happened. Somewhere between exhale and inhale there was a long not-breathing, and the rain on my face, and the sun warming me through the jumper, and the dark outline of the Sugar Loaf in the distance, and the heavy-honeyed furze. I was absolutely content, yet, at the same time, ravenous with want.

I made my way across the yard to the shed where Aidan worked, as if this was where the answers lay, never mind that I hadn't even begun to work out the questions.

The shed was primitive: the door hung askew on rusty hinges; the corrugated iron sheets of the roof did not quite meet at the seams. Aidan had hung a makeshift fluorescent light, dangerously close to the leaky roof if you ask me, so it was well lit. He was wearing a dust mask and goggles, because the air was filled with white dust; his clothes were covered with it. His back was to me, which made it easy for me to remain there unnoticed, watching as he squatted and stood, stepped back then moved forward, tapped intermittently, hammer against chisel against rock. His movements were rhythmic, slow, smooth, sure, the movements of a dancer, a martial artist, an artist.

He only startled when I coughed—the dust—swung around like someone disturbed from a dream. Then, like someone disturbed from a dream, he slowly seemed to wake up. He pulled down the mask and pulled up his goggles. He still looked dazed. His *How are you?* was distant, formal, cold, his mouth pink and moist and obscene in the ghostly mask of his face. His question—could it have been more innocent—provoked a rage in me I hadn't known before. He didn't remember my name. There was dust in my throat. There was no coffee. No running water. I'd had to piss outside in the middle of the night, stung my arse on a nettle. Every kind of grievance I could have dreamt up was his fault, because he had shown me magic and taken it away in the same moment. I had seen behind the scenes and the wizard was nothing special, an artisan, chipping away in the dust.

7.

I have not gone near his shed since that first time. He'll be in when he's in. In the cottage, he has arranged rolled newspapers neatly in the hearth, and twigs. All I have to do is strike a match. It roars into flame. I make a wigwam of turf around it, then I pour vodka into a tumbler and sip at it while I wait. When he comes in I pour another and hand it to him. He knocks it back and returns the plastic tumbler to the table with a down-to-business bump.

    –Are you ready?

He gets busy now, plugging in a radiator, clicking on a

Superser I haven't seen before. I'm warmed by the vodka and pleased at his thoughtfulness. Rachel and Claire never see this side of Aids, Aidan, I correct. He's setting up lights, transforming the cottage into a movie set. I take off my clothes.

–Here. He pats a sort of plinth, sort of pedestal, on which he has placed a squarely folded blanket. I climb on and perch in the spotlight, legs crossed, tits out. Preen a bit. Artist's model, me. After a while I'm bored. After another while, I'm bored and slumped. Still he's click-clicking. Is that not cheating anyway? I imagined intense sketching and brush stroking. And something velour, artfully draped... With photos, you're neither here nor there. I wonder, as he points his lens, if I'm being objectified. I get myself into a subject-object muddle. I remember that I can still speak.

–How much longer?

He looks surprised to see me, he was so involved in his crouching and clicking (objectified!).

–You're doing great.

I'm mollified. I wonder what it would be like to be the one with the camera, him on the plinth. Mmm, nice. Now who's objectifying whom?

Finally, he puts the camera down and stands and stretches. He takes a blanket off the bed and places it around my shoulders. He kisses me on the top of my head and murmurs thanks into my hair. Then he turns the Superser off and plugs out the heater. He stoops to turn off the spots and he's caught for a moment in an up-light. For the first time I see how wrecked he looks. He's a few years older than me anyway, but he looks about forty. From taking a few photographs. Feckssake.

He catches my expression, and for a moment he looks as if he would like to explain it all to me, explain something to me...

–You were perfect, he says finally.

I don't know what to say to Aidan's tenderness. He comes and strokes my cheek, lets his finger trail to the blanket's opening. Then he frowns and looks at his watch.

–A quick one in the Roundwood Inn?

Still in the wasteland of my twenties, I'm happy to put pints first. He fills a mug with vodka and knocks back most of it, handing me what's left to finish.

8.

We clamber over the gate together and fall into his car. It's a Fiat, a rusty blue piece of shit, decked out with big wheels and (he bragged) a huge engine, out of a BMW. The first time I saw it I laughed. Turned out it was a loan from a friend. It revs and roars down the lane and out to the main road. Aidan overtakes an ancient John Deere, waving at the farmer who doesn't wave back. He freewheels down the hill to save petrol, all the way to the car park of the Roundwood Inn.

The locals don't look up when we enter. CS is sitting at the bar. She nods to Aidan, ignores me, not for the first time. I don't blame her. Bottom line is, she's a famous artist, he's in awe, and I'm no one. I pin on a smile, look for a while from one to the other as they speak before taking the hint and my pint and moving over to the window. He could at least toss a packet of peanuts in my direction. When CS finishes her drink and leaves, without saying goodbye to him, without as much as a glance in my direction, he joins me.

9.

He'll be in town for a while, but we won't be able to meet. He'll be with his family. By this, it turns out, he means: his two boys. Oh, and their mother is actually his wife. I react predictably. Why didn't he tell me? Did he not think having SONS was worth mentioning? Did he not think it might interest me to know that he was MARRIED.

–Separated years. It had nothing to do with you.

My mouth may have opened and closed a few times at that point without any sound coming out. Because, unless I thought we were united on a path to the Happy Ring House and a big white dress—and let's face it, I wasn't that deranged —I had to agree, it was nothing to do with me.

I leave without a word. Like a damp firecracker, my anger has volatilised into nothing. Why be angry? He has always been careful not to let me believe... anything, so despite testing myself with a few squeezed tears, I'm not devastated. I don't keep as much as a toothbrush in his cottage.

For the first time, I notice the wool snagged on the barbed wire as I walk to the car, smell the wild garlic. For the first time, I notice Sunday service times on the board outside the little stone church, 9.30 Morning Prayer. I had thought it disused.

Instead of going home to the Liberties, I turn left, past
Eggs for sale and placid brown cows, down into Roundwood.
I follow a sign for Lough Dan. The windy road requires all
my concentration, so by the time I find somewhere to park,
I have all but forgotten why I left Aidan's.

Near the top of the hill, a little wooden gate leads to
a woodland path. Moss grows on the stones beneath the
trees either side. I walk more slowly. Unexpectedly the lake
appears when I round a corner, glittering silver and black
under clouding skies. When I need to rest, a field of ferns
and bluebells invites me in and I lie down among them and
listen to the insects, to a faraway tractor. Yeats' waters and
wild are running through my head. I doze. When I wake,
there's a mist coming off the lake. It has settled on the
cobwebs which lace the ferns, making of them jewelled,
gossamer things. It has settled on me.

10.

He's sleeping on the floor tonight. This should tell me
something but it doesn't. I start a half-hearted fight which
goes nowhere. He gets into the bed, wearily, reluctantly,
probably because it's his best shot at getting a night's sleep.
But who wants a reluctant man in the bed? I want to go
home, but I've had too much vodka. I want to at least get
up, but the fire has died. I stare at the ceiling as the cottage
cools down. He snores softly beside me.

I feel like pushing him out of the bed, back onto the
floor.

I feel like crying.
I do, cry.

11.

It's opening night. I'm going to the show with Rachel and
Claire, even though they don't think it's a good idea. Everyone
except me seems to know what's a good idea. They're
probably right, because it did not end properly between
Aidan and me. I stopped going up there, and he stopped
meeting me in town. I stopped going up there because when
I asked him when I would be getting my invitation to the
launch he said, *Come if you want.*

The room is teeming with people in heels and statement
handbags, carrying programmes which they refer to often
as they approach the pictures. They step forward to read
labels, then step back to appraise the picture or sculpture,
say something sideways to someone else, then fall silent
as if deep in thought. I'm carrying a programme myself. I
don't study it too carefully because it might annoy Rachel
and Claire, but I have had a quick scan to see if I'm credited.
After all, even if he's made them more muscly, and replaced
my head with anvils and other blunt implements, these
drawings and sculptures are made from photographs of me.
I don't get a mention. I'm gratified to see that the ones with
the heads still on are the ones with the red stickers.

–I can't say I'm mad about his take on the female form,
Rachel says.

–Shh.

I recognise CS coming towards us and I prepare a smile,

just in case. She walks past without a glance.

—Come on, I say. You were right. I shouldn't have come.

—Agreed, Rachel says.

They go to get our coats and for a moment I'm left standing on my own beside a sculpture of myself. I stroke my smooth bronze thigh. I'm wondering if anyone will recognise me with my clothes on when I see him, walking backwards, talking animatedly to a group of well-heeled patrons. He doesn't see me until they've arrived at my sculpture, and by then it's too late.

—Paula…

I smile around the group generally, on the unlikely chance that someone might undertake to do introductions. No takers. I withdraw the smile. I've had it with Aidan and his ignorant friends. *Finally*, I can imagine Rachel saying. Or Claire. *Wanker*, one of them would be sure to add, just for punctuation.

—Is this me? I ask Aidan rudely. One of the group, an athletic looking blonde, perks up, waiting for the answer. As if it was her question.

—Um, composite… he mumbles, and guides his posse away.

Bastard. I'd recognise that spine anywhere. I have my own picture, a rolled up x-ray, taken by a chiropractor on Van Ness, San Francisco, the summer of my J1, and currently gathering dust under my bed. That mild scoliosis is on record, and it's all mine.

Later there is a gathering in a pub. I know where to find them because after Rachel and Claire walk me to my bus stop *Are you sure you'll be ok? He's only a wanker*, etc., I circle back and follow the last of the liggers out of the gallery and down to Temple Bar. I take a few breaths outside before I make my entrance.

12.

I'm standing at the edge of Aidan's circle of family and friends, swaying a little. It feels unreal, only in part due to the white wines I lost track of at the opening. I call his name. There's a flicker of something across his face when he turns. Not shame, not embarrassment. Or, maybe embarrassment, not because of the way he's behaved, because I've made things awkward for him. He gestures at the group with his eyes as if to say, can't you see I'm busy. They're looking at me with interest: a couple, maybe his parents, two boys, CS, the athletic blonde his arm is draped around…

He widens his eyes, as if he can't believe I'm still there. I turn and walk away, rigid-backed.

13.

Last year, when I was pulling out of a petrol station in the West of Ireland, I noticed a man walking in. I'd have known him anywhere. He lifted his head. Our eyes met. He looked pleased to see me, a surprise on his Saturday morning stroll to the Spar to get the paper, some milk, maybe. The electronic window of my car wound down. My traitorous finger.

–Paula.

–Hello Aidan.

There were greys through his dark curls, and lines around his mouth and the corners of his yellow eyes.

He has five children to my four, etc.

I didn't tell him that I started writing—*make some art instead of talking about it*—or that sometimes, in the middle of a messy, uninspired first draft I think of him, putting in tradesman's hours in his leaky shed.

We wished each other well, went our separate, middle-aged ways. Did we really drink a bottle of vodka then race down the N11 in his souped up Fiat?

I was thinking, I'm glad I got naked for his pictures.

I don't know what he was thinking.

14.

The picture hangs in the bathroom. He gave it to me to say thanks for posing for him, before we'd stopped seeing each other, before his opening. Nobody notices it. I don't notice it myself. Now, I lift it off the wall and examine it, the first time in twenty years. It's not bad. But is it me? I take it into the bedroom and place it on the floor. I take off my clothes.

With mirrors, I take a selfie. Me taking photo of a drawing of a photo of me. (That's my spine.)

The anvil-headed one with the muscles: composite.

The one on the left: me.

Stasis

Ian Maleney

'I matured at twenty-four.' The sentence has haunted me all year, this year, my twenty-fourth. It's nagged at the back of my head as every decision I had to make came and went. The ambiguity of that word, 'matured,' and the concrete figure of the age, twenty-four, undeniable. I have always wanted to think of myself as mature, though it's hard now to remember what exactly the word has meant to me all this time. Perhaps when I was younger I was surer of what it entailed to be mature, or surer of my idea of it at least. I had an image of it. Now, when I ought to be 'mature,' I have no idea what that means. I have no idea what parts of my life, what personality traits, what decisions I've made, might make me mature. What clothes, shoes, books, habits, which friends? Will I know when I am mature, or will I have to go on wondering? At twenty-four, you can't be mature for your age anymore, not really. You're either mature or you're not. It's time to get serious. My parents were married by twenty-four, and they had me at twenty-five. They had a house too, one they built themselves, and jobs. They had a car. Were they mature? I can't imagine.

It was shortly before my twenty-fourth birthday that I first tried to watch *In Praise of Love*, a film by Jean-Luc Godard, in my old bed at my parents' house. I lasted about half an hour before drifting off. A few months later, once more in my parents house, I tried again. I had by this time forgotten entirely about my first effort, and so the first half hour passed with a weird feeling of familiarity that I couldn't put my finger on. As it happened, I fell asleep at the half hour mark again, around the part where Edgar, a tormented young Parisian, attempts to convince Elle that she ought to act in his new project. His project is about love, but it is formless and he cannot explain it. Elle is cleaning trains in a train station, and is not interested. I woke up the following morning, laptop beside me, curtains open. A clear blue country sky in late autumn. I finished the film first thing, before checking my phone, before talking to anyone.

'Already it's a great deal to see anything clearly, for we don't see anything clearly.'

Edgar, we learn, is an historian. He is refusing to forget history, while trying to face up to the present. The past is his key to a radical self-awareness, which is maturity, or adulthood. The past is your family history, your nation's history, your roots; the way you orient yourself in the world. Touchstones. Love is only possible in adulthood, or only true there, where it's not the lustful, selfish playacting of youth, or the nostalgic reverie of old age. Edgar's project—this play or film or whatever it is he's making—is his way of trying to define adulthood, to find it and dwell in it. He wants to run his hands along its edges, to make it appear in front of our eyes, as clear as day. Young love, old love, and something in between, the most difficult to picture. All this clarity—transcendent, luminous, mature. Impossible. The only one who can see it, who can sense it, has no time for it—she is working two jobs.

Edgar can neither grow nor retreat, focused as he is on his

---

1 Jasper Johns, as quoted in *Merce Cunningham: The Modernizing of Modern Dance*, by Roger Copeland (Routledge 2004).

impossible project, so he remains static. Elle cannot believe in any project—for her, there is no possible redemption—so she removes herself from the picture. She has lost faith, and is lost in turn. Their shared memory appears in colour, blown-out and harsh. Some Americans have come to France with a contract for Elle's grandparents, arriving loud and fast in a low-slung Jag. A studio wants to make a movie about their time in the Resistance. Edgar is there too, separately, to interview them. His interest is in a momentous era in French history, when France was still something to fight for, to believe in. He is looking for the human perspective on the grand movement of history, looking for a way to connect the particular and the universal. It soon gets messy, polemical, careless even. Elle's grandmother makes Godard's point for him—you're young and always waiting to grow up, then suddenly you're old, remembering your youth. There is no in-between phase, no point of clarity or assurance where self-awareness reigns. No adulthood perceived. No sense of the self in history. We're just telling ourselves stories, stories of our own and stories we stole from others. Lying in my old bed in the house where I grew up, this is a story I'm comfortable telling myself.

'Whatever the intellectual does, is wrong.' [2]

'I matured at twenty-four,' says Morton Feldman, in a radio interview with Charles Shere, in California in 1967. He was forty-one at the time, almost half-way through his mature period, which ended with his death in 1987. It was

2 Theodor W. Adorno, *Minima Moralia* (trans. E. F. N. Jephcott, Verso 2005)

shortly before he stopped working for his father. Feldman's conversation with Shere is cyclical, but wide-ranging. There are many long pauses, and many half-jokes that aren't really that funny. You can hear them lighting cigarettes in the studio, the curl of a match inches from the microphone. They're spiralling around this idea, arguably the central assertion of Feldman's career, that he doesn't believe in Hegel, but in God. At first I wasn't sure what that meant. I wasn't sure that anyone he said it to knew either, but they went along with it anyway. So will I.

Feldman says he admires things that are what they are. He admires work that doesn't feel the need to take from history as it wishes, artists who have nothing to conquer. The desire is for a work which is not a synthesis of multiple ideas, not mastery of various inherited concepts, but merely a statement of feeling, unburdened by the looming spectre of all the things it is not. Something elemental, indivisible. Something which is itself, separate, yet illuminating. This is faith. The belief that something can be simply what it is, not an instrument of history, not a composite of base aims, desires and appropriations, but merely an exercise, an expression, of the individual's ability to sense. Pure humanist faith. It's about the difference between conception and perception, and a foregrounding of the latter. It is a belief in an art that is not about the truth as an abstract or constant, just a particular truth rigorously adhered to. *In fidelis deo.*

Learn about a pine tree from a pine tree, and about a bamboo stalk from a bamboo stalk. [8]

At the heart of this is what Goethe called *gehalt*, a 'felt-thought.' Feldman brings it up with Shere in that same interview, using Mondrian as his example: 'It's not worked out, it's felt out.' Feldman's work, particularly from the early sixties onward, is devoted to developing and deepening this intuitive process. It's a fidelity to sound itself, to its needs. Feeling out the shape of each note, its immediate character and its place within the whole, how it reflects what came before and how it influences the perception of what is to come. The form and the content are inseparable, they draw each other out. It's easy to see this approach as an oppositional position taken against the teleological excess, the 'historical anxiety,' of the Schoenbergs of this world, but we must assume it's more than a mere contrarian impulse. It's a wish to be constantly attentive to the demands of the moment, rather than the epoch. Susan Sontag once described an 'inescapable truth about perception: the positivity of all experience at every moment of it.' This is Feldman's desire, positive experience in every moment, watching the present fade and die in the air.

The moment is a more humble measurement than the era, the age, but perhaps harder still to get a grip on. Moments are always slipping away, they're gone before we have time to perceive them. In Feldman we find an attempted embrace of the momentary, an urge to slow it down and spread it out so it becomes possible to behold it. It's about the way the bow hits the string, or how a finger presses a key. It's about

3 Matsuo Basho, *On Love and Barley: Haiku of Basho* (trans. Lucien Stryk, Penguin 1996)

touch, and, really, that's all. There is a willingness to work with time rather than with timing, which is the bundling up and parcelling out of time according to the composer's wishes. Feldman noted that Schoenberg was anxious about how he used his time, while John Cage had no anxiety at all. The desire to define and control time was destructive, almost colonial - a wish to shape the world to one man's wishes. It is intricately bound up with an aesthetic desire to fill time, to cram every perceptible moment with the realisation of the artist's own presence—think of Stockhausen's *Helicopter String Quartet*, the spectacle of it all. To overwhelm time, to dominate it, to stand out from history.

'He insists upon an action within the gamut of love.' [4]

Feldman felt, instead, that nature and human nature were one and the same, so there was no need to differentiate oneself from time (which is the most natural thing imaginable), or from its passing. Feldman's music is an attempt to get on time's level, its wavelength. To open oneself up almost enough to feel—with acceptance, not remorse—the passing of time, the drip of each moment as it becomes the past. A simple, impossible aim. There is an undercurrent of grief in almost all his work, but it isn't mourning exactly, more the sense that what is lost must be so. The loss is not unexpected. Its time has come. Feldman wrote of sound as being 'not unlike a sundial, whose enigmatic hand travels imperceptibly throughout its journey.' His sound was that of a sundial when there was no sun, yet abundant light. The

---

4 John Cage, Silence (Wesleyan 1961)

hand disappears, but time has been transfixed within the image of the sundial, within the sound itself. How can this happen? The artist must cast no shadow, or be everywhere at once. 'How truly omnipotent.'

In his last years, Feldman came back to light again, suggesting that the use of light in painting has less to do with chronology and progress than with the imagination, the feeling, of the painter. Pitch, on the other hand, 'characterises chronologically the history of Western music'—the organisation of pitch defines the time, the era. Feldman set out to prove that 'the chronological aspect of music's development is perhaps over.' Now would come the time for light from all directions at once, for a true diversity. No shadows of greed, of desire, just the immaculate transparency of the artist in love with—at one with—the material, the raw corporeality of sound arranged as music. In Feldman's work, time is static, transfixed, an element of the work itself and inseparable from it. Less enlightenment, more illumination. 'You find it in Matisse,' he said, a couple of years before his death. 'The whole idea of stasis. That's the word. I'm involved in stasis. It's frozen, at the same time it's vibrating.'

'Silence was just a question of how we breathed, as individuals. Silence was taken for granted.' [5]

Silence is not a vacuum, it is an element in itself. It's the passing of time. It's not just the opposite to speech, it's the

5 Morton Feldman, radio interview with Charles Shere (KPFA 1967): https://archive.org/details/MortonFeldmanInterview1967

most vital, the most ideal, part of speech, without which communication is impossible. It's an inescapable presence in every moment and it counteracts the constructed, the pretentious, the inauthentic. For Sontag, silence guarded against 'speech dissociated from the body (and, therefore, from feeling), speech not organically informed by the sensuous presence and concrete particularity of the speaker and of the individual occasion for using language.' Silences make each sound significantly more profound, more surprising, more intensely personal. Works that embrace silence become acts of patterning, something against nothing. Like the colours of the abstract expressionists, sound and silence have a habit of spilling beyond any borders laid out for them. Each speaks to the presence of the other, they egg each other on. They flood the work.

I have an anxiety about time. I make a lot of plans. I erect boundaries and channels, strategic flows to stem the tide. Yet it still seems to pour away from me, and I haven't the balance, the pacing, necessary to move with it, to follow it. So I worry and fret about the future and all that might yet be, while staring constantly into the past, trying to figure out what happened to all the plans I made yesterday. I'll be mature when I can face the present I suppose, but how would I go about doing that? It's always already gone, deadened by habit, by experience. 'The adult has always already experienced everything,' but this isn't the adult I'm trying to be. To hold history but not habit, that's a trick. I have notions about myself still. The way I'd like to be seen, or that I'd like to be seen at all. It would be better to concentrate on seeing, but it's often hard to look past yourself. Fat bastard of an ego, casting shadows all around.

'The only philosophy which can be responsibly practised in face of despair is the attempt to contemplate all things as they would present themselves from the standpoint of redemption.[6]

In that radio interview, Shere said of Feldman's music that it was 'music in which one can wander,' a 'garden of sounds with no paved path which it is necessary to follow.' Feldman replied that the path was his mind; though the path is invisible to the wanderer, it nonetheless remains. The path is a presence that, almost beyond the consciousness of the listener, makes each sound, each flower in the garden, more beautiful, more immanent. If nature and human nature are the same, sound is as imbued with the divine—what some might call the Buddha nature—as anything else. Indeed, because sound itself—as a physicality—lacks an ego, it is more 'divine' than those who order it and use it as a tool in their own sense of greatness. Those who appreciate it only for what it can do for them, not for what it is in itself. Those who value the music for the ripples it creates in the world, rather than the vibrations it causes in the air.

Does it come down to faith again? Total attention, a complete openness to feeling, leaves no room for interpretation, only belief. To believe in the immanence of sound itself, to put oneself in service of a mere vibration —something so slight, so vulnerable, so transient—is an act of immense self-sacrifice. It is to accept the dominance

6 Adorno, *Minima Moralia*

of something without agency, without power in the world, to relegate one's own desires and ambitions in favour of a living asceticism. To quiet the constant machinations of one's ongoing internal *bildungsroman* in favour of pure existence, pure sensation, is this the path to transcendence? The key to living with time? A poverty of spirit leads to the riches of the world.

'And then we shall unwillingly return / Back to this meadow of calamity, / This uncongenial place, this human life; / And in our individual human state / Go through the sad probation all again, / To see if we will poise our life at last, / To see if we will now at last be true / To our own only true, deep-buried selves, / Being one with which we are one with the whole world.'[7]

There is a theory that, it is when we appear to ourselves as least like ourselves, then that is when we are closest to ourselves. We are so good at performing ourselves for others, we don't even realise we're doing it, so we can never know 'our own only true deep-buried selves.' They are too deeply buried, they've rotted away, corrupted. So it's the negation of our notions of ourselves we're after here, to figure out if there's a space within as yet untainted. Or, more likely, if there's anything that is redeemable. We're after the rebirth of the spirit. Sontag said that 'art is more than ever a deliverance,' and I'm inclined to believe this has something to do with the spirit of a work, and the soul of a person. Adorno said that artworks become spirit 'exclusively through the relation of their sensuous elements to each other.' We can share in that

---

7 Matthew Arnold, *Empedocles on Etna* (1852)

spirit, which might begin to redeem what's left of our own, if we can bear to look it in the face.

Feldman's music—like love, like time—defeats the artist, the performer, the audience; even this essay. It seems pat to say it is what it is, but here we are, and that's how he would have liked it, surely. 'If you let it, it supports itself,' said Cage. Letting it is the hard part. Letting be allows for time to pass, for the tinkering hand of desire to fade away. Letting be assumes no ideal time, no ideal light—the work remains the same and every moment is as worthy of attention as the last or the next. The big climax is the first note.

What is important now is to recover our senses. [8]

I've not got a handle on maturity. I can't picture its outline. I am too occupied by it, which is the height of immaturity. I have a sense that it might be the ability to look beyond my own shadow, or to feel heat through the skin. There's probably more to it than that though. It has something to do with 'being one with which we are one with the whole world.' Being not a 'slave of sense' but immaculately, indiscriminately attuned to the senses. To be so porous that I'm clear. Transparent, luminous. For now, I remain a brute.

Progress is out of the question. [9]

---

8 Susan Sontag, *Against Interpretation* (Penguin 2009)

9 Cage, *Silence*

Three Poems

Cal Doyle

DOCKLANDS SEPPUKU

R   AND   H   HALL
in the grain   silos   each broken   wall
meets a piece of sky parcelled out   by
their own   cavities   applied
dentistry   capital gains   conference
H   HALL   AND   R
centres   experiential   retail
extravaganzas   await their   application
as if by paint the gloss   of fresh
ground   beans polystyrene
c-cups   beige   shirts
HALL   R   AND   H
draped   across   greytooth:
R   AND   H   HALL
spins   H   HALL   R
AND   into the   soil
of the   city's   jawbone
H HALL   R   AND
R   AND   H   HALL
drills   its   own   grave

THE GHOST ESTATE

sprawls   throughout   the   arteries
of   the   city: voiceless   flats
nodules   in the   eyeless
throats   of those   who choose
to ignore   the spectral   web
of its belonging   hard cash passes
from pocket to   palm its occupants
Agnieska   Caroline   Nosizwe   Ishraq

accept it   like a deposit   of seed
into   the wart   of a used condom
tossed   over   their   bedside
lockers: *Shadow-Pussy   Nubian Queen*
Lollipop   take to the   stage
polished pole   :   (their lodgings)

in   Blackpool   under   the tidal
gaze   of their owners   and glance
through   a   window   the city

looks   down and   away

DISARTICULATED SKULL OF A TURKEY

lost and found

Cracked and elevated behind the gallery glass
the cranial trophy found half-rotten
in a wetted depression of dirt and moss

and tossed into a box, with the other unclean
specimens of fowl: a pheasant's spinal cord
conducts the other skulls, beaks and wings

in their minor aria of rattle, without a word
or rapturous applause
from the laboratory-bound truck, shifting into gear:

virgin sacrifice

it remains unclear if those soft-bodied
offerings ever appeased Tezcatlipoca,
or the four beautiful maidens ever brought
the boy to climax in the year that he wore

an outfit fit for the centrepiece of a holiday's
dinner table; in the legends his heart
was torn from his chest on the altar
as the maidens stripped and bathed

before the ritual to please the shaman:

a dance of seven scarves, a thunder-clap
to set the gobble of turkeys (translated
from the vengeful-divinities of the sky

trans-atlantic express

into feathered clucks on the ground) off, like searing hot
kernels popping in oil that once drowned the skillet.

Strickland's men would gather the birds into sacks
and ship them north-east on the warm Aztec

current: light relief for men used to drowning slaves
in slop-buckets, on deck, and in their grief craved

a quiet night-time fucking of the dead-men's widows,
and got it too, even if a few disarticulated blows

happy christmas

to their skulls had to be administered:

Necks broken. A feast. Tied wrists

cut loose

Deckhand desertion, sea shanties, a lace
  dress slips to the floor   *gobble*   the bloodied kiss

gobble   a mess

our work is never over

of effluvium without any taste but of a blade that sinks
into flesh to make its point known to the nervous system.
Let's get lost tonight, you and I, into the failing nerve
endings
of our articulated bodies, or where the skull sits thus:
black-boned

(arched as if to snatch to eat any creature that thinks
it might have free passage) and brainless. Nothing is
known
to a bird without the grey mess of muscle, or just a thing
to think   *it's either us or them*

virgin sacrifice

to lay on the block and meet the cleaver.
This must return to smoke and mirrors:

Chants that swell
and reverberate against the pyramid walls

as she disarticulates herself from her ritual
dress and lays along the altar. Clinical,

the priest extracts her soul and sings her name.
In the pen, turkeys gobble, scuttle, feed on grain

underworld (or Ovid high-five!)

never to worry about death, myth, or Orpheus
and his lyre that never hit a flat note

on his mission behind enemy lines,

or that his disarticulated head
had never even known what a turkey was

lost and found

or a radio, for that matter. The driver flicks
between frequencies and follows the signs
out of Hades (along a bank of some Styx)

as the aria in the box continues to rattle.
Left behind is the skeleton, decolonised
of a mind (by proxy of this skull)

a web of bone and mud that doesn't shy
away from the forbidden task of flight –
the wing-beat, angular *gobble*-cry

scattershoots a path into the night
as its estranged skull stares me down: rotten,
black, absorbing all of the light.

Four Bridges/Four Exercises in Re-Construction

Adrian Duncan

1.

In 1977 my father and some of his friends built the house that I was brought up in. It sits within a ribbon of other bungalows alongside the main road out of my home town Ballymahon, in south county Longford.

When I was young there was an open ditch that ran along the rear of each of these houses which was used to drain the expanse of farmland that ran down to it, preventing any flooding to our back gardens. The ditch demarked where our domain ended and where the farmland began. I don't remember exactly when my sisters, my brother, and I started playing in this ditch or whose idea it was to put a plank across it. It was one of those narrow builders' planks that are used for scaffolding platforms, or for running a wheelbarrow up into a skip. It bounced as you walked across. This plank opened up the back field to us and half way up this field to the left hand side was a steel gate leading out through the hedgerow onto a single track cul-de-sac road—which forty years before had continued on to Longford town. Up to our mid-teens we would gather at this gate with the other kids of our age who lived nearby. The kitchen window of our house looked out onto the rear patio which led to the fence and ditch, so our mother—who is a teacher but who then gave up her career to stay at home and raise us—could easily enquire out the kitchen window, if she saw us straying up into the field that always seemed to be full of cows, or sheep, or both, grazing circles around each other. Our clothesline was strung across three of the four edges of this patio. If the weather was dry and windy my mother would hang out the bedclothes, draping them over the line and down almost to the ground, creating a ceiling-less room of white and patterned fabric walls between the kitchen and the field. If the sun shone, this room would become quite brilliant. When we were maybe seven or eight I remember my brother, who is eleven months younger than me, playing with these expanses of fabric in a sort of theatrically coquettish way, wrapping them around his body then emerging out from behind them, then disappearing again in behind another. He has always been able to bring his immediate surrounds to life around him and I have always admired, envied, and tried to emulate his invention.

When I was ten my father had built a two storey, tower-like extension to the right of our original bungalow, it having become too small for our family of six children. The rear bedroom window on the first floor gave an elevated view of the back field. You could see up over the brow of the field to the back hedgerow, and to the left, at the end of the cul-de-sac road, you could now also see the roof of McGrayan's house. Their house was a small council cottage probably built in the late 1950s where Mrs McGrayan and her daughter lived with their dog, a vicious collie called Rex who made cycling up that road on your own a source of anxiety as he would often appear at the end of it, and if you were found as being within range he would chase you back down the road. Being chased down that road on my own with Rex barking and snapping behind me were the first really serious moments of my life, or at least the seriousness of isolation became apparent to me in them.

2.

In 1999, after graduating with an average degree in structural engineering, I started working for Irish Rail. I was given a job with the maintenance division whose offices were located in the upper floors of Pearse Station. After six months I became involved in a bridge replacement on the DART railway line near Glasthule, in south county Dublin. The bridge was typically Victorian—a series of large cast iron beams spanning from buttress to buttress with shallow arches of brickwork between the beams.

We started the replacement on a Friday evening in mid-summer of 2000. There was a senior foreman who smoked John Player Blues continuously, he was in his late sixties, stocky and straightforward and all of the activity seemed to revolve around him. There was an overweight senior engineer who had no confidence and was happy to defer all responsibility to the foreman. There were a number of gangs of labourers, and me, a callow and largely useless figure. The DART power lines were unclipped, laid onto the tracks beneath, and protected. The pipes and cables carried within the bridge were shut off at each end and a mobile crane was installed on the road. The bridge was cut open and demolished with many different sizes of extremely noisy concrete breakers. Dust and fumes billowed into the air and large, dramatic floodlights were dotted around the site and run from generators. Lorries turned up throughout the night taking clattering loads of the bridge rubble away. By midday on Saturday the bridge was gone, leaving a void between the original cut-stone buttresses either side—the surfaces of which were then prepared to receive the new, flat, precast concrete bridge units.

There was a moment of quiet nervousness as the first fifteen metre long precast slab was transferred from the back of the lorry up, over, and down onto the bridge buttresses. The crane dangled the piece in a seemingly weightless way above the supports while it was being guided into place by men with ropes. And after some shunting by other men at either end brandishing crow-bars, the unit slotted down. The chains went slack. Then there was a pause. Then two men stepped out onto the slab. They unhooked the crane chains that clinked and limply criss-crossed each other, then the chains slowly disappeared back up into the smoky, umber-coloured early evening sky, then swished lazily through the air over to the next precast unit on the lorry trailer, where two men stood to receive and re-engage these flailing lines. By the time the whole bridge deck was in place I was given permission to go home.

Six months later I left Irish Rail and went back-packing around south east Asia and Australia. I decided when I returned from these travels that I would work as a design engineer in a clean, quiet, bright, and spacious office. After I came back from these travels in late 2001, I spent the following seven years working as a structural engineer in various consultancies designing structures, only visiting sites very sporadically to see how the construction was progressing. Once the basic structural works were finished I would stop visiting the site and more often than not I did not see the structure as a complete, habitable building. By 2007 having worked in Dundalk and Edinburgh, I was back in Dublin, now a chartered engineer, earning good money and working as senior designer on a number of very large projects in a city that then seemed to have been ripped up and re-built in a way that drily mimicked ambition. At this stage my design work was becoming very abstract and I was becoming completely disconnected from the actual material and labour on building sites. Buildings existed as calculations and sketches, and stick-line diagrams and deflection patterns in computer programs, then as instructions and graphics on rolls of drawings, then in conversations with architects and project managers, then as interconnected smooth planes of concrete jutting up out of a building site, or as Cartesian frames of coated steel beams and columns. By late 2008 all of this disappeared and I went back to college to study fine art, and it is only since I emigrated to Berlin late last year—with my girlfriend and our dog, completely broke— where I got some work as a site-engineer on a building-site in Alexanderplatz, have I been confronted again with the actual day-to-day problems and effort of building. I still do not physically labour, I don't dig, fill, pull, drill, bore, cut, screw, drag, lift, hold, sweat... I have no building skills or physical stamina. I tried building-site labour one college-summer in Boston in 1998, working for my cousin, who gave me a job, and though I could basically fulfil most of the tasks given to me, I hated it, and resolved never to work like that again. Now, in Berlin, I have become curious about the labour on the building-site so I photograph the site far more expansively than before, not just of the things being built but the smaller and more incidental details like, bent pieces of rusting reinforcement bars, wet, setting concrete and cement mixes, stacks of bricks and shards of plywood, the skips filled with twisted and dusty building-site refuse, and other things like the conversational pencil sketches made by builders on the unpainted walls and columns of the structure, or some accidental arrangement of tools, or yellow hardhats, or discarded gloves—it is a curiosity that is shot through with revulsion and pity.

There are two very conspicuous buildings on Alexanderplatz, the enormous T.V. Tower and the large, cuboidal, forty-storey Park Inn Hotel building. Both were built in the late 1960s after the early wire fence versions of the Berlin Wall had been erected. The building-site I work on is a refurbishment of a squat, three-storey reinforced concrete framed building that sits in the foothills and is structurally part of the Park Inn building. Early in the project I looked into the history of the construction of the T.V. Tower and the Park Inn Hotel building and I came upon a photographer called Hans Joachim Spremberg and one black and white photograph attributed to him that was taken from near the top of the then almost complete T.V. Tower of a worker who is clipped out onto the edge of a steel frame working on one of its large connection joints with a long wrench in his gloved right hand. He is in his late forties and is wearing a helmet and overalls and he is laughing. He is suspended out in front and slightly below us, and behind him, way way down, laid out into the distance, you can see the medium-rise social-housing blocks progressing eastward along Karl Marx Allee, like tiny Froebel gifts scattered across an engineer's drawing board. In the photograph this worker is looking at something to the left and below the camera. His head is tilted back slightly as he laughs, but his mirth has a sort of mocking quality to it suggesting that this steel-worker has caught the photographer in the trapeze-like act of photographing him—the steel worker has helped to create the point of view for the photographer to carry out his work of mechanically capturing but ultimately flattening what generated this elevated point of view.

3.

A few months back I found a photograph that had been sitting in an album in my old bedroom in my parents' house. It is of an ex-girlfriend, and I would have taken it in summer 2003, on one of those disposable film cameras. We were in Verona at the time on holiday. We had broken up after two years going out and wanted to get back together again. I was living in Dundalk and she was from Scotland, and I was in love with her. In the photograph she is slim with shoulder-length black hair. She stands in the middle of the frame at a slight angle to the camera. She is standing awkwardly, both of her knees are slightly bent, and her right hand is resting on the top of the stone bridge parapet that runs behind her and on out of the picture frame toward a perspective point from which the composition of the image counter-projects. It is a bright day. To the background you can see the far edge of a wide river, and beyond that the stone buildings of the city as they rise gently up out of the valley. She is smiling. She is wearing a pale-coloured corduroy blazer, a pink silky round-neck top, a light-blue pair of jeans and a white pair of dressy trainers. We got back together, but things ended badly, and I took it badly, and we haven't spoken or made contact since. For years after we broke up I would often dream very vividly of her, then wake up to a keen sense of yearning. I rarely dream of her now and when I do it so vague that I can only guess that I have been dreaming of her by the very specific, if faint, sense of yearning that I feel upon waking. The flatness of the passivity of the yearning is all that is left of it. In recent years I have noticed this happen almost only when I visit my parents on my own for an overnight stay. The house during these visits is quiet and my bedroom still has a lot of my old things in it.

4.

In early 2009, midway through my first year in art college, I went down to a section of bogland between Ballymahon and Lanesborough town. Off this trunk road that runs between these two towns there are a number of turn-offs, left and right that bring you further into the warren of roads that thread themselves through the countryside beyond. Here the land varies in type from marsh, to lake, to bog, to forest, to farmland, to agri-industrial wasteland. Sometimes these land types intersubsume, particularly when the water table is high thus then too intersubsuming their designation. I was looking for one very narrow road that led to a small section of shallow, domestic bogland—an offcut from the deeper Bord na Móna boglands—where during the summers, my mother, my sisters, my brother and I would often foot turf with my grandmother. Before leaving my parents' house I got directions from my mother, but still when I was out driving around I couldn't find the road so I pulled up at a section of bog that I had not been to before, and, because I had just bought a new SLR digital camera for college, I got out and enthusiastically took photographs of the land. By then the day had turned sodden and it was starting to get quite dark. When I walked back up from the section of razed industrial bog I had been stomping around in, I noticed two strange corrugated steel structures in the mid-distance. One was short the other, about twenty meters to the left, was a taller tower-like structure. They both faced away from the bog into a patch of land that was not quite bog, farmland or marsh. I investigated the structures and realised that this was a clay-pigeon shooting rig. The taller structure housed the skeet from where the clay pigeon might be hurled, and the lower structure housed the shooter—it was full of lurid red, spent gun cartridges. I photographed this arrangement on the flat landscape from a number of angles and later that week drew the arcs of a clay pigeon and a bullet onto the photograph. I tried to imagine the intensity of the moment when a clay pigeon is shattered by a bullet.[1] I visited shooting ranges with a borrowed video camera, recording men shooting at clay pigeons. I began to idealise the arcs that the clay pigeon and the bullet made by removing the context surrounding them, until they became two arc-segments on a blank piece of paper. I remember one

1 Single bullets are not most often used for clay pigeon shooting— these shots usually consist of small, intense sprays of pellets from a cartridge.

Saturday night, having spent hours drawing and re-drawing in my notebook these two arcs with separate starting points and a shared apex, realising that this shape looked like a leaf. I then realised that the place in space, time and intention where these arcs meet is in its idea the same place that a leaf-tip occupies just as it stops fully flourishing outward toward the sun. Then I realised that there was another part that ghosts this shape. It is the impossible part of the shape. It brings together its real and imaginary elements. It starts at the back of the point of collision and forks out in two separate curving lines down toward two distinct points of imaginary rest.

A few years later I revisited the clay pigeon shooting rig in the bog and walked out beyond the two steel structures and found clay pigeon fragments that had fallen onto the ground. I put some in my pocket and later with some glue I made small mounded sculptures with them. The colour tones of these fragments varied from a vivid to a washed out orange-red.

Subcritical Tests

Ailbhe Darcy & S.J. Fowler

ODYSSEY

There's no one else to forget for you
the poppy juice, the rooms sweet with milk
where milk could not be
and the sucking bee at its grig those quick weeks.

ailing, a cashewshaped miniature blind
children has been forgotten like a bunker fruit (normally a
lemon)
by those who suffered the thing we're to open
the brand alarm (that is you & I)

were those mewed in shives to mistake
false fruit for fruit, shivelight for light, pleasure
(not neat, not quite cashewsized) for origin,
it won't suffice, our dashed notes (you & I)

but they're also those who taught us that
minor bomb threat (leon) v. half species death
protect your roads, Ailbhe, they're welcome in
my shelter, stockpiled: nootropics, voids, bulletproof
coffee, steroids.

TRUMPET

I want to believe there's something in the bunker,
in the cowslip's bell. Stockpiles of shivery paper,
caffeine, nicotine and romance. and not just romance.
Onion juice and doubled tongues for the scurvy and
amnesia.

I want a double ration: The world to keep going;
the world to end in my time. I don't want to miss it.
To this all economy reduces. To productivity beverages,
to squeezing out more than four lines, to vegetable juices.

ailingr, however, no winter could be arrived at that would
be a greed upon by both the parties, the nations of you
writing
& I writing, & you mothering. there is no romance of the
onion
it is the base of fruit, the Big of vegetable impressions
pressed into glass

when there has been antinatalism over intoning others
lives, there will be proper room for misanthropomorphism
Samuel's contempt, unhidden, for those stupider than he
the box cracked upen, a way forward when all is dead black

REBOUND

That which I leave to sound the house myself
is that what annoys me most. A rhythm
of dark jungle hidden drums. They fork
the hurt of a mess, like the wise themselves

like that refuse itself, that cuts holes
in the annals of brave officers / scientists
there is the question of the why the world
hates you, is not the answer because in smartest

shipshape order, the tocking is the bomb.
Splendid is the radius of this house,
where the only game in town is to be the bomb.
Mom is the bomb, Little Boy is the bomb,

pushing food around the plate. Pushing
wheeled toys with indefinite plastic lifespan.
Evacuating on schedule. Not wasting space
knowing what's left to destroy or the price of eggs.

STAGECOACH

 nothing will happen (ed dorn)
so slowly the rubber ring forgotten
on the handle of skin is removed
the design is intentional, the knowledge lost

Unkind momentum to be buzzing at these four walls
having at the matter's facts, sliding an earwigging glass
over the concrete seeking rumours of let out.
There are things our words will definitely not affect

as ages pass so the remote wisdom
that took generations to accrue dies off
they are our friendship policing
a council of vintage money

Or there is listening to you describe death by a thousand
cuts,
rifling through myself for the correct expression:
'The worst part is the imagination that goes into torture.'
'I think that might be the redeeming factor.'

CIMARRON

here is a home block your dome where
you how is made & you are grown
a simple flaccid real readiness for wars
then you will know it can go   either way

either way we know indignation will not do.
complacency will not do. sincerity will not do.
irony will not do. humour is at best difficult
to arrange with any certainty either way.

here is a dome your know as your home
because of course the earth is jealous
a simple friend won't let you be alone
then you choose it to go one way yours

Rose of Cimarron, coming open in
yet slower motion; slower motion;
peeling open. Yours the splendid
temple of this home and the sucking bee

At eight forty-five in the evening, I stood at the hatch window of the medicine room, doling out little paper cups of pills to the loose queue of patients in the corridor. It was fifteen minutes from the end of my shift, my fourth twelve hour shift in a row. I was jacked tired. Of course, Gerry noticed.

'No snoozing on the job Nurse Nally. What if the right pill goes to the wrong man and the wrong pill goes to the right man? What then?'

His bony old man's head, with his flashy dentures, and his scrappy shreds of black hair that were like the feathers that fringe a rook's beak, poked around the shoulder of Mona, the depressed retired post office owner from county Louth. Mona limped off with her pill, and Gerry stood there in his full glory, in his fluorescent pink, skinny woman's AC/ DC tee shirt hugging his ribs above a pair of drainpipe jeans with a stripe of pretend diamonds on the outside of each leg. He wagged an officious finger at me.

'Now come on, give us those magic beans, as I call them, wha'? Did you make sure the one to put me to sleep is in it? That's the only good one, as I always say to Hegga.'

'Don't tell me she was in again today?' I asked him.

To say I wasn't keen on Hegga is an understatement. She was a hard, jaundiced old woman with hair like kelp, who'd routinely visit him late in the day when the other visitors had come and gone. She would glide into the ward like a silent ghoul and fly straight over to his bed, or out into the smoking cage with him. She always came late, probably because Bert, his brother-in-law and only other visitor, another parasite, came early. Bert… come to think of it, was Bert his brother-in-law at all? Bert was very like Hegga. Maybe he was Hegga's brother?

'Hegga was in,' said Gerry, sucking his meds up into lips like a vacuum nozzle, 'and she still is. She's down in me bed talking to me about some very important stuff, Nurse Nally, about me rights, Nurse Nally. A man who knows things go right to the top needs to know his rights, amn't I right, Nurse Nally?'

According to Gerry, there is a global spying conspiracy that goes all the way up from 'your window-cleaners,' to your 'presidents, prime ministers and captains of industry.' A standard enough thought in places like this, the 'secret system.' It was his main obsession. He'd tell us nurses that he was 'learning new things about the secret system every day, oh yiz'd love to know what I know.' The trade off for his secret knowledge seemed to be that 'spies are always on the lookout for me, spying on me with machines.' 'To battle,' I saw him say to himself once before, as he sat on the stone bench in the smoking cage.

'As long as chatting is all you are doing down there Gerry…' I said.

I was only half joking. On a ward inspection the previous week, Moll, the other nurse, had pulled open the curtain around his bed, to find Hegga tugging him off, 'and him wearing sunglasses,' a detail I had to laugh at. I shouldn't have brought it up. He got all heightened, antsy, a bit all over the shop. He was so beside himself, that he was full of slithery repetitive movements, like a frightened disco dancer who can't stop. It was repugnant.

'Don't come nosing in at me and Hegga,' he said, 'We are having an important chat. A crucial chat. You see, with Hegga's head for things, and my…'

He stopped, and he raised a hand to his mouth, giving me an eyeful of all his rings, Liberace knuckles, imitation stuff though. He had clearly let a cat out of a bag. What was Hegga up to? I had to find out.

'Come on, King Louis, and hurry the feck up, we're growing beards here,' said the reedy auld voice of lanky Sam, the English lecturer.

He was standing behind Gerry and he had become impatient, as had some of the others behind him, the ones who looked forward to the medicine. The patients split half and half, you see, between those who want the medicine and those who don't want the medicine.

'Hold on one sec now, Sam. Wait…' I said to his glowering head, as he stepped up to the hatch.

As old Sam's pill disappeared into his maw, Gerry took advantage by slipping away, back to his bed and Hegga. I decided I'd go nosing after them once I had finished with dispensing the tablets, for I'm a nosey nurse, as you have seen; Nosey Nurse Nally is what some of them call me. I'd go down, suss out what the story was, then head home, for some heroic sleeping. Just me marinating in the leaba, until my next shift. When I had finished up and locked the hatch, I walked as lightly as I could across the ward to get near to his bed, which had its curtain pulled around it, as I expected it would, at the furthest end. He had asked for the specific bed three months into his stay which was thirteen months and counting. He'd have it for another week, when he'd be due a rotation on account of another patient's request. He originally asked for it because the sink was at that end, and he used the sink a lot, to wash his y-fronts with a bar of Imperial Leather soap. He didn't trust the hospital laundry with them. 'Me DNA is on them,' he explained to me once, and now he's worked out the further problem that his DNA might be collected regardless, out of the hospital's pipes—'that's the system for ye, always one step ahead.' As I traversed the ward, I flung a quick look around at the other patients. A few were already asleep, and there was that relative quiet you'd sense after the medicine but before the sleep talking, which can be a real frightener with them all talking out of their separate lonely hells at the one time. I stopped at the foot of the bed next to his. It contained the sleeping lump of a new patient, a big miserable youngish fella called Barry. He had arrived in the night before, lashing sweat like someone with a disease, holding his stomach, crying like a baby.

'No. Leave me alone,' he said, startling me, but it was only the sleep talk, thank God.

I sat on my hunkers and pretended to read his medical notes. It was the perfect spot to eavesdrop. Because the main hospital lights had been dimmed for the night, the lamp beside Gerry's bed threw his and Hegga's shadows on the curtain. It made them big, and somehow like spider shadows or insect shadows in how they moved as the pair of them talked.

'Listen to me, you'll take it, no listen, take it, take it, take it,' he said, and his skinny arm stuck out of his shadow to pass something to Hegga, who wouldn't stop moving, pacing.

The weird shape of her zig-zagged around the curtain the way a bug moves on cow shite. She took what ever it was that he gave her, then whispered something to him, but I could not make it out. It sounded like a hiss.

Gerry continued, '...when the Power Invest money comes in, I am going to buy a DeLorean. You might know the car Hegga, the time traveller's car from *Back To the Future*. There is only one man... so far, mind you, so far... one man in Dublin with a DeLorean...'

I had heard this story before. According to Gerry, the DeLorean belonged to his nemesis, the man who he was possibly swapped with at birth, who he would oftentimes say was 'a powerful man, a rich man, and an influential man, you might call him the mirror opposite of me.'

Hegga seemed to hiss again.

'Who's there?' she said.

I leapt out of my skin. I nearly went running. It was all I could do to remain rooted there, as her arm's shadow jumped up Gerry's curtain, pulling it open enough for her and Gerry to see me. I immediately looked at my feet. I just couldn't look her in the face. To the sink instead, I said, 'visiting hours are over, Hegga, you'll have to go.'

Without saying a word, she got up and left, passing through the edge of my sight because I still refused to look directly at her. Her shape went sideways, like a fast crab in the dimness, towards the green light of the exit sign, and the door where a security guard would be waiting to wave her on her way. Why didn't I confront her? I'm not sure. A force of some kind stopped me. I confronted Gerry instead.

'Here tell us, Gerry,' I said, pushing the curtain open and

sitting down on the plastic visitor chair beside his bed, 'what is 'Power Invest'? Is Hegga taking advantage of ya?'

'Take that big fucken nose of yours out of my business, Nurse Nally... You must think that you're Big Brother's little brother or something, but you're only a cog. A cog!'

He was fuming, sitting there on top of his sheets with his bed tilted the way he liked it, so that he could 'observe and report.' There was still a smell left by Hegga on the air. It was a wet outdoor smell, like rained-on cardboard. Under his skinny arms, I could see that sweat was soaking through the AC/DC top. It must have felt cold, he was shivering as well as everything else.

'I'm only looking out for you, Gerry,' I said.

'Hegga is not taking advantage of me,' he spat, and up he craned his old crow head until it was right up in my grill, 'you are lucky, Nurse Nally, that I don't tell Hegga everything. Everything I really know about this place, about its secret system. Oh hoh, there'd be trouble then... because unlike you and me Hegga is powerful, very powerful...'

In my pocket, my mobile phone made its noise. *Bloop bloop.* My immediate superior, Doctor Bob, perhaps, or worse again, my landlord. Throughout my life, I've had a ghastly and strange amount of trouble with landlords.

Gerry nodded his head slyly towards me, and said, 'is the person in charge checking up on you? Or is the person in charge of the person in char...,' and then, just like that, he stopped.

He had lost his chain of thought. In dispensing the prescriptions of Doctor Bob, Moll and I administered a lot of them a drug to stop florid thinking, and that was the main thing it did to their thoughts, snip at them before they completed. I suppose a psychiatrist would say it stopped them from getting out of hand, like cutting down weeds, or flowers. He then looked as if he were about to laugh or smile. The crow's feet appeared either side of his eyes, and his mouth opened wide enough for me to see the four or five worn teeth that sat behind his dentures like yellow olives. His visage carried a green tint, light thrown from the distant exit sign. The peculiar way he considered me. Pity maybe it was. He said the weirdest fucken thing.

'It's a hard and sorrowful old station for the likes of you, a nurse. But a pair of new shoes might be just the thing. A pair of new shoes might just make you happy.'

Before I could open my gob, he reached for the box of cigarettes he smoked. The same malodorous brand they all smoked. They smoked them because they were cheap and I hated the smell of them. Whenever I cleaned them up from around the smoking cage, I'd imagine that the tiny blue trademark sticker on their butts was made by mould, and that it had mould's rotten unnatural auld taste. He tapped the fag box open and poked in it with his orange and brown fingers, until he found what he was looking for, rolled up next to a half-smoked fag, a fifty euro note.

'There you go,' he whispered to me, and so close and so soft was his voice that I could be sure that nobody else on the ward heard him as he crushed the note into the pocket of my nurse's uniform, 'There you go. I don't need it. Go buy yourself a nice new pair of shoes.'

I looked over my shoulder. Everyone was in a world of their own. Nobody was watching. I took his money.

'Our secret, don't tell Mammy,' he winked, and he picked up his sunglasses, which he wore over his eyes when he slept, and he put them on.

Our secret. I laughed, and I coughed. I was pretending already that nothing had happened between the two of us.

'Well, I'll be on me way,' I babbled to him, 'I'll tell nurse Moll things are fine with you. You've a visit from Bert to look forward to in the morning. Cheerio, Gerry.'

With my head held low, and my breaths coming hard, I took off in Hegga's footsteps, towards the nurse's station where I would finally clock off on the computerised system. As I went, one of my hands groped madly at the fifty euro note in my pocket, balling it up, saturating it with sweat. I did not turn back all the same. I carried on through the corridor, and inside the pocket of my uniform, it was as if the note grew dense and heavy, and the heaviness grew cold and sucking. All the same, I did not turn back.

A Writer's Guide to the Dialectical Landscapes of Dublin

Therese Cox

One overcast April day in Dublin—is there any other kind?—I wandered down the long slope of Ringsend Road into Barrow Street, in search of something I couldn't quite place. A flâneur's impulse had led me to this intersection of this not-so-foreign city, though I didn't then have the vocabulary I do now for what I was up to. *Faffing about*, my Irish friend would have said. *Idle exploration*, I'd have conceded.

Barrow Street is a narrow enclave of Ringsend, a working-class area on Dublin's southeast side that I had knocked about only once before, many years back, a bleak November afternoon to bake Thanksgiving cookies with a chaplain from Belfast and an expert in sixteenth-century conceptions of sin, both of whom I had met singing in the Trinity College Chapel Choir. It was the late nineties. I was alone in Dublin and homesick. My mom had airmailed me a turkey-shaped cookie cutter from Illinois in the hopes I could enjoy my first Thanksgiving away from home baking. The three of us—myself, the chaplain, and the sin expert— rolled out a slab of sugar, eggs and flour on the counter with a Jameson's bottle, while Palestrina motets filled the cramped but cosy home.

Seven years later I remembered this all—the warm smell of unbaked cookie dough, the hollow purity of soprano voices—as I gazed at the squat buildings of Ringsend, my hands in fingerless gloves buried in my pockets. A cat's cradle of telephone wires hung down over houses huddled under the shadow of the concrete silo of the abandoned

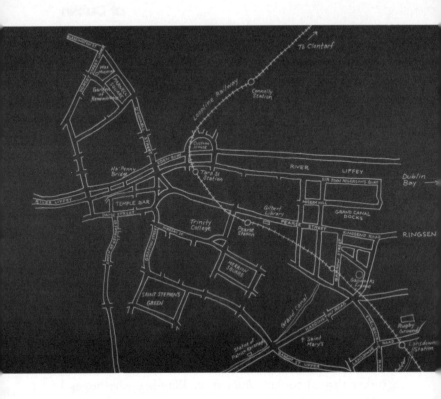

Boland's flour mill, which I'd just passed, eyeing its shattered windows. An unmistakable air of dereliction attached itself to the faded building site signs, and beyond the barbed wire my eye fell on a series of row houses on the far side of the road. Identical in size, they stubbornly asserted their individuality in their painted stucco-and-brick facades and oddly stuck-on numbers.

One house in the row snagged my attention, though I could not have explained why. It was ordinary in every aspect. It had neither the memorable glued-on name of its next-door-neighbour (St. Jude, patron saint of hopeless causes), nor the particularity of the brass door knocker down the road shaped into a delicate lady's hand. This one had only a dark grey ground floor and an upper floor of fine red brick to distinguish itself, yet I knew in an instant that *this was the building I had come to see*. It was not, as one might expect, the house where I had once rolled out cookie dough with a bottle of Jameson's; it had nothing to do with the Palestrina. The only sound was the faint rush of passing cars, their sharp petrol smell stung my nostrils. I had stopped on the footpath, struck, just then, in that flash of a moment with an *memoire involuntaire*... Peering up at the blackened window, I saw in my mind's eye a distinct image of a teenage girl's face pressed up against the glass; it was a cold Saturday night, and after the boredom of her brother's epic game of Risk that raged for hours downstairs, she was at her bedroom window, silently awaiting the arrival of her dream suitor on a silver Vespa in the street below. Fumbling for a pen from my coat pocket, I took out my Moleskine notebook and assembled a sketch. I drew three windows and one door—a child's rendering of a house, missing only the slanted roof and smoking chimney—then coloured in the dark red brick. I labelled it with definitive strokes: *Greta's house. 18 Barrow Street.*

The house—this place I recognised instinctively, this memory that flared up in a sudden moment of insight— was not mine. Greta, the girl whose face pressed up against the glass, was not me but rather existed in a novel I hadn't yet written. Yet I knew this place; in it I saw my character's history, an alternate imaginary Dublin existing with just a thin fabric separating it from the real city before my eyes. What made me so sure? 'The past,' as Proust writes in the Overture of *Swann's Way*, 'is hidden somewhere outside the realm, beyond the reach of intellect, in some material object (in the sensation which that material object will give us) which we do not suspect.' In that whiff of petrol fumes and that glimpse of a half-grey stucco, half-red brick building, I'd found my flash of the past in the present, what Walter Benjamin describes in the *Arcades Project* as the dialectal image. I was transported.

'A landscape haunts, intense as opium.' Mallarmé's words, mediated through Benjamin, are just as potent for a fiction writer in the twenty-first century as they were for the historical writer. This idea connects a whole lineage of haunted-by-landscape writers, stretching out like smoke across the centuries, a long plume of a notion that intoxicates, a bit of skywriting over the Atlantic. What haunts a writer about a place is intensely personal; try to get her to pin it down and you're left either with vacuous generalisations or particularities so...*particular* they seem ill-suited to the task. Cities and monads are a complex mix. Blake sees heaven in a grain of sand, the Surrealist novelist Louis Aragon sees the Black Forest in the Meudin industrial area, I'm left cataloguing the meaning of life in a litany of waste spotted floating along the Grand Canal Dublin. The landscapes that linger in the mind—and heart—do so for reasons that seem to defy reason. Giedion suggests the flâneur is drawn to 'despised, everyday' places and structures—that, I think, is more like it. Something must account for why I'm mucking around Ringsend, or a nearby post-industrial abandoned dock in Dublin, sketching broken chain-link fences and calling it 'research.' It is research, of a sort. But I never expected to look like this.

Eight years ago, I decided to write a novel set in Dublin. I didn't really want to. I was, at the time, confused and annoyed by what was happening to the city I once knew so well. This was proprietary to the extreme. I'd lived there only briefly for a spell in my twenties, chain-smoking and crash-coursing my way through twentieth-century epics in a cramped flat in Rathmines, having decided to live 'the writer's life.' Tired of Illinois, I would make a go of it in Ireland, a country that, based on past jaunts, I'd decided fit me like a pair of beloved old Doc Martens. By the time I revisited Dublin in the summer of 2002, I'd been away for four years. In the interim the city had succumbed to the influence of the rising Celtic Tiger. I'd left it a lovably scruffy place, more town than city, somewhere you could still busk—as I had done— for your daily bread, and arrived back to find a brash yet uncertain capital bolstered by a bold new economy, a giddy city overtaken by the chirp of mobile phones and the gleam of Eurotrash gastropubs. The city centre felt alienating with the shiny new pyramids of the Ulster Bank building and glass-fronted effrontery, and when the Bewley's café on Grafton Street—my favourite writing café back in those last few months of the twentieth century—at last closed its doors I no longer knew the temperature of the place. I found myself pushed on my walks further and further to the outskirts, trying to find my place or any place, really—in the cosmopolitan labyrinth.

Walter Benjamin suggests the flâneur's philosophy hinges upon encounters with estrangement and surprise; perhaps it's possible that Dublin's newly bustling city centre weighted too heavily toward estrangement and not enough surprise. The ruined corners were more hospitable precisely because of their inhospitality, and a lonely impulse of delight drove me to the forgotten bits—the alleys, the abandoned railway sheds, the decommissioned graving docks—just as it once drove Yeats' Irish airman to the clouds.

I wanted to write about the new Dublin because I wanted to get at the heart of something I didn't understand. Certainly, a booming economy was good for the people—decades of grinding poverty was nothing to get nostalgic about—so what was I doing mooning over romantic bits of rubble, complaining about the good old days? My own sense of place felt threatened by the influx of money: old cafés and corners I'd grown fond of fell away, and as buildings were changed utterly to make room for new ones, my romantic connection to the city was endangered. Why not write about it, why not set a book in Dublin in the late nineties—freeze it there—with some sort of epilogue set in the present day, so I could wander between the two cities in my mind and try to make some sense of it? Underlying it all, I decided, would be echoes of the Dublin of a hundred years ago that Joyce wrote about in his fifteen *Dubliners* stories. I would take elements of these stories, I reasoned, and pitch them forward into Dublin at the turn of the next century. In this way I began constructing, in my mind, a dialectical landscape, an allegory, one I'd create partly by writing and partly by travelling.

Robert Smithson's 1973 essay 'Frederick Law Olmsted and the Dialectical Landscape' makes the case for New York's Central Park as a zone that is in constant dialogue with its geological past. Look at a rock tunnel, cast your eye over the ridges and curves of the Gill and find yourself transported to a time long ago when the land was covered with glaciers and Pleistocene ice sheets. Landscape artists and architects, keen to a sense of environment, can work this notion to uncanny effects. I witnessed one of these well-orchestrated dialectical flashes most recently on a trip to Dublin where I stood on the south bank of the Liffey in the newly refurbished docklands area, on a plot of land that fifteen years ago was little more than a dusty, briny space called Misery Hill, a name found nowhere but on old maps.

Misery Hill—where a shiny Libeskind now holds court, the spiky jewel set into the crown of the surreal, over-designed plaza filled with what look like red light sabers jabbed in the ground—used to be a whole lot of nothing, with the exception of an old brick chimney and massive gasometer that used to stand on Sir John Rogerson Quay. Torn down in 1993, the gasholder is still visible in some old footage of Dublin's skyline, notably in the Phil Lynott 'Old Town' video, and it also features in the memories of my novel's narrator, Greta Gardner. It's a dialectical image that returns her to a childhood memory, one made all the more poignant by the fact that she's running to get away from a volatile lover—the moment of danger. With no grand building or glazed architectural rendering yet replacing the gasometer, Greta still looks on the derelict, empty place and experiences, when the wind is blowing from the right direction, an uncanny flash of the past rising up 'in the now of its recognisability.'

Standing on the south quays, looking north past the Libeskind over the widening mouth of the River Liffey, you can't miss the ostentatious new convention centre called, unimaginatively, the Convention Centre with its enormous cylinder-shaped façade. It's gone from gasometer to glazed can of Pepsi: the choice, it would seem, of a very new generation. But are these objects, these buildings one feels compelled to describe, as Louis Aragon proposes, *interior boundaries* of one's self, or are they opposite—things that unlock the limitless, the profound, and the mystical?

Objects are of course of central importance in Joyce's *Dubliners* short stories: think of the coin Corley presses into the palm of Lenehan at the end of 'Two Gallants' or the feather in the hat of the plump lady in 'Counterparts' who gives rise to violent emotion in the beaten-down Farringdon. In the *Dubliners* stories, such objects often give way to that favourite old chestnut of creative writing classes everywhere—the epiphany, a dialectical image worn smooth from overuse. But it is not in the *Dubliners* stories, instead in *Ulysses* where Joyce truly unlocks the enormous transformative power of the object, and he does it by naming so many specific, verifiable objects and places found throughout the city so as to inspire an urban scavenger hunt—hence Bloomsday on June 16th, when readers take to the streets to create their own re-enactment of an imagined past. What is so limitless and exciting as a bar of lemon soap? Nevertheless, it's that same imaginary bar of soap— an emblem of the one Bloom buys for Molly—that compels enthusiasts every year to drop by Sweny's pharmacy for a whiff of that lemon scent, a mass-manufactured Proustian madeleine for the smart set. (Full disclosure: I, too, have bought the bar of lemon soap on more than one of these occasions. It's very good soap—but no epiphany.)

There is most certainly a preservational impulse to all this obsessive documentation. Although writing fiction, I found myself wanting desperately to capture the true spirit of Dublin at a certain moment in time, and to capture the spirit, I knew I had to capture the buildings, streets, and street furniture as they existed at that moment—as it might never exist again. Compare this with Louis Aragon's *Paris Peasant*, his own cataloguing of the Paris arcades, where he describes the 'writing mania' behind the endeavour. Page after page he reprints in his novel, with painstaking accuracy, text from placards, from advertisements, and menus, mysterious messages in old telephone directories, signs in dirty windows, box office hoardings and other ephemera from the Paris streets, unearthing the secret repositories for modern myths. He implicates himself and the pages that he 'inexplicably blacken[s]' with 'frantic attempts to describe… these winding byways now crouched under the threat of the raised pickaxe.' The pickaxe of Haussmann is raised, the pen slips in quick underneath it to fill the space.

My field notebooks are filled with signs for places that no longer exist—Miss Coquette's on South William Street, Caroline Records on Richmond Street. I've also captured endangered words like those of a prank plaque on the O'Connell Bridge mourning a fictional priest named Fr Pat Noise, one the council's been threatening to take down for ages—much like Aragon writing of the arcades in the Passage de l'Opera before Haussmann's bulldozers mowed them down. The more I saw places were threatened, the more important it was for me to get things right. Joyce, writing *Ulysses* in exile, obsessively consulted Thom's 1904 *Street Directory of Dublin* for details of shops, pubs, street furniture, and when such documentary material, or his own steel-trap memory, was not enough, he penned letters to his Aunt Josephine to pose pedantic questions about the city: was it possible to leap down to the basement window at 7 Eccles Street without concussing oneself?—'I require this information to finish a paragraph,' Joyce insisted, before he could finish the description of keyless Bloom's leap in the Ithaca episode. Here I was, the American exiled from Dublin, writing letters to friends there about the phrasing of a sign at the train station in order to complete a scene. I lurked on Irish architecture discussion forums and pored over the details compiled during my annual research trips, fixated on the minutiae to the point where I no longer knew why I was doing it. In the end, I aimed to work all of this into a book that would combine the two—to use Aragon's term for it again—'a mishmash of inventions and real facts,' but for the purpose of stirring up an emotion I knew as all too real. Call it the uncanny, call it the dialectical image: it was there, and if I dug back through the wreckage of today's future ruins, I might capture it at last—or for a second.

The image that flashes up in an instant is the history of the story the novelist wants to tell—the 'true picture of the past.' Reasonable protests—from family members who can't understand why eight years is not sufficient to finish a novel, or why so much research goes into something so fictional—insist there is no such thing as a true picture of an invented past, but these do little to convince the novelist otherwise. The flash excites as it enervates. The dialectical image compels a rescue mission. The flash is an imperative: write your way to the meaning of this, write to the heart of the matter. It explains plane tickets, hotel bills, six, seven, eight field books. It craves more of the same, creates the desire to find it yet again. The flash does come again, but never where it's expected, never the same place twice: in the public lavatory of the Dublin City Library; along the manky banks of the Grand Canal;. at night, on bicycle, in an abandoned lot near Newmarket where an ice cream truck in January plays 'Greensleeves.' And of course, there's the dialectical image that hit me as I looked up at a sparkling new convention centre and recalled an old gasometer that once overshadowed the quayside. Then I remembered: not my memory. Greta's again. *Fuck sake!*, as the girl would say.

After the flash, the writing moves at a slow burn. It calls up smells of sulphur, of smoke, the aroma of coffee I keep at arm's length from my notebook mixing with that of Dublin's remembered petrichor, its fag ends and vinegar crisps, the bilious green stench of the Liffey at low tide. There's no accelerating the process of writing a novel, at least not in my workshop, only deceleration by degrees, sentence by sentence, image by image. 'How long shall I retain this sense of the marvellous suffusing everyday existence?' Louis Aragon writes in his 'Preface to a Modern Mythology.' For the flâneur, its answer comes in two parts: as long as one can walk the streets of the landscape that haunts him, and, presuming one wishes to prolong the sense—as long as one can write.

What I saw on Barrow Street one afternoon I will spend the next three, four years of my life weaving, unweaving, writing and erasing, working with painstaking slowness into a story that I don't discover so much as try to uncover. For it is one thing to recognise it as a picture, as history rising up in the present, it is entirely another to capture it in words. One may not get the image right or even half-right before the image of history 'threatens to disappear irretrievably.' As Benjamin warns in the fifth thesis of the 'Theses on the Philosophy of History': 'The good tidings which the historian of the past brings with throbbing heart may be lost in a void the very moment he opens his mouth.' The good tidings came with the Aer Lingus flight, with the turn onto Barrow Street and the thrill of the scrawl of pen across the page of a field notebook, but that flash was long ago. (That flash is *history*, you could say.) The void that's left is the space of writing. The throbbing of the heart, as days turn to weeks, weeks to years, begins to feel like less of an asset to the novelist (the fake historian!) and more a curse.

Pages pile up of bad writing, wreckage, of flotsam and jetsam. It's not all bad. There's a faint glimmer here and there with this or that *mot juste*. But drafts accumulate. Crumbled papers pile up around the feet of my angel of made-up history, who can't flee the unholy mess fast enough, body pointed toward the future, his face drawn back, time and again, to the past.

The writing of the novel unfolds into a hybrid of half-real, half-imagined experience. The Johnny Cash on the radio is real, as is the young fella outside I spied out on a cigarette break, holding a bright green coffee cup. I change the names. I play fast and loose. It is not the historical past that leaps like a tiger into the present moment. It's the imaginary future—the book that has not yet been written flashing up in the mind of the writer. The writing is the chasing-after. The writing is the afterthoughts.

Awakening: that word so ripe for the Surrealists, so beloved of the seekers of the dialectical image. Is the flash of a dialectical image, is this awakening, the same as a flash of artistic inspiration? Is it naïve to conflate the two? And if they are not interchangeable, do they ever run on the same track, or at least a parallel track to the other? Thus far I've been mingling the dialectical image alongside writer's inspiration as if the two were one in the same. But is it disingenuous to import the idea of materialist history to imagined history? Is it capricious at best; at worst, dangerous? A bad year of writing, surely, is no state of emergency. (The writer didn't quit her day job.) There is no moment of danger because the threat Benjamin describes—'that of becoming a tool of the ruling classes'—is simply not at stake. Surely what could be at risk if I misrepresented my made-up character's invented history? What could possibly hang in the balance?

Would not an image, or series of images, be the proper way of working out an dialectical image? After all, 'History,' writes Benjamin, 'decays into images, not into stories.' Wouldn't a proper response, then, be to embrace the image and ignore this messy business of narrative altogether?

Let's save the writer the trouble of all this impossible transcoding.

One solution to this, of course, would be simply to record each image as it crossed my path. To be a *bricoleur*. To do what Benjamin did with the *Arcades Project*; what Louis Aragon does in *Paris Peasant*. I'll be Aragon describing the casks and spigots and barrels of the Certa café, I'll run down the complete list of drinks on the menu and post wholesale into my field book the street signs complete with longitude and latitude. Michael Taussig proposes in *I Swear I Saw This: Drawings in Fieldwork Notebooks, Namely My Own*, 'can a fact like a kidney be a story, and if so, what sort of story?'

Here's one I never tire of telling. The sign, like the green sign that Robert Smithson describes in his 'Tour of the Monuments of Passaic,' that 'explains everything,' is posted on a tall sheet of metal outside St. Patrick's Cathedral, in the fair green park where, on a rare sunny day, kids cavort and civil servants on lunch breaks smoke on benches and eat sandwiches:

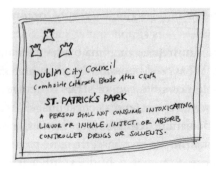

I can't tell how many times I've tried to work this damned sign into the book, with no success, putting the wording of the sign into the book through the mouth of the characters, or commenting on it in some way, before I realised that I didn't need to do a single bit of interpretation, that the story was all right there, in the very image of the sign, in those three verbs: inhale, inject, absorb—the story of Dublin's streets, of its heroin problem, of the city council's polite but ultimately useless attempt to control and contain the menace to society that is public drug consumption. To try to improve on it was to ruin the story, was to mess with an image where the past, present, and future of the park was stated so pithily.

Surely a novel like that, comprised of the language of Dublin City Council ordinances, its plaques to fake figures, its peeling planning permission signs and newspaper headlines (Dublin may have flashed the claws of the Celtic Tiger, but in the *Irish Times*, *Cow knocks down four in Ennis* is still page two news), would clarify things. What if I were to write a book that would exist, as Louis Aragon wrote of his own project, as a 'new kind of novel that would break all the traditional rules governing the writing of fiction, one that would be neither a narrative (a story) nor a character study (a portrait), a novel that the critics would be obliged to approach empty-handed.' I have that book already, but it isn't a novel and never will be: it's my field book. Or field books, more correctly. The field book not as a supplement to the novel but a replacement, or a work in its own right. I like to consider this picture drawn near the graving docks near Ringsend, good for nothing but itself, ripe with the sweet scent of the sense of the useless that Aragon so cherishes, ripe for what it offers when I breathe deeply and inhale and it takes me right back to those ruins.

Ireland is a land of ruins. *What land isn't?* I can hear my own cynical reply. But Ireland, like Benjamin's allegorist, holds particularly fast to the ruins. I recall a certain surly travel agent who refused to allow two twenty-something young women the unalloyed excitement of booking a bus ticket to go see the Paleolithic site of Newgrange in the midlands west of Dublin. 'Why do you want to go there? It's just a bunch of rocks,' he chastised my friend Rachelle and I. 'But the history!' I protested. 'And the castle!' The travel agent scoffed his retort: 'What's *left* of it.' Even the city of Dublin, even in these sleek post-Celtic Tiger days, holds proudly to its Viking past, its medieval walls—if you can ignore the Viking Splash tours, which dispatch helmeted hordes of tourists through the streets in yellow amphibious vehicles. Layers of history are everywhere evident in Dublin, and you don't have to walk far to find a wall to scratch at. Look at your hands as you walk away from that building, that wall: the dust and asbestos and stone crumble at your touch.

With so much history at our disposal, so many rich material objects, where, then, might we find the dialectical images of Dublin—those that speak not to the idiosyncratic leanings of an Midwestern American fiction writer but to the people, to the city—to history, in other words? Or in this have we confused the dialectical image with Jung's archetypal images—a distinction Adorno and Benjamin insisted we absolutely *not* do? Can't we identify our images and take a tour of them, a Zozimus Ghost Bus through the past? Or if there is no universal, then isn't it true that the dialectical image is subjective, personal? 'Observation,' Flaubert remarks, 'is guided above all by imagination.' Wandering the streets of Dublin, matching postcard images from the past with buildings of the present, becomes its own form of writing. Like the poet who hung a note on the bedroom door that said 'POET AT WORK,' I ought to hang a lanyard and press pass around my neck that reads 'WRITER AT WORK' when I walk through the dialectical landscapes of Dublin.

Today, a hoarding with an advertisement promising new lifestyle experiences flutters, torn, in the cold January wind. The wind blows over the Celtic Tiger burial grounds, a dream abandoned just at the moment it began to come to light. The economy, so buoyant, has crashed just as suddenly. 50% of working architects have lost their jobs. Queues for the dole office wrap around the corner. Sleek, glass-fronted shops and restaurants with catchy one-word names like Gruel, Nude, and Lemon are mostly deserted. The Insomnia Coffee Co. closes up shop at five p.m., the long ropes of the mop swirling in circles on the floor, the chairs hoisted onto table tops, their spindly legs pointed upwards in the air while outside an addict begs for change with a battered brown Bewley's paper cup. What will survive?

'We have so many fictions and images,' artist Hito Steyerl writes, 'that have already realised themselves in the world that we basically live in a junkyard of fictions and images. Like decommissioned planes in the desert. We live in a junkyard of wrecked fictions.' It's hardly a reassuring image, but if it is true, we can no longer ask the impossible of our ideas, those decommissioned planes of ours: obsolete and discarded, such things must no longer be asked to fly. The best we can hope for is salvage, is to admit repossession barter for parts. Why agonise over the right fiction, the right image, when any old spring or wing or wing nut will do? I struggle with the Conceptualists, with the 'Allegory without Melancholy.' The image is more than the ink, more than the paper. The image is dialectical—it springs up in lived experience. Walking through Dublin, I am engaged in a writing, in a protest against routine: the writing of a book read by nearly no one—why? Is it because such a task—to represent the dialectical image with poignancy and accuracy—is essentially impossible, save a rare Proust?

And so the novelist's so-called freedom from what Nietzsche calls 'the tyranny of the actual' is actually no such thing. The 'blind power of facts' command her still. She wants to use the history for life and action and not for atrophy, not for avoidance. Nietzsche's 'On the Advantage and Disadvantage of History for Life' reminds us that to live and to act requires a certain degree of forgetting, that 'the unhistorical and the historical are equally necessary for the health of an individual, a people, and a culture,' yet how to cultivate the forgetting? Is writing a forgetting or a remembering? Beckett, writing on Proust, said: 'The man with a good memory does not remember anything because he does not forget anything. His memory is uniform, a creature of routine, at once a condition and function of his impeccable habit, an instrument of reference instead of an instrument of discovery.' The novelist practises the habit of memory, only feels compelled to invent a prayer, perhaps to St. Francis: *make me an instrument of discovery*.

Writing changes location. From scribbling through my fingerless gloves into a Moleskine on Percy Place to a longhand afterthought penned at a flat round table in the Mespil Hotel, I work the images into the world I've half invented. Years later, the book still a half-finished thing, I now sit at a keyboard in Brooklyn, illuminated by the blue glow of the screen, doing new things with old words. I am still trying to get back to the flash at the heart of what happened as I walked down Barrow Street in Ringsend, Dublin one day, and saw in that squat stucco row house a recognition of more than an invented past—but the imperative for a future work—and another, and another, and so on into infinity.

And yet to look upon the building site of a new book might awaken the same sensation Smithson describes at the sight of new construction, at that 'zero panorama' containing plenty of what might be called potential stories yet feel intuitively like ruins in reverse, skyscrapers of language and narrative rising up before my eyes, petrified before they ever came to life. A hopelessness seizes up in me. I recognise what Aragon saw in a blue accordion labelled 'PESSIMISM': it's that dear old companion, the sense of the useless—the best incentive to writing that I know.

I want to return to Proust, who describes the denouement of the cup of tea, thinking of how it compares to my attempts to return to Dublin, year in, year out, to try to capture the moments that seized me with such power:

RINGSEND

Places, dreams, adventures

WINDSURFING

GRAND CANAL DOCKS
GRAVING DOCKS

I drink a second mouthful, in which I find nothing more than the first, a third, which gives me rather less than the second. It is time to stop; the potion is losing its magic. It is plain that the object of my quest, the truth, lies not in the cup but in myself. The tea has called up in me, but does not itself understand, and can only repeat indefinitely, with a gradual loss of strength, the same testimony; which I, to, cannot interpret, though I hope at least to be able to call upon the tea for it again and to find it there presently, intact and at my disposal, for my final enlightenment. I put down my cup and examine my own mind. It is for it to discover the truth. But how?

It's a question that—along with landscape—haunts the writer. The experience of the madeleine contains in it not only a sensation but an invitation—or more than an invitation, an imperative. It is more than seeking—'Seek?' writes Proust. 'More than that; create.' And so the writer—the writer of fictions, the chronicler of useless histories—concludes, her own words fading into the background, giving way, once more to bricolage, to allegory. There is, it would seem, more than one way to traverse a dialectical landscape. But no matter how new the territory looks at the outset, one feels one is brought back, time and again, to a familiar terrain— one such as one saw, one day, in that flash when all of time stood still.

Two Poems
Translated by Will Stone

SALZBURG BY THOMAS BERNHARD

You luminous towers in the clear morning,
you warm wind, you ancient tree.
Into space reaches the cathedral's cupola
and casts peaceful shadow, without pain.

Above the lanes and the capitals. –
in calm courtyards the young vine spreads
Thousand fold are the sun's rays
in the soft chimes of a pure spring.

So the light trickles over the flat roofs
flashes like flame and soon is stone.
The whole city drinks from the sun's tumbler.

And rejoices further in the green leafage,
moving as one into the heavens
and in the doves' murmur turns to music.

THE WALK BY FRIEDRICH HÖLDERLIN

You woods, handsome flanks
Painted there on the greening slope,
Where I lead my vagabond's step,
Repaid with sweet rest
For every thorn sunk in my heart,
When darkened is the mind
That paid from the very start
In pain for thought and art.
You lovely images in the valley,
Garden and tree, for instance
And the little bridge, the slender,
The brook one can barely make out
How beautiful out of the clear distance
Shine these splendid pictures
Of a landscape I gladly visit
When the weather turns mild.
The deity amicably escorts us
With blue to begin with,
Then after with clouds prepared,
Made rounded and grey
With fiery lightning and rolling
Thunder, with the charm of pastures,
With beauty, the gushing source
Grants the primordial image.

Initiations: On Grisey's Music

Liam Cagney

'Putting truth and untruth together a shot may be made at what this hybrid actually was like to look at.' – James Joyce

One Saturday night a couple of summers back—it was the sweaty summer of 2013—needing, as you might expect, some respite from the months on end of PhD work lathering my mind with a big yellow sponge of stress, at my friend Simon's invite I went to this garden party in Stokey—Stoke Newington—a 'gold party' whose hostess Elene, this Greek girl Simon somehow knew, black afro and almond eyes, had told everyone they should come dressed in gold, *as much gold as possible!!!*, as *wonderful wildlife of gold!!*, in typical London turns of phrase written on the Facebook event page. As my friend Emmet and I, both in our normal clothes, passed through the kitchen of her house and into the back garden, our noses filling with the waft of joints, our ears with the sound of Italo Disco—disco, for some reason, being really in in London that summer—I spotted Simon's blonde head plonked on a stool beside a black-haired guy in front of a background of millions of coloured Xmas lights garlanded from tree to tree and branch to branch, and to the side of them our hostess Elene, prancing around wearing a little gold top-hat, a gold sequined dress and a fake gold beard. Emmet and I pulled up two stools beside the lads and sat down. Throughout the night the four stools would slowly sink into the mud, and occasionally one of us would fall over. Simon's friend turned out to be Rob, the tall Rob I'd heard about ('Rob Gob'), who, when the hostess Elene pranced over to quiz us about our goldless clothes, turned around and told her that since he cried gold, shat gold, and had gold running through his veins, decorating himself with some gold ribbon or other raiment would be like trying to tint a gold bar with a yellow highlighter—drawing our gold hostess Elene's silent ire, her hatted afro turned and went back to the kitchen, dipping a little gold key into a little bag of powder.

Some chat ensued, distracting us from the cheesy music blaring from the speakers, and then, naturally enough, since the four of us played in bands—Emmet and I in N, N minus, Simon and Rob in Night and Fog—it drifted to what our favourite piece of music currently was, I saying, as Emmet and Simon got up to try and find some beer, that my favourite piece of music in the world—and actually my favourite piece of music by anyone in the history of music, and therefore, you'd have to appropriately conclude, in the history of the universe as well—was *Jour, contre jour* (*Daylight/Against Daylight*) by the late French composer Gérard Grisey, who was the inventor in the 1970s of a genre of classical music known as Spectral Music—a piece of music that lasts twenty-two minutes or so in performance, Rob, I said, that was written in 1978 and that's scored for an ensemble of thirteen players accompanied by a pre-recorded electronic part played on tape over the auditorium's speakers—something of a landmark in twentieth century musical art, I went on, and yet, as has been the common fate of that unsmiled-on domesticated toad that goes by the name of twentieth century Western Art Music, a work that unfortunately remains completely unknown to everyone other than a few academics, who can hardly be said to be deserving of such a fine and downright mysterious piece of musical art, I pointed out, since, snobs to a man and nerds to a man—and men to a man, too—they themselves can only treat such a piece as *Jour, contre jour* (as they do Grisey's oeuvre in general) with a knowledge that is actually unknowledge and a comprehension that's clearly incomprehension, with the shrivelled-up imagination produced by too many years spent behind the doors of the academy, gathered round together in sterile-smelling seminar rooms to prod *Jour, contre jour* and other such works with sticks, prodding and prodding it *Jour, contre jour* (I took up a stick and prodded) much as you might prod roadkill found at the side of the motorway—a dead animal birthed by speed and abandoned by time. I immediately had to repeat this long statement to Rob because he hadn't actually heard me over the thumping disco beats. As Rob subsequently nodded in understanding if not quite in agreement, being aware through Simon of my passion for the music of the so-called spectralism school of French music and the music of Grisey in particular—the subject of my PhD, the reason I was hanging around London—nodding despite the fact that he himself (Rob) was unfamiliar with the music I was talking about (as we both knew), I immediately qualified this sweeping statement about *Jour, contre jour* by admitting that on a fundamental level this choice for my favourite piece of music in the world was by necessity a completely arbitrary one, like a card drawn at random from the pack, as they say, because, I said, it's based not on the inherent value of the music in question (like such a thing exists) but on my own personal taste, the day of the week, my interests, my choice of profession, the fact that I exist as opposed to not existing, that I'm still living and not yet dead, how I was brought up in my toddler years, my playing second clarinet in the Donegal Youth Orchestra a bit later, the nature of the insecurities I've developed since then, the degree of my vanity, the degree of my paranoia, the degree of Grisey's obscurity, my predisposition for the psychedelic, my desire to appear cultivated and intelligent (I was counting these various conditions on the fingers of first my left and then my right hand as Rob, his stool sinking, observed), and not least, I said, on the fact that *Jour, contre jour* is a piece of music I know as opposed to one I don't know—because last spring, I went on, at the Paul Sacher Foundation in Basel, Switzerland, the main archive in the world for 20th Century classical music, I studied for weeks in a deep trance-like state of concentration the Sacher Foundation's *Jour, contre jour* 'dossier', a large folder that holds within its modest cardboard covers the totality of Grisey's sketches for *Jour, contre jour*, Grisey's draft musical manuscripts, his written notes, and the fair copy of *Jour, contre jour*'s score, and which therefore records to a degree that's as precise as will ever be humanly possible the actual process by which Grisey, over the course of several months in 1978, composed *Jour, contre jour*. In the luminous light of the Paul Sacher Foundation's reading rooms, I said, in a silence of such resonant immensity it seemed to climb out the window all the way down from the Münsterplatz to the waters of the Rhine, which, flowing below, are visible from the prospect of the reading room, it was revealed to me through close scholarly scrutiny Grisey's initial concept for the piece, which Grisey idly sketched one afternoon when he was at a Parisian bistro having a coffee, a little pen-drawing on a paper napkin—a paper napkin Grisey subsequently to care to keep and preserve—a little pen-drawing of a musical piece that would enact in sound, over the course of a series of insistent, glistening chords cascading in waves of increasing and then diminishing harmonicity, the course of the sun in the sky (I pointed upwards), from the sun's first appearance on the horizon at dawn to the sun's death at dusk—the whole piece of music being experienced as "the interminable wait for the night," as Grisey wrote hastily beside the drawing on that fateful little paper napkin, with which after having his coffee he also wiped his lips. The masterful way in which Grisey—who was undoubtedly the finest French composer of his generation and literally a wizard, outshining all others, of what has been called the 'literate tradition' in Western music (that is, music that's notated, I said, music based on training in what the French traditionally term *écriture*)—executed with his toolkit of musical notation that initial concept of a piece based on the sun's journey in the sky speaks loudly of what, in my more hackish moments, I've come to think of as the 'sensory success story of spectral music.' 'The first principle of spectral music,' Grisey once said, I told Rob by way of explanation, 'is finding the optimal correspondence between concept and percept—between the concept of the score and the percept of the experienced music.' Without even going into the music's technical side, without even going into, that is, how Grisey models his chords on the internal spectral structure of sound, it's this principle of the optimisation of concept and percept that *Jour, contre jour* achieves so awesomely.

But let me fill you in a bit about Grisey, Rob, I went on, to help you understand just where I'm coming from. Grisey was born in 1946 and raised near Belfort, a small city in the east of France near the borders with Germany and Switzerland, a territory annexed at different times in history by the Germans since it's the gateway to the Rhineland. As a child Grisey was an accordion virtuoso. 'Gérard. As a child Grisey was an accordion virtuoso. *'Gérard Grisey, jeune accordéoniste extraordinaire!'* proclaimed posters on walls and ads in local newspapers all over the country, as the boy performer toured around to general wonder. Grisey won prizes nationally and internationally in the accordion world cup. He could basically play anything anyone asked him to at any moment, at the proverbial drop of a hat, and he would improvise amazingly at length upon any musical motif, however crude or stupid, someone might happen to be humming at any given time. As soon as the tune had left that person's lips, as if by some power of acoustic transmigration it would emerge again from the happy bellows of Grisey's Hohner accordion, whence it would pour and pour in manifold ways for minute upon euphonious minute like water from a Versailles fountain, all sparkly and ornate and unspeakably lovely, into his astonished listeners' ear-vessels, which were very grateful for it indeed. Little Grisey's accordion music's balming properties were far and wide spoken of. Grisey got his maroon-coloured accordion, Rob, I went on, from his granny, whom he loved dearly and whose little lullaby songs were Grisey's first musical memory. On a darker note, Grisey in later years used to say that had he not been given that famous maroon Hohner accordion by his beloved grandmother at that exact moment in his life—as an Xmas present in his fifth year—he most likely would have committed suicide very soon after. It was either suicide or the accordion. And this was the beginning in Grisey's mind of the idea of music as a death surrogate—music as death's stand-in—which of course informs the notion of the 'interminable wait for the night' in *Jour, contre jour*, a piece that's nothing if not a death surrogate in audio action. In the posthumous edition of Grisey's *Collected Writings* there's a black and white photo of Grisey as a young blonde-haired boy sat holding his accordion, which is almost bigger than his body. This young boy with the blonde curly hair and a little smirk on his face sits proud as punch on a high chair, dressed in his Sunday best, staring directly at the camera, posing on the chair holding to his body his accordion, cradling that huge mass in his outstretched arms. Growing up as a kid Grisey was a well-known fixture on the Belfort streets, the little blonde boy who wandered around with the big maroon Hohner accordion that was almost bigger than his body, playing pieces by Rameau, J.S. Bach, Ravel and others, impromptu, by memory, without a note out of place, with occasionally even the odd original composition of his own thrown in, according to the diktats of his expressive inclinations (how he felt, in other words). And in a way, Rob, I said, Grisey's whole oeuvre as it developed from this point on, an expanding and contracting oeuvre, a focusing and breathing oeuvre, can itself be considered, if you like, as some sort of metaphysical 'accordion'—though that's a bit speculative on my part, in fairness.

Anyway, let me get on with my story. Flash forward to a few years later, I said, and after spending some lonely years studying music in Trossingen, West Germany, at the Hohner Academy, 'the home of the accordion' as it was known throughout the world, the *omphalos* of the mid-twentieth century 'Renaissance of the Squeeze-Box,' Grisey applied to join Oliver Messiaen's famous composition class at the Conservatoire national supérieure de musique de Paris, the Paris Conservatoire, a class which in the lore of French intellectual history is right up there with that grey grandiose windbag Jacques Lacan's roughly contemporaneous psychoanalysis seminar—a music composition class where all the giants of twentieth century Composition had studied in the late 1940s, rubbing shoulders, wagging tongues and furrowing brows to solve the problem for the rest of the world as to 'the future of music,' as they said, giants of men such as Pierre Boulez, Karlheinz Stockhausen and Jean Barraqué, who all used dressed in identical flannel suits and smoke their pipes in tandem as they thought about music— the future of music—the *being* of music— literally legendary figures, Rob, and true gentlemen one and all. So it came to pass that the boy Grisey applied to join this class in Paris. And in applying to join Messiaen's legendary composition class, this young kid Grisey, with what I'd describe as Rimbaudean precocity and impudence, wrote a Passacaglia for solo accordion that when Messiaen, who, though a passionate man, was always formal in that typical French intellectual way, received and turned the pages of its somewhat roughly inscribed pencil-written score, sitting at the desk in his office, humming quietly to himself the melody and bass by turns as bar by bar he read through the piece from the first page to the last, upon reaching the last note of Grisey's Passacaglia he leapt up with a start from his hard wooden chair, ran to the window of his office at the Conservatoire on the rue de Rome, and, throwing up the heavy window frame, shouted at the top of his baritone voice out the window, with tears streaming down his rosy red cheeks, *Elle est retrouvée! Elle est retrouvée! Elle est retrouvée!*—It's been rediscovered!—and just kept on shouting that phrase over and over—*Elle est retrouvée ! Elle est retrouvée!*—It's been rediscovered!—up into the sky for literally an hour without a break, hands gripping the window frame, tears taking to the air in all directions, his glasses half fallen off his face, decorum gone quite athwart, shouting and repeating the phrase over and over like some insane man-bird, until all the birds outside on the rooftops started joining in and squawking along in this huge bizarre chorus on the rue de Rome, to the disbelief of the passersby down on the pavements below, so shocked, amazed and excited was Messiaen by this Passacaglia for solo accordion that had been written and sent to him by the enigmatic blonde Rimbaldean Belfortean Grisey, which in Messiaen's mind—the mind of a devout Catholic—at once acquired a Theological significance, like a scene frozen in a tableau in a stained-glass window showing a boy on the horizon holding an accordion with the rising sun behind him, a moment auguring nothing less than the explosive announcement of an entirely new epoch in the history of mankind, which was of course an embarrassing exaggeration on Messiaen's part.

So it was, Rob, I went on, that Grisey, the humble rural accordionist, was taken on as a composition student at the Paris Conservatoire by Messiaen, who even at that time, in the late sixties, was a major musical celebrity, a 'flamboyantly composed' man, well known in fashionable society, esteemed as one of the greatest and most famous composers of the twentieth century, 'a colourful Catholic composer' as the Anglophone press used to call him alliteratively, a man also renowned for his many-hued shirts. And like his new Master—indeed, I added, it's one of the bonds that fused them—Grisey was himself, too, a devout Catholic, though none of his family had been—a young man of private spiritual fervour, who, once he had moved to Paris, used to go along with his girlfriend Jocelyn, soon to be his wife, every weekend in his best tuxedo to the Greek Orthodox service on the rue Daru, the reason for their trip being the much greater weight afforded by the Greek mass to symbol and ceremony, the mass being a solemn, drawn-out, antiquated affair quite in line with the young Grisey's tastes, and which was not without an impact on the development of Grisey's musical style, I added. Now, Grisey himself, Rob, I said, who was by nature a solitary and a thinker, was certainly not in the dark as to the nature of his talent and his vocation, a combination he always referred to when writing in his journal as his 'gift,' which was less a matter of having a knack for stringing together black blobs and scribbles on manuscript paper than of having an aptitude for *thinking through to the Beyond of that act*—to the Beyond of what writing in music actually is, an awesome abyss opened in every single musical act, lying elsewhere than on the manuscript page, there if we attune our ears to hear it. Thus Grisey began to write works, whose incredible sophistication belied their author's still young age, to which he gave mystical names such as *Charme* (1969), *Initiation* (1970), and *Perichoresis* (1971, revised 1973), the last of which, Rob, I said, is a term in Christian theology signifying, to the limited extent that earthly words can, the mutual indwelling and intersecting—I gesticulated for this with my hands—of the three distinct personae of the Godhead. So that's *Perichoresis*, I said, holding out my right hand. *Initiation*, on the other hand, I said, holding out my other hand, is a piece scored for baritone voice, double bass and trombone. And *Initiation*'s score comprises hundreds of small sections of musical notation and other performative symbols which its performers can arrange in one of any number of different orders. While *Initiation*'s notated score, a melee of black marks, appears like the finished draft of some great feat of engineering, an engineering project of such immense graphic complication as would cause Isambard Brunel's face to turn pale, from the point of view of how it sounds—and forgive that oxymoron—*Initiation* is very much of its time, in other words, a late 60s-esque acid freakout. Sober technical sophistication here clasps palms with delirious aural druggery. The baritone part is made up of strings of nonsense vocables—*is-si-tok*, *tu-ku-tu-ku-tu*, *a-vle-ke-te*, and that type of thing—which Grisey spent months and months compiling, sat in the *Bibliothèque nationale* poring over books on phonology, acoustics, information theory, linguistics and so on. The effect of *Initiation* when you witness it in performance, as I did once at a festival in Strasbourg a couple of years ago when I was over staying with my Donegal friend Cormac, whom you don't know, is of something happening that is at once both *extraordinarily ridiculous* and yet at the same time *imperative to be taken seriously*, as if pornography were used for sex education or the Old Testament as a *Seinfeld* script. Intoning solemnly those complex vocal lines, the baritone comes across like a young man who's been struck with severe Alzheimer's. And yet to write that insane vocal part, with its all gurgling and click-click-clicking and plosives, which sound completely random, all those multifarious vocal inflections, the young precocious Grisey engaged in the most sophisticated research and made the most complex calculations. To facilitate his compositional yearnings, Rob, I said, to allow his musical dreams to come true, Grisey, who by this stage had long curly hair and always wore a caftan when strolling about Paris, applied himself in fact to the study and the mastery of sophisticated mathematics in several branches: trigonometry, calculus, set theory, number theory, Boolean algebra, and so on. This was to supplement his musical training, which in Messiaen's hands had seen him progress from that humble maroon Hohner accordion to a mastery of composition across the glittering gamut of Western instruments. And when, as I have, you've seen the sketches for Grisey's works in the collection held at the Paul Sacher Foundation in Basel, Switzerland—pages upon pages, stacked as high as the ceiling, of inscrutable sums and calculations, which blow all over the reading room any time a gust of wind should enter through the window coming up from the Rhine below—you realise that Grisey's craft was indeed as much that of an engineer as of a composer, a musical engineer. But a musical engineer of what? Simon now asked, he and Emmet having returned and handed us our beers. That is exactly the question, Simon, I replied, swigging from a manky bottle of Sol, exactly the pointed, curious question, I said, pointing—an engineer of *'what-we-don't-know.'*

The author points out that not all of the details in the above are true.

April Truth

Ilya Zverev, translated from the Russian by Anna Aslanyan

For Korney Chukovsky

It was only quarter to eight, maybe only twenty to, when suddenly the phone rang. Mum and Dad had never been called this early, but Mash sometimes had. She ran out into the hall in one stocking and snatched the receiver.

'May I please speak to Masha Gavrikova?' asked a polite, one could almost say, a man's voice. Mash could swear she knew no one with such a polite voice.

'Speaking.'

'Mash…' This was accompanied by a sigh of relief (it took Kol some effort, of course, to deliver that long polite opening). 'Miss English says, bring your deck. To record pronunciation. Ryasha will pop round to yours in a minute.'

Everyone called her Mash, even though Lyudmila, their Miss Russian, said it was vulgar and rude. But it wasn't rude —just as it wasn't nice when they called the other Masha, Mussy. It's just that one really is a Mussy, a purry pussycat, but this one, she's a real Mash, one of us lads.

Even back in Year 4, she was the best in the class at satchel fighting, and she wore her beret at a daring angle, askew, slanting all the way down to one ear (so much so that Yura Fonaryov even asked Miss Physics what physical laws held it in place). And whenever Mash put a kettle on, she always turned the gas full blast, so that a minute later the kettle lid, too, was askew. They were right to rely on her to get the deck.

'Mum, we need the tape recorder,' she said firmly. 'For English.'

Mum threw up her hands and called Dad. Dad came out of the bathroom with a full beard of soap growing from right under his eyes.

'What is it now?'

Dad had a PhD in philosophy and, naturally, looked at everything from a philosophical perspective.

'On the one hand, Mum is absolutely right: the tape recorder is not one of your toys, you can't tote it around as you please,' he said to Mash. 'But, on the other hand,' he said, this time to Mum, 'a tape recorder is certainly necessary for one to perfect one's foreign language skills.'

He always knew how to say something in a way that made it almost impossible to object. If he simply said *for a lesson*, Mum would probably refuse. But *to perfect one's skills*!

Mum cherished the tape recorder. When some boring guests came, such as Dad's fellow philosophers—his colleagues from the department, people you couldn't think of anything to talk to about—they'd put on a tape. They had special tapes for that, with the kind of ditties you wouldn't be able to hear on the radio, no matter how hard you tried to tune in. This one, for example:

A topknot, a topknot, a curly little topknot,
Oh, how you billow in the wind, heigh-ho!

'There is a certain bravado here, unbridled, reminiscent of the vast steppe,' Dad would remark at this point. And no one would object.

Anyway, despite all this, Mash was allowed to take the recorder. Just then Ryasha—also known as Vova

Ryashintsev—arrived.

'What ya want me to take then?' he said, sounding rough, in the manner of Chelkash, the protagonist of Maxim Gorky's book. 'This 'ere?'

Ryasha tried to be a proper lad, as rough and battle-hardened as Kol. He too would say *bloody 'ell!* and spit without parting his lips. However, he never really succeeded in any of those things, since he was a spindly four-eyes, plus really spoiled by his highbrow upbringing imposed on him by his parents, dentists with a town-wide reputation.

As they came into the classroom, both holding on to the leather handle of the heavy music box (Mash wouldn't allow this walking catastrophe to carry it by himself), a wail swept all over the desks. Kol, unable to contain his happiness, jumped onto the teacher's desk and yelled:

'April Fool on you two—time to cry, boohoo!'

Usually a brief *April Fool on you* would do; but on this occasion two fools were fooled at once, so Kol took the trouble to put on his poet's hat. And that hurt even more.

'This witticism of yours is, if I may say so, of the lowest possible calibre,' Ryasha said in a trembling, educated voice, but then, pulling himself together, barked: 'Ya scum, I'm gonna smash your stupid mug in…'

Mash said nothing. She put the deck in the far corner and looked out of the window, as if nothing happened.

Meanwhile, the class was yelling and dancing and going wild:

> Ap-*rul* Fooool!
> Ap-*rul* Fooool!

They didn't stop until the next victim appeared in the door.

'Ouch! You've got paint on your sleeve!' Lyosha Semyonov shouted to her.

The victim also went *ouch!* and started twisting her arm trying to see her own shoulder from above.

'Ap-rul Fooool!' the class shrieked.

April Fool's Day continued outside, too. By the school gate, under the WELCOME red banner (which, seen from this side, read the other way around: EMOCLEW) there stood a cordon. A few boys, the more enterprising types, were hoping to intercept someone—someone who hadn't been tricked by anyone yet—and show the fool what day it was today.

Sometimes they succeeded. Mash saw them suddenly start jumping up and down with joy, dancing around some unfortunate, who was looking about, bewildered.

Apart from the story with the deck, there were a few other significant achievements. Leo Makhervax, a crazy young naturalist, was shown a picture of a little bird cut out of a Polish magazine, and told that it's a zoological mystery, a *Papio nightingalis*, which can be found in the south of Galápagos Islands only, and sings in a man's voice.

'Galápagos Islands are generally full of surprises,' Leo said. 'This is the only place where you can find giant tortoises.'

He was credulous and really did know a lot, which made the trick somewhat less impressive. The first prize, therefore, went to Mash, who, after recovering from the shock, managed to trick the best student Sasha Kamensky, their know-all, a tall, skinny boy with bushy eyebrows, who spoke in a condescending tone to everyone, even to the headmaster, even to the General Colonel of Armoured

Troops who came to the school on the eve of Armoured Trooper's Day. Mash approached him:

'Come on, Sasha, tell us where these lines are from: *The penny of life has dropped, an ink-stain on the blank sheet.* Can you at least guess the poet?'

He moved his lips, big and soft, reminding Mash of the horse she had seen in the country last summer, and said:

'Of course it's Mayakovsky. Early. Possibly from 'The Backbone Flute.' Yes, oh yes, of course it's from there…'

And then he started explaining what particular idea the poet wanted to convey in these lines. Unfortunately, he never managed to bring his explanations to a conclusion because Mash snorted with laughter and ruined the whole thing, for which the class condemned her, justly and unanimously.

Already by the first break any tricks whatsoever became impossible. Everyone, including Year 1 kids, had grown vigilant. Everyone expected nasty surprises and trusted no one. Whatever was being said, everyone listened with a sceptical face: *OK, fine, natter away, you won't catch me on this.*

Instead of bringing benefits, deceptions began to cause losses. Because some would forget about April Fool and say things they really knew and meant. That was Kol's undoing: he was told that some grown-up guy was waiting for him downstairs. He laughed right into the messenger's stupid face: to try and catch out him, Kol, on such a trifle! But there really was a guy who came to see him. It was the famous stamp collector Lyonya from School No 29, whose visit the aspiring philatelist could never even hope for. But that did not transpire until much later.

However, it was Yura Fonaryov who drew the shortest

straw. He got a note from a girl whose name I dare not mention here. She wrote that she wanted to go out with him and invited him to the cinema tomorrow. The film she suggested, *Dingo the Wild Dog*, was on at just one cinema, somewhere in the sticks, a place called Lower Cauldrons or some such. But it was this film she wanted to see on their first date. And Yura knew why. Because the film was subtitled *A Story of First Love*.

He cartwheeled out of the classroom and then walked on his hands a bit along the corridor, mindless Year 4 kids racing around, one of them nearly stepping on his hand.

'CNASCA!' shouted the Year 4s. 'CNASCA!'

Yura grabbed his bully by the scruff of the neck and enquired in a severe tone what his cheeky behaviour and this odd cry might mean. The kid turned out to be timid. He explained, wistfully and reverentially, that he pushed Yura by accident; as for *CNASCA*, no one has a clue what it means. But the word does exist! He hopped along to his classroom and, after a bit of brown-nosing, persuaded his classmate whose turn it was to guard the door that day to let him sneak in. After rummaging in his desk for a minute, he shoved the last page of his Year 4 textbook into Yura's face. It did indeed say: *Printing Works No 5 CNAS&CA*.

'Well, what did I tell you? Does it exist?' he asked, this time in a cheeky tone.

'It does,' Yura said. 'It's abbreviated. Perhaps it means Central Nutrient Additives Stabilisers & Catering Agency.'

'Ha-ha!' the kid said. 'April Fool!'

And Yura was stung by the thought that *her note*, too, like everything else today… It would have been horrible! Firstly because, you know why, and secondly, because he'd been tricked. No, no, it can't be, she handed it to him herself, and at that moment she had her eyes... no, she didn't have any eyes—they were lowered, she only had her eyelashes. She also had her cheeks, though, burning bright. But what if she was simply worried the trick wouldn't work?

In desperation, he dashed to his bosom friend Leo Makhervax.

'Let's think logically,' Leo said, trying to tuck his fingers into his stiff, dishevelled thatch, as impenetrable as a jungle. 'Why didn't she hand her epistle to you on the twenty-eighth of March, say, or, conversely, the day after tomorrow? Coincidence? Fine! But why this particular cinema in Lower Cauldrons, out there in the sticks? Another coincidence? Fine! I've got a copy of *The Week in Cinema*. OK, it starts next Monday, but still...' (A five-minute pause.) 'See, *Love and Tears* is on. Suppose the schedule could change on Monday. But look, what a mocking title: ...*and Tears*. Coincidence?'

Then Yura saw her—the one whose name I dare not speak—at the end of the corridor and, before Leo had time to go *Fine!* once again, he made a dart towards her and, laughing bitterly, threw down that very note.

'No way—you won't catch me out! April Fool.'

But she didn't laugh: her lips curled, while her eyes —now that they weren't needed, they were where they were supposed to be—her eyes brimmed with quivering tears. Either she is a great actress (unlikely as last Christmas her performance in a school play, where she had the part of Old Man Khottabych, was a fiasco), or he is an ass. Yes, he is an ass! A wretched, stupid, self-destroying ass. Need to ask

Leo, this smart alec, damn him, if self-destroying asses exist. Well, if Yura exists then they clearly do.

On the way back from school Mash had to lug the deck on her own. When she approached Ryasha, he turned away and spat without parting his lips, but it landed on his own sleeve, which made him really mad.

'I'm not a lackey to ya, am I. It's not like I've been 'ired to drag your bloody stuff around.'

Mash pushed him with her shoulder so he bumped into a wall a bit; then, keeping her pride, she picked up the deck and hauled it outside.

Mash was snub-nosed—accordingly, her nose was naturally turned up. In addition, she tended to hold her head high and walked in a special athletic way, which revealed a proud and independent soul. The whole thing was rather spoiled by her plaits. Two chestnut plaits, quite normal, their only remarkable feature being that they were the last remaining ones in the whole of Year 6.

All the other girls had already had their hair cut and now sported the backs of their heads looking boyish and stubbly. Mash dreamed of following the trend, but was bound by a word of honour. Back in the day when the down-with-plaits movement was first taking over the minds of 6A, 6B and 6C girls, Mum made her promise she would keep her plaits. The most recent rebellion at home happened just yesterday as she fought for the oath to be quashed.

'But why do you want to cut off your nice little plaits?' Mum asked with the air of a martyr. 'Why, oh why?'

'All our girls have cut theirs off, every single one. Because it's more original like that.'

'And what do you think this word means, *original?*'

'Like everyone's, fashionable,' said Mash confidently.

'I'm afraid it's the other way around,' laughed Dad. He even went and brought Mash a green dictionary volume, *K to S.* 'Would you care to see for yourself?'

After shaming his daughter in this manner, he spoke again, this time sticking to the point:

'As Russian folk wisdom has it, "Until you've promised, be strong; once you've promised, be strict."'

Next time Mash will, of course, be wiser, she will be strong and promise nothing. But now that she's promised she has to be strict...

She stopped by the school gate to catch her breath; at the end of the day, the deck is heavy if you carry it by yourself. And then someone touched her plaits. Not yanked, no, just touched them. But still, bearing in mind her foul mood, they could count themselves dead, provisionally.

She turned around abruptly. Before her stood Yura Fonaryov, sad and solemn.

'Listen, Mash!' he said in a voice one usually puts on to recite that poem by Nekrasov: *From exultant idle talkers/ Whose hands are steeped in blood.* 'Could you explain to me the point of all this idiocy, this animal brutality...'

He picked up the deck and, decisively waving her hand aside, carried it by himself. She said, April Fool's Day is a wonderful day, full of fun, and look, she's been tricked worse than him—well, how was she to know about the note?—but even so, there's nothing brutal about it, it's great to have a day like this when you can deceive everyone and have a really good laugh…

'Yeah, sure, you've been tricked worse than me,' he said, sounding bitterly ironic. Just like my mum's friend, he thought, that inconsolable widow who had her fur coat, skunk or something, stolen at the wake. 'No one's ever been tricked worse than me…'

Mash didn't pester him with questions; he'll tell her himself if he wants to. But Yura had gone off in a new direction now, passionately trying to prove that, since there is a day when everyone can deceive everyone else, then, for the sake of justice, there has to be a day when no one can deceive anyone! Does there have to be such a day or does there not?

'Yes, there does,' said Mash. 'And we all need to agree and declare one particular day—for instance, tomorrow, the second of April—just such a day. So that everyone takes an oath, and no one can tell a lie, not a single false word.'

'Neither with voice nor with gaze,' Fonaryov added solemnly (and I can see why he added that).

Instead of doing his homework, Yura spent the whole evening penning the oath. He was generally pretty good at penning things, and even *showed some promise of literary talent*, as they wrote back from the *Ogonyok* magazine, where Yura's mum used to send his poems on the sly. He remembered with sadness his first verses written, perhaps, in Year 2:

> Red fire
> Red red flags
> Red belts crisscrossing
> The machine-gunner's chest

> Red all around
> Engulfed by a flame
> The Commissar's heart
> Is all aflame!

Now, burdened with much knowledge and experience, he can hardly achieve the same freshness of perception. Anyway, having left behind poetry, that sin of his youth, he was now working in prose, writing a novel about love and fidelity, set in the Far North. Sadly, though, he was writing it all too slowly (hindered by an artist's demanding nature and high workload—it's Year 6, so what would you expect).

By half-ten the oath was nearly ready. The style could do with a bit more polishing, but Yura's father sent him to bed. Father worked as a traffic controller and valued discipline above all else.

…By the first break the idea had completely taken over the masses. Even Kol, who didn't want to take an oath cos we've got enough of 'em bans and rules. Even Sasha Kamensky, who didn't want to stoop to an oath he hadn't thought of himself. Even Ryasha, who never did anything Kol didn't do. Even this lot, in the end they all solemnly declared that they 'recognise the second of April as April Truth Day and swear by their conscience and the conscience of their class (meaning 6B), under the people's vigilant eye, to speak the truth and nothing but the truth on this great day, and not to deceive, nor pull anyone's leg, nor make anything up, nor make any false statement, nor lie, be it with word or voice or gaze.'

During the second period, Ariadna Nikolaevna, their

Miss Physics, young, pink and clean, asked if everyone had done their homework.

'I haven't,' Fonaryov said, adding heroically, 'I haven't even tried to.'

'Ohh!' Ariadna said. 'Why the heck are you so proud about it? You're going to get a *U*, not a medal.'

That she, instead of being formal, as befits a teacher, said *why the heck* in such an intimate manner, just like a student —that pleased everyone a lot. Whatever you say, she's a great girl, our Ariadna, a wicked teacher!

'What about you, Makhervax?'

'I copied someone else's,' Leo boomed gloomily.

'Really?' Ariadna began fiddling with her blouse collar and blushed so much you felt really sorry for her. 'Whose was it then?'

Silence.

'I'm asking you: whose homework was it?' cried Ariadna, severely yet quite plaintively.

'Mine,' said Sasha Kamensky, proudly flinging up his eyebrows.

'Who else have you given your homework to copy?'

'Me,' rose someone.

'And me,' rose another.

'And I copied it from him,' went a third.

'And me,' someone raised his hand in the back row.

'And me!'

'That's it!' groaned Kol. 'She'll get us with her bare hands.'

Ariadna, however, wasn't going to get them with her bare hands. She suddenly shut her eyes tight for some reason, and then she smiled, her face turning into a little girl's, all cheeks and dimples.

'You folks,' she said, 'you must have made a resolution to start a new life from today on. Is that it? I've tried it several times myself…'

Ariadna sighed and, for some reason, didn't tell them what it had all led to. But most importantly, she didn't torture anyone with any more questions, instead going straight on to a new topic, Archimedes' principle. The class had already heard of this principle, as featured in school folklore: 'Chuck a body into water, it'll never sink an iota.' But it turned out the folklorists were wrong. Because if the body's density is greater than that of water, it'll sink alright.

'By our next lesson please make sure you do both sets of homework, this and the previous one.' Saying this, Ariadna Nikolaevna even tapped her delicate finger on the desk.

'Grrrr!' growled the class, indignant at the very suggestion that anyone could possibly let Ariadna down, now that she had shown such generosity of spirit. Never ever! The sky would sooner fall on earth, parallel lines would sooner meet in a single point, Spartak FC would sooner lose to the despicable Dynamo…

In the long break, Yura Fonaryov reprimanded his best friend Leo Makhervax: why didn't he answer Ariadna's question, nearly breaking the oath as a result?

'I'd rather break a hundred of your oaths than be a snitch,' Leo declared gloomily. 'No oath should make you a slave.'

And the best minds of 6B began arguing about this interpretation: is it fair, doesn't it provide a loophole?

Indeed, their class was such a motley crew. While some folks were already kind of grown-up and pondered the meaning of life, others were like mere boys, like Bandar-logs from *Mowgli*, like some sort of Year 5s; they raced up and down the corridors, yelled, fooled around and never pondered the meaning of life.

An exercise book with *Girly Secrets* written on it was going around, being passed from desk to desk. The more backward girls, taking advantage of April Truth, compiled some moronic questionnaire in it.

'Who do you like? How do you like Batalov? In which film do you like him best? Are you ever in a bad mood?' The answers also rivalled each other in their stupidity. Some lofty soul (probably Mussy) went as far as writing that she likes 'such strong, manly, high-minded and beautiful people like the *Magnificent Seven*, (oh dear: *such people like*), that she finds 'Batalov adorable in all his films and especially in real life,' and that, on top of everything else, she sometimes feels 'a certain sadness inside, albeit full of light, and the heart aches, ever so slightly, with a vague longing every girl would recognise: for something big that could embrace so powerfully…' (this one she clearly lifted from some book somewhere).

Kira Pushkina, the chair of their Young Pioneer detachment's council, said it wasn't the done thing for Young Pioneers, that kind of questionnaire. You need to ask completely different questions: about cosmonauts, about your cherished dream to go to the taiga and about your favourite book character, the polar explorer Sanya Grigoryev, whom you consider your ideal.

And Mash, who never ever agreed on anything with Kira and even thought that she got her glorious surname by some egregious mistake—Mash said, all of a sudden, that Kira was right. Founding April Truth Day for the sake of this poxy rubbish—why even bother!

The founders of this great day, when they first came up with their idea, couldn't even begin to imagine what problems and troubles it would bring about, how many shocks and crashes, nay catastrophes, it would cause.

Mussy, hurt over her questionnaire, went out into the corridor and started cruising around like a ruthless felucca in the Mediterranean, Algerian pirates at its helm. She would stop every boy she happened upon, wait for some witnesses to approach and, aiming at him with her eyes, these murderous muzzles, ask something along the lines of:

'Go on, tell us, how do you like Masha Gavrikova?'

'I think she's a good friend and a progressive Young Pioneer,' replied her first target, poor Ryasha. The fact that Kol sent him to none other than Mash for the deck was, rest assured, no coincidence.

'Are you in love with her?' Mussy fired off.

'Like 'ell I am,' said Ryasha in a lazy tone, blushing like a banner.

But the witnesses, who seemed to have liked this game, stared at him, demanding an answer and sighing with reproach.

'Well, I mean, I like her well enough, of course. Compared to other girls…'

After making sure that Ryasha had been bled dry, Mussy went in search of her next victim. The third one happened to be Yura.

'Are you in love with—?' In a loud, cheery voice she named the one whose name I hadn't had the heart to tell you. 'Are you?'

A happy crowd jostled around them, and there, by the wall, stood *she*. Not very near, but still, close enough for every word to be heard.

'Are you in love or not? Did you get a note or did you not?'

If he, the founder, says *No!*—that's the end of April Truth. If he, Yura, says *Yes*—that's the end of love. What love can survive being pilloried in this way?

Yura stood there, his head held high, silent like the Young Pioneer hero under torture in S. Mikhalkov's poem.

Scattering the crowd, Sasha Kamensky fought his way to Mussy. He knitted his famous eyebrows menacingly, and said:

'Go on, Mussy, ask me quick, what do I think of you?'

'Well, what do you think of me?' she asked coquettishly, tilting her head to one side. What a pussycat!

'I think you are vile!' Sasha said. 'And you, ladies and gentlemen, you too…'

It's unclear why he addressed the crowd in this strange manner, using the words one comes across in plays about the life of pre-revolutionary merchants, which everyone was forced to go and see at the Maly Theatre. However, they produced an extraordinary effect. The crowd immediately dispersed or, rather, ran off haphazardly. Mussy batted her eyelashes for a while, gasped for air, then said:

'Not funny. Anyway, look at you: skinny like a stick.'

And Yura, all these terrible worries over, went straight over to *her* and asked what show they were going to.

'The one at quarter past four,' she said. 'Will your parents let you go?'

'I'll tell them we have a school meeting…'

She gave him an intent look and smiled.

'Ah, yes, of course, it's April Truth…'

Never mind. He'll go to the cinema with her anyway! Remembering his father, who worked as a traffic controller and valued discipline above all else, Yura added:

'Whatever the cost.'

By then a whole crowd had gathered in a corner, engaged in polemics over whether or not Yura was right to have remained silent. And Leo, his wonderful basso booming over everyone's voices, kept saying:

'That was a matter of a woman's honour! He had no right to tell. What are you, little children? Have you never read books?'

None of the polemists were little children, and all of them had read books. Any objections, therefore, were dropped. But still, it turned out that some rules for telling the truth were necessary, after all. Because, on the practical side of things, everything seemed to be too complicated somehow, and always different…

Failures and catastrophes kept multiplying. Someone suddenly found out about a horrible, if long forgotten (Year 4, 2nd term) act of treachery committed by a close friend, who caved in during a cross-examination under oath. Then it transpired that the class newspaper *For Excellence in Study*, which had been awarded the first prize at a competition run by the Palace of Young Pioneers, was drawn not by Grisha Gukasyan, one of their lot, but by his father, a set designer at the Operetta Theatre. Finally, the mystery of Skillful Hands, the team led by Kol, was revealed. It had been the most tight-knit and orderly team of all, its work kept totally secret. Guys from other teams, Art Lovers and Young Historians, had always supposed, on the basis of some dropped hints, that they had been building a working model of a ballistic missile and something known as a 'kerosene locator.'

However, when they put the heat on Kol, he admitted under oath that at their sessions the famous Skillful Hands had simply read spy novels published in the Military Adventure Series. The novels were procured by Ryasha, whose father provided dental services to a certain editor from Military Publishing.

The chair of the council, Kira Pushkina watched in silent horror as reputations collapsed and glories faded. She suggested, out of a desire to save whatever could still be saved:

'If this is how things stand, let's at least call our April Truth Day a special event. We as Young Pioneers have almost no good deeds left. Let it be an initiative by Right-A-Wrong, a collective farm worker who has appealed to the people's conscience.'

Yura Fonaryov, crazy with his private happiness, roared with laughter and, hinting at Kira's rank, said:

'Every nation gets the government it deserves!'

After all, it wasn't for nothing that he belonged to Young Historians. And Mash, a member of Art Lovers, said nothing —instead she simply came over and shooed Kira off the desk:

enough of your pointless nattering on this great day.

The main catastrophe happened during the fifth period, Russian Literature. With an all-school Maxim Gorky event approaching, Lyudmila Prokhorovna promised to talk about some of the great proletarian author's works which were part of the Year 8 curriculum, no less.

Who wouldn't be flattered to be promoted to Year 8 for an hour? Especially seeing that they were all sick and tired of those stupid essays titled 'Work Hard, Play Light' and summaries based on the painting *The Three Warriors*.

'A. M. Gorky, 1868–1936,' Lyudmila said solemnly and looked around, scanning everyone through her thick glasses, as if expecting something. They knew what she wanted and made inspired faces, like those in the photo 'Moscow Writers Meet the Staff of the Resin Elastic Factory.'

'Song of the Stormy Petrel,' she went on, more solemnly still. After leafing through the book for a while, she found the required page:

> High above the silvery ocean
> Winds are gathering the storm clouds,
> And between the clouds and ocean
> Proudly wheels the Stormy Petrel,

(not to be confused with a thunderbird, mind you—we've already discussed this compound word)

> Like a streak of sable lightning.

She got to the end and said:

'Now take out your exercise books and write down after me: 1) gulls, the intelligentsia unsure of whom they should side with; 2) grebes, creatures afraid of a coup, the middle class; 3) waves, the masses; 4) thunder and lightning, reactionary elements trying to silence the people's voice; 5) penguins, the bourgeoisie; 6) Gorky, the Stormy Petrel of the Revolution. Done? Now put your pens down. Tell us, Kalizhnyuk: what are the gulls?'

Kol sluggishly got out from behind his desk, thought a bit, grunted a bit.

'Whatsit called…I mean, them folks as got education…'

'Do you mean the intelligentsia? Correct. You can sit down now.'

Then her eyes fell on Mash, who was cringing to death listening to this analysis.

'Gavrikova!' Lyudmila shouted. 'Why are you fidgeting like this? Perhaps you are not interested?'

It was a rhetorical question (they'd already done them, like in that poem by Nekrasov, for instance: *Oh Volga, oh my cradle! Has anyone ever loved you as I do?*). Rhetorical questions are asked for no reason, just like that, there is no need to answer them. But everyone's impatient eyes were on Mash.

'I am not interested!' she said, sounding exactly the same as Galileo did when he stated, some time ago, 'And yet it moves.'

'Perhaps you are not interested in going to school in general?'

'In general I am interested.'

'Is it just my lessons, then?'

'Yes.'

Mash could only pray for Lyudmila not to be an idiot and

not to ask this question of everyone else. Because then —it didn't bear thinking of what would start then. But Lyudmila was beyond praying for.

'Perhaps none of you is interested?'

'None of us!' the class yelled. 'None of us!'

Lyudmila kept banging on the desk with her briefcase for a long time, but the class kept yelling:

'Not in-teres-ted! Not in-teres-ted!'

Maria Ivanovna, the deputy head, came into the classroom running.

'What's going on here?' she asked sternly.

Mash, considering herself the guilty party, said:

'Lyudmila Prokhorovna asked us if her lessons were interesting. So I replied…'

'We replied,' the class yelled. 'All of us…'

'Go home at once. And don't expect to be treated leniently. This kind of disruptive behaviour won't go unpunished.' She spoke sternly, but sounded somewhat unconvinced; many thought she didn't sympathise with Lyudmila all that much, but shouted just the same, out of duty. 'Shame on you all, shame on the whole 6B! Whatever next?'

An emergency meeting was held in a little park opposite the school.

'Who wants this freaking truth when it only makes things worse for everyone?' Kol said.

It was a rhetorical question. But he got an answer. The answer came from Yura Fonaryov. Yura was really pushed for time (he still had to pop back home, dump his satchel and wangle some money) but he couldn't leave—oh no.

'Truth makes things harder, not worse. But in the end, it

makes things better.'

'In the end? What about tomorrow, when they draft in our parents? What's it gonna be like then, better or worse?'

'Does your old man beat you?' Sasha Kamensky asked Kol. He sounded miserable, clearly being no stranger to beatings.

'Nah, but he'll start moaning: *When I was your age I used to eat millcake, I used to wear patched rags, I used to plough with cows*. Why doesn't he give me a cow so I can plough, it's better than him going on like that…'

'It's OK: tomorrow will no longer be April Truth, we'll get away with it, one way or another,' said Ryasha, who had a lot of power over his parents. 'It'll blow over. We'll admit our mistakes…'

'You mean, tomorrow it's back to lying again?' said Mash, terrified. 'So all our troubles will have been for nothing?'

'Let's at least write to *Pionerskaya Pravda*,' Kira Pushkina suggested. 'Let's start a contest. To be nominated as The Conscientious Detachment.'

'Shut up,' said Kol. 'We really need to oust her to hell. But it would be a real shame to go back to telling porkies tomorrow —that would mean all this aggro's been for nothing!'

…In the evening Mash was reading about Archimedes' principle. Dad, lying on the sofa in his braces, was also reading.

'What's in the evening news?' Mum asked him.

'Nothing much… Mrs A. L. Penniless is divorcing Mr M. S. Penniless…'

'I can't blame her,' Mum said in a meaningful way.

'You and your hints,' sighed Dad.

The phone rang in the hall.

'That will be Kovalevsky,' said Dad, his voice full of vengeful triumph. 'I'm sure you've forgotten to put in a word for him.'

'Masha, I'm not in!' Mum shouted.

Mash had already obliged on similar occasions, many times, but today was April Truth Day.

'Hello. Yes, she is. Mummy, a phone call for you.'

'Tell him I've only just left, gone to the Popovs, a minute ago.'

'I won't lie!'

'Is this the way to speak to your mother!?'

Mum put on her special welcome-dear-guests face and picked up the phone.

'Mikhail Petrovich, dear, I was just going to call you. There hasn't been any progress yet…'

Mum came back into the room, breathing heavily, her eyes sparkling in the manner of the actress Mordyukova, and shouted:

'So I'm a liaress, in your opinion? Is that it?'

What a strange word to stumble on. It probably doesn't even exist. But poor Mummy, of course…

'No, I don't think you a liaress. It's just we in our class have decided not to lie anymore. So there was nothing I could do.'

'And I, in your opinion, was going to lie!?'

Mash just didn't know what to say to this, because Mum was, after all, in, and did, after all, ask her to say that she wasn't… She looked at Dad helplessly.

Dad proved to be on top of things, as ever. After all, he had a PhD in philosophy, and could find an explanation for anything and everything.

'You've misunderstood. Mum just didn't want to upset someone. It happens—it's called a white lie.'

'To make things look white? Or to look white yourself?' Mash was horrified at her own words; whatever she does or says today, everything sounds kind of rude, even though she doesn't mean it that way at all.

Mum started crying, and Dad said that Mash was still too young to judge things like this, let alone to subject adults to biased interrogations. Anyway, it's time she went to bed as even the most virtuous ideas do not exempt people from their responsibility to go to work. And her work is school, and you have to get up at half seven for school.

When Mash went to her room, Mum and Dad started arguing in a loud whisper. He said, Masha is a grown-up girl now, it won't do to throw scenes like this when she's around.

'Yeah, right, and when I'm not, it's OK?' shouted Mash from her room. 'I can hear everything. Honestly, you people!'

'Eavesdropping is shameful,' said Mum, closing the door.

But Mash wasn't eavesdropping—she just couldn't help hearing.

She already regretted everything that had happened tonight. Indeed, why did she snap at her poor old folks? They don't know, do they, that today is the second of April. Or rather, they do—this they do know; it's just that the grown-ups were never part of the April Truth treaty and they never took the oath…

1963

Five Poems

Michael Naghten Shanks

IN LONDON, IT IS

curious how showering with baby wipes in a toilet cubicle
the night after whiskey healed the wounds
cratered into you by jägerbombs
makes you think of a David Foster Wallace essay.

Tonight, you'll eat spring rolls
while walking through winter air
that comes from you and is already behind you
because you're feeling late and moving too fast.

Fingerprint grease on the pages of your poems
will historicise the moment.

EXPERIENCES

have I been stung by a wasp outside
the italian takeaway under the neon sign that spells
out R O M A in pink and blue
and reminds me of miami in the 1980s
or did I tell you about the guy who was watching
the shawshank redemption on his macbook
in the emergency room
while I waited for my mom after she had stopped
breathing in the ambulance and anyway
how authentic an experience do you think you can have
in the cavernous college hallways
below a multinational coffeehouse
because sometimes you just want to eat chicken
without a side order of reality

FRAGMENTS OF S

is a montage a picture of pixels of moments of you
with two red bulls and *the world's favourite love poems*
on the green of hampstead heath with fresh strawberries
covered in white chocolate your arm around your sister
'this is england' styled bad poses in the ladies' dressing
room
deep red lips contrast the bright blue dress you wear
offsetting auburn hair darkly painted fingernails captured
blurred in the motion of rat-a-tat-tatting the teacup
as white as the bubbles next to your red-raw skin
but brighter than the santa claus bath bomb
before the explosive effervescence you lie seductively
with a panda bear sweater green and pink dinosaur socks
on top of your bed your legs crossed your eyes closed
pretending to sleep for cinematic romance with no sequel

I AM YOUR REFRIGERATOR AT 3 A.M. WHEN YOU ARE HUNGRY

I could not consume the stars above the beach in
Enniscrone
or stop the soot of London mixing with Camden coke.
In different seasons, love is ice-cream: we want to lick
our favourite flavour all year, even if it makes us sick.
I give you a call and you come over. We watch
a Werner Herzog documentary, *Cave of Forgotten Dreams*,
about simple drawings of extinct animals. One of us says:
Do you think the artist ate the art or the art ate the artist?
We know the beginning and the end before we press play.
We consume designer drugs not designed for us; our
bodies
separated by a punnet of mixed berries the colour of our
bruises.
You sprinkle sugar over everything; the clumps of sugar on
my sheets
remind me of the stars above the beach. We both have our
flaws to share. We eat the air's empathy-flavoured existence.
In the morning, you'll say: *I just ate a special K cereal breakfast
bar when what I really wanted to eat was pepperoni pizza.* I'll say:
*I want to be ten years older eating dauphinoise potatoes for dinner and
apple pie with cream for dessert.* In a month, you'll confess your
sins
over Sunday lunch, across the table in a café, croissant
crumbs will stick
to our forearms. Tonight, you stroke the scar on my thigh
inscribed by a firework. You touch my scar to touch my past.

You comfort my past when you fear you cannot comfort my present.

You comfort me to comfort yourself. When we wake, you say: *I spilled the sugar.* I say: *I know, I could taste it on your elbows.*

INFINITE ASMR

Look into the pitch-black pool, the crystalline screen,
at the multiple open tabs: twitter, facebook, youtube and
gmail.
Listen to the female voice you have selected
to guide you through this experience.
[For best effects wear headphones.]
Ignore new notifications and suggested updates.
In 360 degrees, her dulcet and whispered words
will begin to blur boundaries.
Allow your fantasy to permeate her veiled face.
*'…as you listen to the echoing crinkle of your loved one's footsteps
receding into the distance…'*
Refresh your world.
Former followers rarely return.
Please don't be so foolish as to think they'll name a flower
after you.

The Cardinal & the Corpse

A Flanntasy in Several Parts by Pádraig Ó Méalóid

I n *At Swim-Two-Birds* Flann O'Brien writes,

> I reflected on the subject of my spare-time literary activities.
> One beginning and one ending for a book was a thing I
> did not agree with. A good book may have three openings
> entirely dissimilar and inter-related only in the prescience
> of the author, or for that matter one hundred times as
> many endings.

It's hard to resist the temptation to mimic that opening in
writing anything about Flann O'Brien in my *own* spare-time
literary activities; to have several beginnings, and any amount
of endings.

To start with: I have a particular place in my heart for
the work of Flann O'Brien. Everyone in Ireland, give or
take, knows that his real name is Brian Ó Nualláin, or Brian
O'Nolan in English. Except that that's not entirely true.
The family surname, although it was always Ó Nualláin in
Irish, was originally Nolan in English, not O'Nolan, the
O' being attached in the aftermath of the Gaelic League's
pushing for a revival of Irish language and culture in the
1890s. So even from an early age Flann was used to a certain
mutability, a certain slipperiness, in his external identity. He
would later write as Myles na Gopaleen, a name looted from
Dion Boucicault's 1860 play *The Colleen Bawn*, and also from
Gerald Griffin's *The Collegians¹*, but he also wrote as Brother

1 Gerald Griffin's 1829 novel, *The Collegians*, on which *The Colleen
Bawn* was based, novelises the true story of the murder of fifteen-
year-old Ellen Scanlan, who was killed by the banks of the River

Barnabas, Lir O'Connor, George Knowall, and many more names as well, some of which are known, but with yet more undoubtedly still waiting to be discovered. What we do know—or at least *think* we know—is that, except for some very early newspaper work in the Irish language, it seems that he never wrote under any of the variations of his own name.

Flann O'Brien's first novel, *At Swim-Two-Birds*, published by Longman, Green & Co. in March 1939, attracted praise from the likes of Graham Greene, who was working as a reader for Longman's, and later from a self-exiled James Joyce in Paris, just two years before his death. At the age of twenty-seven O'Brien's star seemed to be on the ascendant, and he assured all his friends in Dublin that his next work, the as-yet unnamed and unpublished *The Third Policeman*, was better. However it was rejected with the note, 'We realise the author's ability but think that he should become less fantastic and in this new novel he is more so.' His agents tried a few other publishers, but nobody was biting. He covered this up by telling his friends that it was no longer in his possession, misplaced variously by stupidity, loss, or misadventure: he had left it behind in the Dolphin Hotel on Essex Street; it was lost on a train; it had blown away, a page at a time, out of the boot of his car whilst driving through Donegal. The truth was, however, more prosaic: the manuscript sat in a drawer in one home or another for over a quarter of a

Shannon in 1819. However, it's probably true to say that the book, and the subsequent play, are at best *loosely* based on the original murder.

century, until it finally saw print after his death, and secured his legacy forever.

To add to his troubles, Longman's premises were destroyed during a London bombing raid by the Luftwaffe, destroying all unsold copies of *At Swim-Two-Birds*.[2] A potentially glittering literary career that at the beginning of 1939 had seemed unstoppable had less than two years later been ground to a halt.

O'Brien had not stopped writing, however: he began his *Cruiskeen Lawn* column in the *Irish Times* on 4th October 1940, originally as An Broc (The Badger), but from the second column on as Myles na gCopaleen, a name further tweaked to Myles na Gopaleen in the 1950s, under which name it ran until his death in 1966. He also published a short novel in Irish, *An Béal Bocht*, under the name of Myles, and had a play, *Faustus Kelly*, performed in the Abbey Theatre in 1943, but it would not be until 1961 that he would have another novel published in English, when MacGibbon and Kee published *The Hard Life*, followed by *The Dalkey Archive* in 1964, for which O'Brien cannibalised parts of *The Third Policeman*.

The Cardinal and the Corpse, a 40-minute semi-documentary made in 1992 by Christopher Petit and Iain Sinclair for a late-night slot on Channel 4, described quite accurately by one commentator as 'a show about books and bibliophiles in London,' muddied the pseudonymous O'Brien waters further. When I first watched it, I had no idea what was

---

2 Sales up to that point only amounted to two hundred and forty-four copies, allegedly.

going on in *The Cardinal and the Corpse*, or who most of the people in it—with the exception of Alan Moore and British science fiction writer Michael Moorcock—were. It seemed to be another story with several beginnings, several different threads running through it, none of which I had the slightest understanding of.

The documentary has three main streams, or 'quests'[3] as they were called, but it was the third one—The Flann O'Brien Sexton Blakes—I became fixated on the more I watched it. In the course of the action, we see husband and wife book dealers Gerry and Pat Goldstein rummaging through tables of books at one of the London markets. Pat Goldstein pulls out a handful of pulp novels, looks at them, and says that they are 'Sexton Blakes by different writers.' During the remainder of the documentary, we manage to get enough of a look at these to at least see the titles of several of them: *The Cardinal and the Corpse*, *The Case of the Alpha Murders*, *The Riddle of the Blazing Bungalow*, *Broken Toy*, *The Blonde and the Boodle*, *The Frightened People*, and *Espresso Jungle*. We also see one of the standout characters in the whole show lurking in the background, a book dealer called Driffield, who is making a mysterious phone call where he tells the person he is speaking to, 'I'm down here with Pat and Gerry. They just picked up some Sexton Blakes. *The*

3 Quest 1: The Journals of David Litvinov; Quest 2: The Barrett Magus; Quest 3: The Flann O'Brien Sexton Blakes. The first of these was definitely fictitious, as far as I'm concerned, even though David Litvinov had existed, but was dead since 1975. At least with the second quest, I knew both Alan Moore and the book he was searching for were real, or at least as real as an occult text and a comics writer can be, I suppose.

*Cardinal and the Corpse...*I remember you telling me once that Flann O'Brien had something to do with that.'

Later on, the Goldsteins have sold their finds to The Charing Cross Road Bookshop, where we see Driffield skulking behind a bookcase, emerging once the couple have left, to buy the Sexton Blake books for himself. Then he's on the phone again saying 'I've got some things you might be interested in. Flann O'Brien originals...not recorded in the bibliography. No one's ever seen them other than me. Stephen Blakesley—*The Case of the Alpha Murders, The Cardinal and the Corpse.*'

Had Flann O'Brien written these? If so, why hadn't I heard of them before? There was a lot I hadn't heard of, I was finding, and Drif had specifically said that they weren't in the bibliography. I did the only thing I could: I went looking on the internet, back then in 2009. A search for *'Sexton Blake / The Cardinal and the Corpse'* returned nothing, leading me to believe that they'd made the whole thing up, and that should have been that. But for some reason it wasn't. I looked at the thing a few more times, and did a few more searches. Time marched on, and more and more information found its way onto the internet in the meantime. When I finally had enough sense to do a targeted search for just *'The Cardinal and the Corpse,'* I got a result. There had been a book called *The Cardinal and the Corpse*, and the author was given as Stephen Blakesley, just as they'd said. Perhaps there was something to it, after all. To cut a long story of late-night Googling mercifully short, I figured out that an author called Stephen Blakesley had produced eight titles, between 1946 and 1952. Some of these were actually Sexton Blake titles, too. So at least some of what was in Sinclair & Petit's TV programme was true, after all.

Sexton Blake was a fictional detective who lived in Baker Street, as did Sherlock Holmes, and while in December 1893 *The Strand Magazine* was publishing Sir Arthur Conan Doyle's *The Final Problem*—in which Holmes apparently fell to his death at the Reichenbach Falls—issue six of *The Half-penny Marvel* published *The Missing Millionaire* by Hal Meredeth, the very first appearance of Blake, the same month.

Sexton Blake worked as a consulting detective, had a sidekick called Tinker, a faithful hound called Pedro, and a bullet-proof Rolls-Royce, named The Grey Panther. He was a bit more of a physical detective than a cerebral one, though, and this may have been part of his appeal to his intended Penny Dreadful audience. Before long there were Sexton Blake stories—either stand-alone stories or serialised ones—appearing in *The Half-penny Marvel*, *The Union Jack*, and *Pluck*, and numerous others. Blake was hugely popular, and there have been something in the region of 4,500 stories written about him, by around two hundred writers, an awful lot of them under various pseudonyms and generic house names.

So, what evidence is there that Flann O'Brien wrote Sexton Blake stories? On the face of it, there appears to be lots of it, overwhelming amounts of it, actually, both from himself and others. First of all, there's a letter he sent the then popular writer Ethel Mannin in July 1939, along with a copy of *At Swim-Two-Birds*. The correspondence, although brief, is in itself fascinating, with references to various side characters who may or may not have been mutual acquaintances of Flann and Mannin. Once she had read the book, though, Mannin didn't like it, and said so, prompting the obviously thin-skinned Myles to write back to her, full of bluster, including these closing paragraphs,

> It is a pity you did not like my beautiful book. As a genius, I do not expect to be readily understood but you may be surprised to know that my book is a definite milestone in literature, completely revolutionises the English novel and puts the shallow pedestrian English writers in their place. Of course I know you are prejudiced against me on account of the IRA bombings.

> To be serious, I can't quite understand your attitude to stuff like this. It is not a pale-faced sincere attempt to hold the mirror up and has nothing in the world to do with James Joyce. It is supposed to be a lot of belching, thumb-nosing and belly-laughing and I honestly believe that it is funny in parts. It is also by way of being a sneer at all the slush which has been unloaded from this country on the credulous English although they, it is true, manufacture enough of their own odious slush to make the import unnecessary. I don't think your dictum about 'making your meaning clear' would be upheld in any court of law. You'll look a long time for clear meaning in the Marx Brothers or even Karl Marx. In a key I am preparing in collaboration with Mr Kevin O'Connor, it is explained that the reader should begin on p. 145 and then start at the beginning when he reaches the end like an up-&-down straight in Poker. The fantastic title (which has brought a lot of fatuous inquiries to bird-fanciers) is explained on p. 95 and is largely the idea

of my staid old-world publishers. My own title was 'Sweeny in the Trees'. I am negotiating at present for a contract to write 6 Sexton Blake stories (25 to 30,000 words for £25 a time) so please do not send me any more sneers at my art. Sorry, Art.

Many things that would preoccupy O'Brien throughout his life are evident in that letter: his desire for literary acceptance, his preoccupation with money, his difficult relationship with James Joyce, and of course his strange obsession with Sexton Blake. O'Brien's choice of Ethel Mannin as a possible champion of his work is certainly a strange one: her forté was mostly sentimental popular fiction with a left-leaning feminist tinge, very far from what *AS2B*[4] was, and her liberal views—she had affairs with both W.B. Yeats and Bertrand Russell—hardly coincided with O'Brien's own highly conservative Catholic worldview, or his evident misogyny.

O'Brien next mentions Sexton Blake over fifteen years later, in 1955, when he writes to the Stephen Aske literary agency in London, suggesting that he would write Blake stories for them to place on his behalf.

> This letter arises from a chat I had the other day with my friend Marten Cumberland, who gave me leave to quote his name. He told me of the market for Sexton Blake stories and suggested I get in touch with you. I am interested in trying my hand at this sort of work.
>
> I have read the Sexton Blake stories in my day and can, of

[1] O'Brien was referring to *At Swim-Two-Birds* as *AS2B* in his correspondence from very soon after it was published in 1939, so I shall too.

course, refresh my recollection with the current stories. I am sure I could do this job particularly as Cumberland said he thought the plot would be supplied. Anyhow, I should like to try. I would be willing to supply two chapters as a sample for nothing.

Sadly, there is no record of a reply to this.

Flann next talks of Blake in 1962 (*AS2B* had been republished by MacGibbon & Kee in 1961, soon followed by *The Hard Life*) in an interview for BBC television's *Bookshelf* with Peter Duval Smith, which included this exchange:

PDS: I believe I'm right in saying you've written several Sexton Blake detective stories?

FOB: Yes, I have.

PDS: Are you proud of them?

FOB: I am very proud of them, very proud indeed.

PDS: How many did you write?

FOB: I've written five…

He again confirmed that he had written Blake books in the *Cruiskeen Lawn* column in the *Irish Times*, in a three-part piece starting on 27th February 1964, where he laments the publication of the last book in the Sexton Blake Library:

It is sad to find how a friend, intending to be kind, can bring down gloom and sorrow. A few weeks ago one of my Ladies of the Bedchamber at Santry (a purely honorary office) called to a newsagent to collect my usual compendium of reading matter, and in due time delivered to me *Lady's Home Journal*, *Osservatore Romano*, *Our Boys*, *Which?*, *Fanny Hill*, *Studies*, *Die Zeit*, *News of the World*, and – *The Last Tiger*, a

Sexton Blake story by Wm. A. Ballinger.

It was that last item which shocked me deeply because (a) the book announced itself to be the last of the Sexton Blake series, the great detective having just retired, and (b) because I have myself belonged to the arch, arcane, and areopagitic coterie of authors who have written Sexton Blake stories for Fleetway Publications Ltd, London.

Oh, do not laugh, reader. I am very proud of that achievement, and it is barely possible that the Editor might get permission to reproduce my story serially in these columns.

Those four mentions of his writing Sexton Blake stories —in 1939, 1955, 1962, and 1964—are the only ones I can find—which is not to say there aren't others yet to come to light—but in themselves they certainly show that, over that twenty-five-year span, and possibly before it, Flann O'Brien was both interested in Blake, and either had written stories for the series or, for whatever reason, kept up the pretence that he had written them, for at least a quarter of a century.

Why was Flann O'Brien so obsessed with the idea of writing Sexton Blake stories, which ones might he have written, and, finally, did he actually do so?

To understand the *why* of this conundrum, this insoluable Mylesean pancake, we need to know something of his circumstances. O'Brien is often lumped in with James Joyce and Samuel Beckett, as the third member of the trinity of modern Irish literature, but he really wasn't like them, in many ways. Joyce and Beckett were Dubliners, born in the affluent suburbs of Rathgar and Foxrock, respectively, but Flann was an outsider, being from Strabane in the divided six counties of Northern Ireland. Whilst Flann longed to be a Dubliner, the other two turned their backs on their native city—and country—settling in mainland Europe. Any chance he might have had to migrate, to become a true European ex-pat, was destroyed by World War II, his failure to find a publisher for his second book, and his role as the family's sole earner after his father's death in 1937. He was bound to the life of a civil servant, tethered to his own perception of himself as a failed novelist. One other thing, both cause and effect, feeding back on itself, was his voracious alcoholism, which took hold of him early, and undoubtedly contributed hugely to his too-early death at the age of fifty-four, just when it seemed he might actually be making some sort of a comeback as a proper writer.[5] As a result of several of these things, O'Brien was always looking

---

5 To the very end, Flann never got over his animosity towards James Joyce. In his last book, *The Dalkey Archive*, he has Joyce wishing to join the Jesuits, and claiming that he never wrote any of the books that were attributed to him, which echoes Gerard Griffin's later life in all sorts of interesting ways. In the end, he has Joyce being offered the job of washing and mending the priests' rotting undergarments, rather than an actual place in the order itself. When writing to Cecil Scott of publishers Macmillan in New York in January 1964 he says, 'The intention here is not to make Joyce himself ridiculous but to say something funny about the preposterous image of him that emerges from the treatment he has received at the hands of many commentators and exegetists (mostly, alas, American).' However, when writing to Timothy O'Keefe in September 1962, when he's still working on the book, he confided 'But Joyce. I've had it in for that bugger for a long time and I think this is the time.'

for more ways to make money, and the Sexton Blake stories seemed perfectly suited for this. They were hugely popular, and the rights were owned by the publisher, rather than the original writer, meaning that there was a huge potential market there, if he could but get his foot in the door. It also seems likely that he had read the stories in his youth. If he based various names he used on Griffin's *The Collegians*, then it is also likely that he chose the name of Sergeant Pluck, the man who first utters the line *'Is it about a bicycle?'*, from the old Penny Dreadful title *Pluck*. And his very fascination with *The Collegians* does seem to show an interest in crime fiction, as does the fact that there is a volume of Sherlock Holmes short stories amongst the books in his library, as preserved in Boston College's John J. Burns Library.

But there might have been an even more fundamental reason that Flann wanted to write crime fiction, besides the need for money and the seemingly easy Sexton Blake market he was so taken with. When O'Brien's father died they found amongst his papers a crime novel he had written, and which had been accepted by publishers Collins, but which never saw print, as the elder Nolan was unhappy about their payment terms. The incentive to write crime novels didn't stop there, either, as Flann's brother Ciarán had two books published by An Gúm, featuring an amateur detective, Parthalán Mac Mórna.[6] Flann's own crime novel, *The Third Policeman*, had

6 The first, *Oíche i nGleann na nGealt* (*A Night in the Valley of the Lunatics*) was published in 1939, the same year as *AS2B*, and the second, a collection of four stories, *Eachtraí Phartalán Mhic Mhórna* (*The Adventures of Parthalán Mac Mórna*) in 1944. According to John Cronin, writing in *New Hibernia Review* in Winter 1999, Parthalán Mac Mórna was 'a kind of Hibernian Sherlock Holmes, who

failed to be accepted in the gap between the publication of his brother's two books, and this may have added a certain spur to his desire to produce something in that genre.

As soon as that interview with Peter Duval Smith on BBC TV went out in April 1962 people began to speculate about which titles he might have written. The June 1962 issue of *Collectors' Digest*—a magazine devoted to British story papers—had an article referring to the interview, and asking 'Detective Inspector Lofts' if he could find out. DI Lofts—an entirely imaginary and honorary rank—was actually W.O.G. Lofts, or Bill to his friends, a tireless cataloguer of boys' papers and related matters, and in his time probably the greatest living expert on Sexton Blake's labyrinthine maze of writers, pseudonyms, and house names and had, at the time of that article, been the SBL's editor since November 1956. If anyone was likely to know the answer, it was him. He replied to the request:

> I can only offer the following suggestions:
>
> 1. He did write Blake stories—but they were all rewritten by a regular writer.
>
> 2. He was the man who wrote stories by 'Stephen Blakesley'—in the current series, the name of the author being given as F. Bond—but of whom no details are known.

---

presides over a tale of rural mystery and intrigue. Parthalán is an intellectual, an unmarried recluse, who lives in a remote cottage, plays Chopin on the piano, affects a pipe, and applies Holmes-like sagacity to the solving of various mysterious happenings.'

3. He certainly has never written any Blake stories under the editorship of W. Howard Baker, for Mr. Baker knows all his authors personally.

4. Being a true Irishman it is possible that the mention of writing Blakes is real Blarney!

There was that name again: Stephen Blakesley. Who was he, and what had he written? It turns out that there are eight books by Blakesley, from three different British 'pulp' publishers: Bear, Hudson published *Terrell in Trouble* in 1946, Piccadilly Novels published four titles, two each in 1946 and 1947—*The Proctor Case, A Case for the Cardinal, The Cardinal and the Corpse*, and *The Case of the Alpha Murders*, and the three remaining titles were published as part of Amalgamated Press' Sexton Blake Library, one in 1951, and the other two in 1952: *The Riddle of the Blazing Bungalow, The Trail of Raider No. 1*, and *The Man with a Number*. Was Stephen Blakesley yet another pseudonym of Flann O'Brien? And, if so, why was Bill Lofts giving the authors name as F. Bond? In an article called 'De Me,' published in Queens University Belfast's *New Ireland* in March 1964, O'Brien had quite a bit to say about the use of pseudonyms by writers:

> In twenty-five years I have written 10 books (that is, substantial *opera*) under four quite irreconcilable pen-names and on subjects absolutely unrelated. Five of those books could be described as works of imagination, one of world social comment, two on scientific subjects, one of literary exploration and conjecture, one in Irish and one a play (which was produced by the Abbey Theatre). On top of

that I have produced an enormous mass of miscellaneous material consisting of short stories, scripts for radio and TV, contributions to newspapers and magazines, and even book reviews. This is work and can be very rewarding financially, often surprisingly so. But is it insufferably hard work? Not necessarily.

No author should write under his own name nor under one permanent pen-name; a male writer should include in his impostures a female pen-name, and possibly vice versa. A literary agent (there are probably 50 firms in London alone) is essential for the financial realisation of a writer's worth, particularly for the dissemination of his works abroad in translation, but the practitioner of the literary craft who is crafty will have several agents unknown to each other, each dealing with him under a particular pen-name which is not disclosed to the agent to be a pen-name.

He repeated the assertion that a writer should have one pen-name hidden inside another in his reply to Bill Lofts:

So far as Sexton Blake is concerned, I cannot help you very much, as it is such a long time ago. I should point out that in innumerable writings on a great diversity of planes— and subjects, I have never once used my own name. I have countless pseudonyms, and for reasons of my own it is sometimes necessary for me to mislead publishers.

We can at least say that neither Stephen Blakesley nor F. Bond are necessarily impediments to these books being by Flann. Can those names yield any further clues, though? Flann was occasionally given to leaving little hints embedded in his pseudonyms, as we saw with his use of names from Griffin's *The Collegians*. The Irish for Dublin is *Baile Átha Cliath* (pronounced Blaw-KLEE-ah), very similar to Blakeley, so not a million miles from Blakesley. Is that a hint, for those who wish to see it? Surely there has to be something in the similarity between that surname and that of Sexton Blake himself, too. And his other name here: F. Bond. Could it be possible that the middle three letters, BON, stand for Brian Ó Nualláin? Probably not—but you just never know, do you?

If you are conducting a criminal enquiry, at least the ones you read about in books, you look for means, motive, and opportunity. And you look for evidence, which will allow you to tie all these together. Flann O'Brien certainly has plenty of motive to want to write, and to write Sexton Blake stories in particular. He had the means, as he was an accomplished writer, by any measure you care to use. Did he, though, have the opportunity? Did the editors at the SBL ever accept or publish any of his work? At the outset, there seems to be plenty of evidence to suggest that he did. There are a huge amount of references to his having written Sexton Blake books, sometimes even including the possibility of them being under the name of Blakesley, in books and articles, and online blogs.[7]

Nonetheless, nobody seemed really sure. There were, after all, a few snags, the most serious of which is the time-frame of it all. If, as he told Ethel Mannin in 1939, he was

7 In Brendan Lynch's *Parsons Bookshop: At the Heart of Bohemian Dublin, 1949-1989*, Peter Costello and Peter van de Kamp's *Flann O'Brien: An Illustrated Biography*, and an article in *The London Magazine* in 1988, to pick three examples from my researches, to represent many more instances.

negotiating with the SBL to write books, why was he writing to ask Stephen Aske to place stories for him in 1955? If he didn't start writing the stories before 1955, then what about all the books published under the name of Stephen Blakesley between 1946 and 1952? It did seem as if the mystery would remain unresolved, without even a satisfactory explanation as to why the story was so prevalent, yet so untested. Even the National Library in Dublin have three SBL Blakesley titles attributed to Flann O'Brien listed in their catalogue.

Writing in *The Spectator* in January 1988, in an article called 'The Mysteries of Flann O'Brien,' John Wyse Jackson, having reviewed all the evidence he had to date, finished by saying,

> Thus far, therefore, the story of the mysteries of Flann O'Brien. Perhaps O'Nolan wrote them, or perhaps he wrote other, earlier ones. [...] Pity the poor bibliographer. All helpful correspondence will be gratefully received.

Although Flann's own claims sometimes don't seem to ring true, he nonetheless maintained his position that he had written Sexton Blake stories right the way through his life. It was a situation that his fellow Dublin resident Erwin Schrödinger would have recognised—both solutions were potentially true, and we could only know which by metaphorically opening the box. At this point, however, we were unlikely to find any new information...

Until, that is, a British writer called Jack Adrian wrote a letter to the *Times Literary Supplement* in November 1989:

Sir, – The problem of whether or not Brian O'Nolan (Flann O'Brien) wrote Sexton Blake stories—mentioned by Denis Donoghue in his review of Anthony Cronin's biography of O'Brien, *No Laughing Matter* (October 27– November 2) —has bedevilled researchers for nearly thirty years. I think it's possible he did. What I'm sure he didn't do is write them, or anything, under the name 'Stephen Blakesley'—although I fear the canard that he did may well, in the first place, have emanated from me.

In 1962 a colleague of mine, Bill Lofts, wrote to O'Nolan, who proved evasive on exactly which Blake novels (out of fifteen hundred) he'd written, when, and under what pseudonym; follow up letters were ignored. All of the Blake authors had by then been identified, their pseudonyms penetrated—except for one writer: Stephen Blakesley, who wrote a handful in the period 1951-3 (*The Riddle of the Blazing Bungalow*, *The Trail of Rider No. 1*, etc). No trace of him has ever been found, no Blake writer remembered ever seeing him and, in any case, payments for the books themselves were discovered to have been made to an 'F. Bond,' which might have been the real name of the author, or an agent or—as it was then (1962) suspected—a cover for Brian O'Nolan.

In the late 1970s I discovered that cheap paperback originals (non-Blake) by 'Blakesley' had also been published in the period 1945-7 (*Terrell in Trouble*, *The Cardinal and the Corpse*, etc). I mentioned the Flann O'Brien /'Stephen Blakesley' theory to a friend, who then passed on the good news to a runner for a number of London Modern-Firsts dealers. Within a couple of months no Blakesleys were to be found anywhere, unless you had a tenner or more to spare—and

> this at a time when the average early-1950s Sexton Blake usually sold for 25p.
>
> The snag is, the Blakesley books simply don't read like Brian O'Nolan. That is to say, they don't read like a witty and clever writer hiding his true style under a veneer of junk, or even a man verging on alcoholism (as O'Nolan was at that time) banging out the first thing that came into his head, for money. There are no little touches, no penetrable (to those in the know) jokes. They are distinctly run-of-the-mill. Significantly, the main characters in most of the Blakesley thrillers (Blake or non-Blake) have a habit of settling their differences in a particular area of Britain—the industrial Midlands, where I suspect 'Stephen Blakesley,' whoever he was, came from originally. In any case, 'Blakesley' only wrote three Sexton Blakes, not five.

I'm not sure if the quibbles about the quantities of SBL books Flann claims to have written are important, but one sentence immediately jumped out at me: 'I mentioned the Flann O'Brien/'Stephen Blakesley' theory to a friend, who then passed on the good news to a runner for a number of London Modern-Firsts dealers…' As far as I'm concerned, there's only one person who fits this description: it had to be Driffield, from *The Cardinal and the Corpse*. Was the entire thing, from beginning to end, a scam by a canny bookseller, to sell largely worthless books for vastly inflated prices, based on some very dubious circumstantial evidence? Did *anyone* know the truth?

One day, not too long ago, I spotted Micheál Ó Nualláin, the only surviving member of the twelve siblings, and eighty-six years old himself, waiting for a bus out to Monkstown. I should go and ask him, I thought. But did I want to? Did I want to actually solve this, to know for sure if it was true or untrue? I'd already done a ridiculous amount of digging, involving visits to both the National Library here in Dublin and the British Library in London, much correspondence with lots of kind and helpful people, and spent far too much money buying books that ultimately expanded, rather than diminished, the mystery here. If I asked the question, all that would be as nothing. I thought about it, and watched his bus arrive, watched him get on it, and wondered if I'd made the right decision, not approaching. And I decided that I definitely should have asked him, because I might never get another chance.

Fortunately, I got another chance. A while after that first existential encounter, I saw him again at the bus stop. This time, reader, I asked him. 'I don't think so,' said Micheál, 'but you wouldn't know. It's the kind of thing he'd do, though.'

None the less, research is ongoing.

The Belly of the Whale

A Captain Ruggles Novelette by Adam Biles

The hardest battle a Limey commando has to fight is against the ghosts of his own mind!

I

Captain Dylan Prometheus Ruggles, British army first airborne division, was born at twelve hundred feet, through a slit in a sky measled with stars. A naked manikin, a hand span in height but fully matured, a search-and-destroy mission hardwired in his genes. A foundling, a celestial bastard, an orphan charged to the universe's care. A military experiment. A character in a bad novel.

Not yet burdened with consciousness, Ruggles drifts amongst the starscape as his body protracts and sprouts. A rootless tree possessed. Skin stretches, gives, wrinkles. Bones lose density, knobble and arc. Hair greys in chalky streaks. From his backpack a cord winds loosely, umbilically, back to the birthing slit; a vertical wink of light against the inky darkness. His mind loops with partial thoughts and unanchored memories.

When his mouth ejaculates, 'I…' gravity interrupts with a jolt. He drops, but only to the length of the cord. A yank at the pack, a whip crack, and the furled membrane of a parachute blossoms over his head. A ridged silk placenta softening his descent, a canopy barring the heavens from view, barring his retreat forever.

Easing earthwards Ruggles feels himself into his body,

into the world. The air at this height is cold and his bare skin crawls. His feet throb, laced into paratrooping boots—calf-high, beetle black. The ground below flashes with toy explosions, phosphorescence in the gloomy, uncharted sea. Distant mechanical thunderclaps rumble asynchronously with the flashes. His mud-green trousers flap and snap in the breeze, his combat jacket ripples. Nascent thoughts run first *Dulcie*, then *search-and-destroy*.

At eight hundred feet he can make out treetops and hedgerows and a river. In a clearing he sees three rows of huts, long and thin, witheringly institutional. Padding his uniform he feels a folded map, a book of some sort and a packet of Woodbines. He plucks one, crumples it against his tongue, chews it into a wad, then stuffs the pack into the band of his helmet. His kaleidoscope mind sharpens.

Spiralled and tossed like a dandelion seed—'angels' Dulcie calls them—his trajectory the whimsy of the eddying air. He's headed for the trees, for the huts, for the trees again and then for the banks of the river. At three hundred feet, the wind's final caprice snaps him back into line with the huts and whisks him into the final plughole vortex.

He sees fences now, and a watchtower. Beyond he sees two monstrous figures, nightmarish sentries, five times the height of any man. Giants. Their *Stahlhelme* shoving skywards, two raging steel *glans penes*. He pedals against the void, swims. Imagining himself a bird, he flaps. No use! Fortune, that mischievous bitch, has played her hand, marked him as a prisoner. A hundred feet, seventy, fifty. A tube of light from one of the watchtowers sweeps across his path. Thirty, he slackens his legs for landing. Fifteen, ten, five.

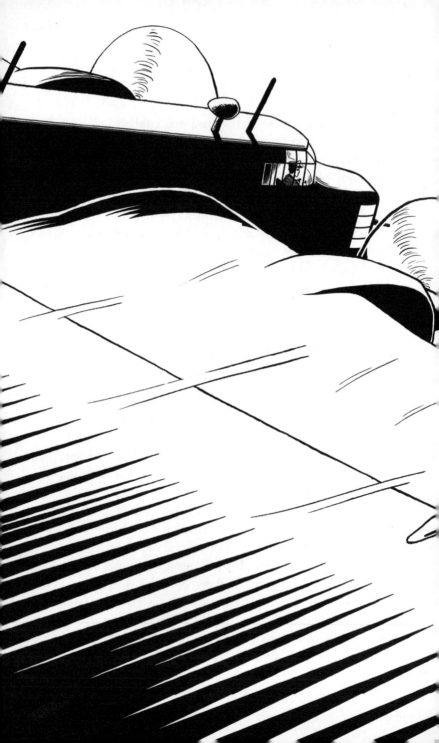

Contact.

His feet sink into the churned soil and—he could swear it!—the earth ripples, pulses with concentric circles. The huts judder, skip, and for the briefest moment, a single frame spliced in this disaster film, his mind mocks him with a vision of England, of tumbling hills, of a strange manor house, of an ambulance, its back doors leering open.

His body crumples and he loses consciousness. Far, far above the white slit blinks once, flexes as though smiling, then closes forever.

II

Captain Ruggles awoke naked in a puddle of cold urine. The smell, camphoric and sweet, tickled his nostrils but was not unpleasant. He was alone in a small cell, barren and not much larger than a closet, with a barred window at one end and a door at the other.

His thoughts were muggy, as if he had been asleep for some time, or drugged, and his throat pricked. No matter how far he rambled through his mind's outlying regions, Ruggles couldn't locate any scrap of intelligence concerning what happened to him after he had landed, how he had been stripped and transported to the cell, and by whom. The forgotten events simply would not be located, as if they had been detached from his memory, torn out, victim to a coupon-cutter's need for ('Thorough and gentle, no shock!') Ex-Lax pills. Otherwise he was unhurt, tired certainly, but that was to be expected after the previous night.

What rotten, rotten luck that the wind had sabotaged his mission before it had even started. He knew that the Krauts had some formidable allies, but if they had now inveigled Zephyrus into the Axis, the war was as good as lost.

Whatever was going on, his priority was to contact HQ. To let them know he was alive, that the mission had been an abysmal failure, but that he was fit, and ready to do whatever they required of him from his newly compromised position. He was also keen to make contact with any other detainees, to pool intelligence and orchestrate an escape. But all of that would have to wait—at least until he could find a way out of this cell.

The shriek of a whistle warbled through the window, piercing to the heart of his ruminations. The window had been built high up into the wall, giving the cell a disjointed aspect, accentuated by how it tapered towards the door. A room conceived to taunt its occupant with its unabashed, chew-up-and-spit-out, machinal inhumanity.

Despite being a stately six-foot-two, Ruggles was a good twenty inches shy of being able to see through the window and out into the yard. Still, twenty inches are nothing to a man of military bent. A quick spring and grab manoeuvre saw him hanging from the bars, his body right-angled, a perfect weight distribution between his ropy arms and equine legs, planted five feet up the wall. His soldier's body could be twisted to almost any request Ruggles made of it, make any habitat its own. Just then, he had channelled the grimping powers of the koala in its eucalyptus tree, and felt at home at once. He could dangle so for hours if need be. He could even allow himself to free one hand to disentangle and scratch his slingshot genitals, perhaps the only part of his body over which he had limited dominion.

The yard was populated by his fellow inmates, harlequin-like in their tattered fatigues. What struck him at once was the good number of women—almost unheard of on the battlefield. None of the Allied powers recruited women to serve on the front line, as far as he knew. He had heard the rumours of the American Vixen Assassin Squads—what red-blooded Tommy hadn't?—but he had never actually believed in them. Hadn't they just been conjured up by propagandists to inject fire into the bellies of the lower ranks—the delicious, though distant, prospect of encountering one of these burlesque princesses being enough to harden the wavering resolve of any tail-starved squaddie. But if so, where had these damsels in the yard sprouted from, and why had they not been segregated from the men?

Neither was the physical condition of the detainees encouraging. They were being put through their paces by one of the camp guards, an insipid slapstick of stretches that even the most vigorous among them struggled through like sorry old acrobats. Where was the Anglo-Saxon vim that the newspapers back home bragged of every day? Had that—like the Vixens—been merely another flake in the confetti shower of desperate propaganda scattered from the bunkers of Whitehall?

He turned his attention from the yard and out past the high wire fences. On the horizon he again saw the tall figures that, in the delirium of his descent, he had taken for giants, horrifying progeny of the Nazi laboratories. In the truth-loving light of morning, he saw them for what they were—the skeletons of ruined smock mills, with timber caps he had mistaken for *Stahlhelme* and shattered sails in place of the bolt action rifles. He had thought he was being dropped into ██████████████████████, but now suspected the pilot had veered off course and chucked him out somewhere over Holland. More rotten luck. While he spoke French with ease, *il parlait nederlandais comme une vache espangole*. A hobbling reality that any escape plan would be obliged to grapple with. Releasing the bars, he kicked off against the wall, turned a double somersault in the air, and punched his feet into the floor—a perfect stuck landing.

His uniform was folded in neat squares just beside the door—jacket, trousers and handkerchief piled in order of size. He picked them up, pressed his face into them and inhaled the scent of industrial springtime. Someone had taken, laundered and pressed his fatigues. What a strange thing for Jerry to have done! He had been instructed in the queer old-maidish tendencies of certain Nazis—a quality that somehow made their equally reputed sadism shimmer with enhanced grisliness—and he attributed this quirk to that. Their perverse spirits being excited in direct proportion to the dapperness of their torture victim. It made sense in a way: the more dignified, the more human, the captive, the further he could be dragged down and debased. Still, this treatment could perhaps be the quirk of a single, prudish guard, a man repulsed by the sight of grime, a fairy perhaps, and if this were so it might be something Ruggles could later use to his advantage.

He slipped into his fatigues, looser than he remembered them. The jacket bagged about his abdomen and the trousers, its buttoned waistband limp, hung from his hips as though pegged on a washing line. He tugged on the collar and checked the name inked inside. Ruggles, D.P.—his uniform alright. He lifted his jacket at the waist and went to pinch an inch of skin, but was shocked when four pallid inches came. The grotesque attenuation of his body meant he would have to start reckoning on his delirium having endured more than the eight or so hours he had previously assumed. But how long? Two days, seven, forty? Really, he had no way of knowing, and such ignorance was dangerous for a soldier. When the balance of a war might tip in a matter of days, none of the intelligence he had been briefed on before boarding the Whitley could now be assumed to hold.

'So'—Ruggles thought—'in this vile snakes-and-ladders conflict, I have paratrooped directly onto a serpent's head and slithered down to…' Well, he couldn't even be sure he was back to square one. At least with square one, you knew where you were and what lay ahead. Ruggles was lost, compass-less and alone on this vast bomb-pocked tundra. And worse, no matter which direction his honed soldier-sense might wish to lead him, he was cooped up in this prison camp, as flightless as a pinioned bird.

Ruggles waited for a long time, how long he couldn't fathom, and when still nobody came, he permitted his heavy head to loll and sleep to rise over him once again.

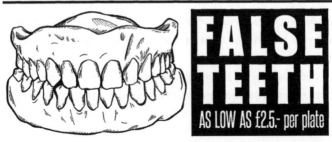
III

The young girl's voice warbled as if being channelled through a tin whistle.

'Daisy, Daisy, give me your answer do…'

Prising open his eyes, Ruggles lifted his head.

'I'm half crazy, all for the love of you…'

'Dulcie?' His voice barely scratched the air of the cell.

'I'm sorry Daddy,' said the girl. 'I didn't mean to wake you.' Ruggles shook his head and batted away the girl's apology.

'Dum-de-dum-dum marriage.'

'I can't afford a carriage.

'But you'll look sweet, upon the seat of a bicycle made for two!' Ruggles lifted his leaden arms and clapped. The young girl, who until this moment had been sitting in a chair across the cell from him, stood and bounced a dainty curtsy. Ruggles ground the backs of his bruised wrists into his eyes. His vision cleared and he swallowed back a thrust of emotion.

She was here. His angel. Her robin's-egg eyes, her ruddy cheeks, her gossamer hair, that chipped tooth, cried over for days then worn proudly as a badge of creeping maturity. All here.

'Pinch yourself, Daddy,' she said and laughed again. He did, on the back of his hand. She was right to recommend it. Such apparitions were the stock-in-trade of dreams or heat-oppressed minds. The feeling of fingernails scoring crescents into flesh was blissful. He was awake, percipient. This was no dream, no hallucination, then. She was here. She had come for him.

'Dulcie,' he said again, for he could think of no other word nor had any desire to do so. Dulcie crossed the cell and took his head in her arms. Ruggles lolled into her grasp, allowed his head to be cradled against her ribs. She toyed with a tongue of his hair, twisting it about her fingers.

'It's so good to see you Daddy. It's been so long.'

'I know. I know,' trying not to sob in front of his daughter. 'But Daddy's got some things to do right now. Important things.'

'What things?'

'Just…' He flicked at the air with his hand. 'Just this. The war. England.'

'What war, Daddy? There is no war. Not anymore,' a hairline fracture to her voice.

'No war?'

'No, Daddy.'

'No Germans?' He could feel her small body trembling against his skull, then the patter of tears on his crown. His angel was crying.

'No Germans either.'

Ruggles' mind waltzed. Someone must have been trying to protect the poor girl, hiding the truth from her these four long years.

'But the Germans...' he tried again.

'*Shhh*,' she said. 'That's enough of all that now. It's that kind of nonsense that got you transferred here in the first place.' Was that impatience edging into her voice? A voice that, come to think of it, was not quite the voice he remembered. He wriggled from her embrace and eyeballed the girl. She looked like Dulcie, more or less, though perhaps her chin was a little more pointed, her skin a little more mottled than...

'Who are you?' he thought or said. The girl took a couple of steps away from him.

'I can't take all this. Not at the moment. ███████ ███████. I need my Daddy back.'

'Who are you?' No doubt he had spoken this time. The whole cell trembled with his frustrated insistence.

'Forget it! Just fucking forget it!' she shouted. 'Forget me. You're halfway there already.' As Dulcie said this, the skin of her face turned a very dark grey, powdered and cracked, becoming a kind of living sculpture of baked earth. Then, like a column of unflicked Woodbine ash losing its battle with gravity, the apparition collapsed in a tsunami of dust, engulfing Ruggles and revealing what had been imprisoned inside: an intense blue ball of gyrating light, a Catherine-wheel apparition, spitting sparks and smoke as it whirled in the gloom of the cell. The brilliance of the light forced Ruggles to squint, but he could have sworn that as the light burnt itself out, the smoke took on different forms including the silhouette of the Führer, a defiant smile contorting his monstrous gargoyle's kisser.

Ruggles lay on the floor, his rib cage waxing and waning, double time, matching his sawing breath, and clutching a black and white photo of a young girl, smiling in front of a swing.

IV

How long after this Ruggles was released from the cell was impossible to know, but released he finally was, billeted to Cell Block B.

The ruinous condition of his cellmates was quickly confirmed. They were a miscreated, dilapidated squadron, if ever he had seen one. And more distressing even than that was the presence of Karmacharya, his old Hindoo friend, so far from his natural habitat. It had been many years since Ruggles had seen him, not since a disastrous mission they had undertaken together in the Kush when he was still a Private. And what a toll the years, or the prison, had taken on him—he was almost unrecognisable! Whereas before his thick, dark hair had shimmered like celluloid, now it hung in lustreless hanks. Even worse, his eyes, once so sharp, so alive, so possessed with his fascination with the world, stared blankly, as if at nothing. But worst of all was that he gave no indication that he recognised Ruggles, as if everything they had lived through together had been wiped from his brain's slate.

He was further disheartened to realise, that there was not a single one of his fellow prisoners he could count on to be physically or spiritually robust enough to act as his batman, when the moment came to orchestrate an escape. The camp had broken them. It wasn't just that their bodies had cracked and curled in on themselves, prematurely aged, for even here that could be corrected with a little discipline. It was their spirits that he most despaired of, their hangdog passivity and pitiful cooperativeness with the regime. What fight they once may have possessed had been catheterised from them, sucked out by the guards like a wolf laps marrow from the bones of its kill.

Ruggles inhabited this predicament, this Gordian knot writ prison-size, for more than a year, isolated in his struggle. At times he was again the victim of cruel hallucinations, taunted with visions of rural England, of manor houses and oak trees, and of devils dressed up in gross parody of family members and friends—though never again Dulcie—urging him, as he had been urged in that first cell, to give up the fight, to lower his dukes. But he never caved, always resisted, cast the evil spirits out with insults and violence. And after a while he was victorious... they simply stopped coming.

During the months that followed, some of his cellmates disappeared, and new ones arrived, but the tight-knit quiescence held.

Then, at the end of his thirteenth month in the camp, everything changed. One grey morning, when he was tumbled back into the canteen after another night in solitary, Karmacharya had vanished and a new prisoner sat in his chair. A woman, but with a masculine, donkey-like hardiness. She wore the uniform of a Tommy, and wore it well. In this lowly private, Ruggles at once intuited the Answer, the Knot-cutter, the Yin to his Yang. An alliance with this woman, Ruggles saw, was his best, his only chance of freedom. The question was, would she see this herself?

•

Will Brit soldier Ruggles pull off a spiffing, can-do escape? Will he convince the reluctant lady Private to join him? And what became of the ailing Hindoo? All this and more, only in the next issue of:
Air Souls!
On newsstands the 5th of EVERY month.

Appendix

35 Bungalow, Ballymote, County Sligo, courtesy of Oliver Farry

42 'This selfie, painted by Hildegard von Bingen, shows her transcribing her visions: '*Therefore speak these wonderful things and write and say them in the manner they were taught.*" Joanna Walsh

98 Self-portrait, courtesy of Paula McGrath

154 Hand-drawn map of Dublin, courtesy of Therese Cox

166 St. Patrick's Park sketch, courtesy of Therese Cox

172 Sketch of Ringsend, courtesy of Therese Cox

188 Courtesy of the Ilya Zverev Estate. *gorse* is grateful to Maria Zvereva and Evgenia Kozhina for their permission to publish the story. Translation © Anna Aslanyan 2104

238 This work-in-progress is an extract from the novel *Feeding Time* by Adam Biles, which will be published by Galley Beggar Press in 2016

240-241 © Stephen Crowe 2015

247 © Stephen Crowe 2015

250 © Stephen Crowe 2015

Contributors

SHEILA ARMSTRONG grew up in the west of Ireland and now lives in Dublin. She has been shortlisted for several awards and has been published in various journals. She works as a freelance editor and is currently writing her first collection of short stories.

ANNA ASLANYAN is a journalist and translator. She writes for a number of publications—including *3:AM Magazine, TLS, The Independent* and *The National*—mainly on books and arts. Among her translations into Russian are works by Peter Ackroyd, John Berger, Tom McCarthy, Jeffrey Eugenides and Zadie Smith. Her translations from Russian into English include contemporary short stories and a collection of essays *Post-Post Soviet? Art, Politics and Society in Russia at the Turn of the Decade.*

ADAM BILES is the author of *The Deep / Les Abysses, Grey Cats* and *Feeding Time.* He lives in Paris, but not like that.

LIAM CAGNEY is an author, critic and musicologist from Donegal. Publications his writing has appeared in include *The Moth* and *The Lonely Crowd* (fiction), the *Daily Telegraph* and *Sinfini Music* (criticism), and *Music and Letters and Tempo* (musicology). As a musicologist he has presented papers on spectral music in different countries and is the recipient of several grants and awards. He's currently writing a novel.

THERESE COX is a writer, performer, teacher, and artist living in Brooklyn, New York. A Chicago native, her fiction has appeared in *The Brooklyn Rail* and she was a finalist in the 2012 Irish Writers Centre Novel Fair. She has written online for *New York Irish Arts* and the *Anti-Room* in addition to her blog about typography and cities, *Ampersand Seven.* Therese is currently a PhD student in English and Comparative Literature at Columbia University in New York City.

AILBHE DARCY's first collection of poetry, *Imaginary Menagerie*, was published by Bloodaxe Books in 2011. She lives in Germany.

CAL DOYLE's work has appeared in *The Penny Dreadful*, *Southword*, *The Stinging Fly*, and elsewhere. He lives in Cork.

ADRIAN DUNCAN is working on a novel; adrianduncan.eu, papervisualart.com (co-editor).

OLIVER FARRY is a Paris-based writer, journalist and translator. His work has appeared in the *Guardian*, the *New Statesman*, the *New Republic* and *The Stinging Fly*, among other publications.

S.J. FOWLER is a poet, artist, martial artist and vanguardist. He works in the modernist and avant-garde traditions, across poetry, fiction, sonic art, visual art, installation and performance. He has published six collections of poetry and been commissioned by the Tate, Highlight Arts, Mercy, Penned in the Margins and the London Sinfonietta. He has been translated into thirteen languages and performed at venues across the world, from Mexico city to Erbil, Iraq. He is the poetry editor of *3:AM Magazine* and is the curator of the *Enemies* project.

ANDREW GALLIX teaches at the Sorbonne in Paris and co-edits *3:AM Magazine*. His work has appeared in publications ranging from the *Guardian* and *Times Literary Supplement* to *Dazed & Confused*. He divides his time between Scylla and Charybdis.

DAVID HAYDEN has been published in *The Stinging Fly*, the *Dublin Review*, the *Warwick Review* and *PN Review*, among other places. He is working on a novel and a book of short stories.

DARRAGH McCAUSLAND is a writer from Kells, County Meath, based in Dublin. He has previously been published in the *Dublin Review*. He is finishing a collection of short stories and a novel.

PAULA McGRATH's first novel, *Generation*, will be published by John Murray Originals in July 2015. Her fiction has appeared in *Surge* (Brandon 2014), *Eclectica*, *Mslexia*, *Necessary Fiction*, and others. She holds an MFA and an MA from UCD, and a BA in English from Trinity. She lives in Dublin near the sea.

IAN MALENEY is a writer from Offaly, currently living in Dublin. His work has recently appeared in places such as *The Quietus*, *Dublin Review of Books*, *Rabble* and Novara Media. He is a regular contributor to the *Irish Times*.

PÁDRAIG Ó MÉALÓID lives in Dublin with his wife and cats. He gets called a comics historian a lot. He knows more about the British comic character Marvelman than anyone else on the planet, and once had a cup of tea made for him by Alan Moore, who he has been interviewing every few years for quite a while now. He has written for numerous publications, including *The Beat* and *Forbidden Planet Blog*, and has been killed off in various books by various writers, at his own request.

BOBBY SEAL lives in North Wales where he runs a copywriting business. He has a Master's degree in English Literature from the University of Wales where he specialised in the works of Dorothy Richardson. Bobby regularly contributes to the website www. psychogeographicreview.com

MICHAEL NAGHTEN SHANKS lives in Dublin. His writing has featured in *The Penny Dreadful*, *3:AM Magazine*, *Poems in Which*, *New Irish Writing*, *The Quietus*, *30 Under 30* (Doire Press), *New Planet Cabaret* (New Island) and elsewhere. He is editor of *The Bohemyth*.

WILL STONE is a poet, literary translator and essayist who divides his time between the UK and Belgium. His first poetry collection *Glaciation* (Salt 2007), won the international Glen Dimplex Award for poetry in 2008. A second collection *Drawing in Ash*, was published by Salt in May 2011 to critical acclaim. A third collection *The Sleepwalkers* will be published in 2015. His translated works include a recent series of books for Hesperus Press, with translations of works by Maurice Betz, Stefan Zweig and Joseph Roth, and *Emile Verhaeren: Poems* and *Georges Rodenbach Selected Poems*, both published by Arc Publications. Pushkin Press will publish his first English translation of Stefan Zweig's essay on Montaigne in 2015 and an expanded collection of the poetry of Georg Trakl will appear with Seagull Books in 2016.

JOANNA WALSH's writing has been published by *Granta*, Dalkey, Salt, Tate, and in many journals, including *gorse*, and *The White Review*. She writes arts journalism for the *Guardian*, the *New Statesman*, and the *London Review of Books* online. Her story collection, *Fractals*, is published by 3:AM Press. *Hotel* will be published by Bloomsbury in 2015, as will a collection of stories from The Dorothy Project, and a Galley Beggar Single. She is fiction editor at *3:AM Magazine*, and runs #readwomen.

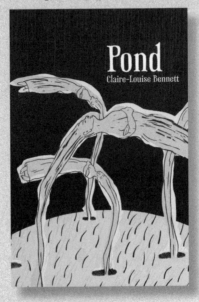

Oslo, Norway*, Lather In Heaven**, Twisted Futures†, Kunst & Grammar‡

Some of the forthcoming publications from Broken Dimanche Press in 2015 by John Holten*, Ann Cotten**, Eric Ellingsen† and Stine Marie Jacobsen‡. BDP is an award winning independent publishing house located in Berlin with a European wide perspective.
Visit our website and online shop at *www.brokendimanche.eu*

Friends of gorse

We would like to acknowledge the generous involvement of the following individuals:

Kevin Barry
Dan Dowling
Jude Fisher
William Fitzgerald
J. Fusco
Cherie Hagar
Fintan Hoey
Niall McGrillen
David Minogue
Doireann Ní Ghríofa
Faith O'Grady
Billy Ramsell
Rrose Sélavy
Jon K. Shaw
Brian J. Showers
Debbie Watkins

And those who wish to remain anonymous.

If you wish to support *gorse*, please visit:
www.gorse.ie